Town Darling

Holly Copella

To Linda and Dave Werner--
More fondly known as "Mom" and "Dad"

ACKNOWLEDGMENTS

Copella Books – First Paperback Edition 2015
Cover Artist: Migaticadesign
SelfPubBookCovers.com/Migaticadesign
Printed by CreateSpace, An Amazon.com Company

PUBLISHER'S NOTE

Chapter One

<u>*The*</u> small, quiet town of Darwood Falls seemed the perfect little town with which to live and raise a family. It was a friendly town where neighbors greeted one another as they passed on the streets. A banner proudly displayed across Main Street read, 'Darwood Falls 98th Annual Fair'. The town fair was an important part of life in Darwood Falls. It was when the entire town got together and showed their unity, and, in some cases, their talents with crafts, baked goods, and contests. A dark-haired, ravishing young woman, Casey Remington, rode her large, gray horse through the streets of town at a leisurely walk. It was a common sight. Casey had been riding her horses into town since she was old enough to ride. Now a grown woman of twenty-one, Casey still used her horse as her preferred mode of transportation on her limited trips to town or just about anywhere. Several people greeted her as she passed and young children ran along the sidewalks waving at her, hoping to gain a free pony ride on the large horse. Casey enjoyed encouraging young children to take an interest in horses. Horses were her passion and her part-time job. She trained horses for pleasure riding and show. She also gave riding lessons on weekends. She especially liked engaging young boys into the world of horses, since most seemed to think it was a 'girl thing'.

Two young boys rode their bikes along the sidewalk, keeping pace with her while waving and shouting to her. She knew what they wanted to see. Casey sent the horse into an amazingly slow canter, which made the horse look like a rocking horse prancing along the street. The clopping of the steel shoes striking the pavement made a rhythmic sound. The boys cheered excitedly. Casey almost certainly established a new, future riding lesson. Casey was certain it was her ability to engage youngster in the world of horses that brought business to her riding lessons. Little did she know it was her girl-next-door beauty that attracted young boys to the world of riding. Casey was the ultimate tom girl, and the thought that young boys or men taking an interest in her never actually crossed her mind. Her world was perfect the way it was, and she didn't need men complicating it for her. She rode into a parking space between two pick-up trucks, dismounted, and tied the horse to a parking meter. She inserted her quarter into the meter and headed for the nearby antique store. The antique store was iconic and charming with beautiful displays beyond large, glass windows.

As Casey entered, she looked at the checkout desk not far from the door. A forty-something year old woman of considerable wealth, indicated by the fur she wore, stood before the desk. Abby Ridgeway stood out in Darwood Falls. Her expensive city clothes, professionally manicured nails, and eye-catching jewelry kept her widely out of touch with everyone else in town. It was amazing she had as many friends as she did. Abby talked with Casey's mother, who stood behind the desk. Casey paused by some trinkets and eavesdropped on their conversation. There was no denying Catherine Remington was Casey's mother. Their features were almost identical. Catherine's youthful appearance sometimes allowed her to be mistaken for Casey's older sister. Casey actually wished she had a sister some days. Her older brother, Grey, was a bit of a pain. As she listened to the conversation between the two women, Casey couldn't help but feel hostility toward Abby Ridgeway. Abby was the mayor's wife, or Mrs. Mayor, as Casey liked to call her. She was a demanding, clinging, snob of a woman, and despite her outward friendliness, she was actually a barracuda.

"Melanie volunteered for the kissing booth this year, and I'm sure she'll win the talent show again," Abby announced cheerfully. "Naturally, Lance will be judging pies and sharing the dunking booth with Sheriff Wiley."

Bragging about her daughter and husband was a daily if not hourly occurrence. With the way she raved continuously about her family and her wonderful life, she wanted the entire town to know she was the woman who had it all. The thought actually made Casey ill. Her daughter, Melanie, was as stuck up as Mrs. Mayor, and her husband was a true politician. He was a snake charmer wrapped in delusions of grandeur and smothered with a 'holier than thou' attitude.

"I'm in charge of the bachelor auction. That's always fun," Abby continued. "And, of course, Melanie's handsome boyfriend, Deputy Tucker, is one of our more popular bachelors again this year. My Melanie has excellent taste in men, don't you think?"

It was almost as if her boasting would continue on forever. Casey wondered how long she had been raving about her daughter, husband, and wonderful life prior to her arrival at the store. Catherine smiled and nodded, almost as if she was actually interested in everything Mrs. Mayor had to say. Casey couldn't believe her mother's level of tolerance for the woman. She wished her mother would tell her off just once. She wasn't sure when her mother decided she needed to start acting like a lady, but Casey found it annoying. She knew her mother had claws, but she rarely used them anymore.

"I didn't see your family on the fair sign-up sheet," Abby continued on with her endless conversation.

Abby seemed to indicate that they should be actively taking part in the fair. Catherine tensed and appeared uncomfortable by the comment. Her claws still didn't unsheathe.

"Things have been a little crazy around here--" Catherine began and was immediately interrupted.

"It's true, isn't it?" Abby gasped while staring at her with a look of surprise. "Brandon's running for mayor."

Catherine appeared surprised by her candor. She fumbled for something to say. "He hasn't mentioned anything to me," she announced then continued with her earlier thought before the interruption. "Grey's been working a lot of hours at the tavern, but I can guarantee Casey will be entering a few events at the horse show. Naturally, Brandon and I will be donating a few antiques for the raffle. We'll definitely do our part for the fair and the community."

Casey realized her mother was beginning to ramble, which would create suspicion. It was time to bail her out. Casey casually approached the desk and touched Abby's fur shawl while staring at it with great interest.

"What sort of animal did they kill to make this?" Casey asked and blinked several times almost innocently.

Abby glanced at Casey and fidgeted. "I'm, uh, not sure."

Casey suddenly gasped with surprise. "Is that--*baby seal?*"

Abby again glanced at Casey, fidgeted, and attempted a polite smile at Catherine. It was probably the longest Abby had been silent since she entered the shop. "I should go. I have a ton of things to do," she announced while seeming tense. "Tell my husband I went to City Hall. I'll talk to you later."

Abby quickly hurried from the shop. Casey was proud of herself. She'd chased Mrs. Mayor out in under a minute. It had to be a town record. Despite Casey's pleased smile, her mother gave her a disapproving glare.

"That wasn't very nice, Casey," her mother scolded.

"Neither is she," Casey bluntly informed her. "All she does is brag about how amazing her life is, how wonderful her daughter is, and how great her husband is." She rolled her eyes with disgust. "I can't wait to see what she brags about after Dad becomes mayor."

Catherine fidgeted. "Your father's intention to run for mayor needs to remain a secret a little while longer, so let's just be civilized, okay?" Catherine sighed softly while staring at the shop door. She looked back at Casey and frowned. "I hate to agree with Abby, but you and Grey should volunteer at the fair this year," she remarked. "We need to show our support."

"Cleaning up corruption in this town should be enough."

"Be polite," she said in a hushed tone. "Lance is in the office with your father."

"Oh, I forgot. We're supposed to keep his corruption a secret from him," Casey teased and flashed a grin.

Catherine attempted to hide her smile so Casey wouldn't be encouraged. "You are a terrible young lady. Didn't they teach you anything in college?"

"Yes, I learned college boys are immature," Casey announced firmly with conviction. "I prefer Dad's old Army buddies."

Her mother's expression dropped into a scowl. "Stay away from your father's old Army buddies."

"Why? They adore me." She grinned while reflecting dreamily. "Remember how I'd sit on their laps, and they'd tell me about their adventures?"

Her mother maintained her frown. "Yes, and it was cute when you were little. The last few years--not so cute," Catherine scolded lowly. "I think you and I need to have 'the talk'."

Casey rolled her eyes. "Mom, please, I've been friends with Dina since forever. She's told me more than I ever wanted to know about sex. I'm repulsed as it is. I certainly don't need to hear more about it from you."

Her mother rolled her eyes and shook her head. She subconsciously looked at the many antique clocks on the wall. Not one had the same time. "Would you rescue your father? It's lunchtime."

Casey nodded and headed for the back office. Her father's office was tastefully decorated with an antique desk and several old lamps. Her father, Brandon Remington, was a ruggedly handsome man in his late forties. He sat behind the hand-carved desk with a false smile plastered on his face. A stocky man also in his late forties, Mayor Lance Ridgeway, sat before the desk and talked endlessly. Casey stopped in the doorway to listen a moment. The mayor was a talker, but he never really said much.

"We're pulling out all the stops for the fair this year," Mayor Lance said. "The talent show is going to be spectacular, and I'm not just saying that because my Melanie is in it. Everyone in town loves the talent show."

"I think it's the legs and cleavage they love," Brandon replied dryly with a matter-of-fact grin.

"Who doesn't?" Lance said with a chuckle.

Casey rolled her eyes at the comment. She hated to think her father thought about such things. Men with their lustful ideas were a big reason why she didn't date. Most men got on her nerves. As she looked at Mayor Lance, it wasn't hard to see why. She knocked on the open door. Brandon saw her, smiled, and motioned her in.

Casey looked at Lance as she entered. "Mrs. Mayor is waiting for you at City Hall."

Lance appeared surprised and quickly stood. "Oh, then I'd better get going." He gave a polite nod to Brandon then Casey and left the office.

Casey watched him leave and appeared pleased with herself. She was getting good at clearing rooms.

Brandon studied Casey and smirked almost knowingly. "Did she really say that?"

Casey shrugged while grinning. "Close enough."

Brandon chuckled softly and shook his head. "I don't know whether I should be disappointed with you or proud."

"It's too close to call," she teased. Her look turned serious. "Mom thinks Grey and I should participate more in this year's fair."

"And that's a good idea."

She rolled her eyes at the thought. "Couldn't I just buy extra tickets to dunk the mayor a few more times?"

Her father had a devious grin on his face as he seriously considered it, brushed it aside, and then smiled uncomfortably. "As much as I appreciate the sentiment, you may want to go the extra mile this year."

Casey was suddenly horrified. "If you're suggesting the kissing booth--"

Brandon appeared alarmed and leaned forward in his chair. "Over my dead body! Leave smooching with guys to Dina." He sank back in his chair and relaxed. "Why don't you and Grey get a couple of friends together and give pony rides to the kids?"

"Pony rides?" she gasped. "They're horses, Dad. Very *big* horses."

"I know you'll think of something." He suddenly grinned. "You know what would really be amazing?"

"Drowning the mayor in the dunking booth?"

Brandon's smile faded into a scowl. "No," he retorted. His smile once again returned. "I'd love to see you and Grey in the talent show."

"What?" she exclaimed. "No!"

"Remember all those skits you'd put on for the guys when they came to visit?" he asked while grinning. "You and your brother were a hit."

"Dad, we were six and ten," she remarked. "Of course the guys were going to love us."

He shrugged. "It was a thought."

It was time to change the subject. Entering the talent show just wasn't happening. "Mom says it's lunchtime."

"Then we should probably head for the diner," he announced. "Word on the street is they're serving strawberry pie today."

"No wonder she's in a hurry," Casey muttered.

Chapter Two

The Boxcar Diner was always busy at lunchtime with dine-in customers as well as business owners stopping by for take-out. It was one of the most chosen places among locals to meet and even conduct business. The restaurant was an old train dining car from the 1920's, which was retired to Darwood Falls in the late 1940's. The wheels and windows were all original, although it had been painted and looked new, in an old-fashioned sort of way. The Boxcar Diner had an addition built out the back to accommodate the masses flooding the diner at lunchtime, but the old train car still remained the main draw for most. Casey, Catherine, and Brandon sat at a booth next to the window in the dining car portion. Most of the seats were the original bench seats from one of the retired passenger cars. The galley had long since been converted into additional seating, with the modern kitchen now operating from the addition. Framed photos of the train in its working condition from decades past hung on the walls, providing decoration as well as conversation pieces. An attractive, blonde waitress in her early twenties, Dina Crawford, approached their table with coffee and iced tea.

"The usual, Mom--Dad?" Dina asked.

Brandon eyed Catherine and raised a curious brow. "Did we have another child I don't know about?"

Catherine ignored his comment and smiled at Dina. "Yes, we'll have the usual."

Dina then looked at Casey and grinned. "Are we on for tonight?"

"First round is on Grey."

"Always good to hear," Dina announced, spun with a lively bounce, and walked away from their table.

Dina had been Casey's best friend since the day they'd met in kindergarten. Their childhood years were never-ending days of games on horseback, trail rides, and playing cowboys and robbers, which sometimes involved Casey's brother, when he had time for his little sister. All that changed when Dina's father took off, supposedly with the mayor's secretary. He was never heard from again, and her mother drank herself senseless. Dina's life crashed after that, and she'd spent most of her free time hanging out at the Remington's farm with Casey. Her mother never abused her; she just resigned from being her mother. At a young age, Dina took on the responsibilities of not only cleaning the house and taking care of herself, but she was burdened with paying the bills and being the only responsible adult in the house. It was too much to ask from a fourteen-year-old. She stuck it out through high school but moved out before the ink was dry on her diploma.

"The tavern again?" Brandon asked while shaking his head.

It was obvious he didn't approve of his daughter hanging out at the local bar, but with limited entertainment in town, there was little else to do most evenings.

"We considered going cow tipping, but Dina prefers cowboy tipping," Casey teased. "What else is there to do in this town?"

Her father frowned his displeasure. "We need to have a serious talk about that place."

"I know what sort of place it is, Dad."

Although Darwood Falls was filled with mostly law-abiding, wonderful people, it had a dark, seedy underbelly most refused to talk about. As if on cue, a wealthy man in his late forties, Ernest Harford, approached their table. Ernest was part of that seedy underbelly. He was the richest man in town and imposed his wishes upon everyone like some schoolyard bully. His brother-in-law being the mayor certainly didn't help the town escape his clutches. Catherine and Casey avoided looking at Ernest. Both shared the same opinion of him. They were repulsed by the sight of him. Not that he was physically repulsive, but his arrogance and iron-fisted tactics made him unappealing. Despite his wife and daughter, Brandon attempted to remain polite to the retched man.

"Good afternoon, Remington clan," Ernest announced cheerfully and paid special attention to Catherine, who didn't bother looking at him. Although obviously captivated by her beauty, he didn't seem fazed by her disinterest.

"Hey, Ernest," Brandon replied, being the only one to even acknowledge him.

"I heard a rumor that you might be running for mayor," Ernest announced with a smile that almost mocked him. His directness was a form of control. He liked catching people off guard, believing they would show their true feelings.

Brandon faked a look of surprise. "Oh?" he said with a laugh. "That's news to me."

Casey's father wasn't easily played. He knew how to handle men like Ernest. He'd spent enough time in the military to learn how to deal with all types of attitudes. Ernest was no different from higher-ranking officers who enjoyed pushing around enlisted men. He enjoyed the power.

"I sort of figured," Ernest remarked and laughed. "You'd find that job tedious and boring."

"I don't know," Brandon teased while casually reclining in his seat. "Pie judging sounds like one hell of a perk."

Casey's father was just playing with Ernest now, and, sadly, he had no idea. Ernest may have been wealthy, but he wasn't very smart.

"Probably the only perk as mayor in this hick town," Ernest announced with a chuckle. He appeared pleased with Brandon's response and was ready to move on to things of more importance. "You guys have a nice day." Ernest continued toward the cashier in the main dining area with his check from lunch.

Catherine glared at Brandon with her loathe for Ernest evident in her eyes. "That man makes my blood run cold." Her mother's claws were finally coming out.

Just once, Casey wanted to see her mother verbally hand Ernest his head. She could do it too. She wasn't as sweet and innocent as she'd have people believe.

"He thinks he owns the town because he owns the mayor and the local law," Casey said with a sneer while adding her two cents. She couldn't let her mother have all the fun.

Brandon appeared uncomfortable and shifted in his seat. "Let's be civil. There are big changes coming," he announced. Her father was oddly non-confrontational for a former military man. "Sheriff Wiley's about to retire and our young deputies have more enthusiasm for upholding the law."

"Deputy Tucker, the town stud, is next in line for sheriff," Casey mocked. "He's dating the mayor's daughter. That means he's practically bought and paid for."

"I hope Deputy Holt becomes sheriff," her mother announced, catching Casey's attention.

"Tucker and Mitchell have more seniority than Vaughn Holt," Brandon informed his wife. "Sheriff Wiley isn't going to pass the torch to him."

"And I certainly don't want him as sheriff," Casey remarked. "He has it out for me."

"He doesn't have it out for you," Catherine scoffed. "You just challenge his authority."

"Yeah, because he has it out for me--"

Catherine rolled her eyes. There was no winning with Casey. She was almost as hardheaded as her father was.

"You certainly had no problems with him when he was first hired a few years back," her mother reminded.

"Probably because I was fifteen, and he looked good in his uniform," Casey replied dryly.

"That's an understatement," Catherine remarked and grinned teasingly. "I seem to remember you having the worst crush on him."

"She did?" Brandon suddenly asked. "Where was I?"

"Tinkering on that piece of junk in the garage," she casually informed him.

"Hey, that piece of junk is a 1969 Chevy Camaro Z/28 classic muscle car, I'll have you know."

His words went right over them. Catherine rolled her eyes and looked back at Casey, who shared the same glare as her father.

"I hope you haven't been spreading those rumors around about that non-existent crush I *didn't* have on Deputy Holt," Casey scolded with a look of mayhem in her eyes.

"Of course not," her mother retorted. "But maybe if you still felt that way about him, you two would get along better." Catherine teased Casey with a lustful grin.

Casey glared at her mother with a look of horror. She couldn't believe her mother was suggesting such a thing. "Ewe, you want me to hook-up with Deputy Holt? That's nasty," she remarked. "He's a surly bastard."

"Casey," her mother gasped then glared at Brandon. "This is what happens when you expose her to your military friends."

Her father appeared humored and unruffled by the comment. "You should hear yourself sometimes. Get a few drinks into you--"

"We weren't discussing me," Catherine scoffed and shut down the entire conversation.

Brandon laughed softly. Casey just rolled her eyes. She'd be more concerned about her parents' bouts of banter if they didn't cuddle and act like teenagers on the couch in the evening. The way they went at it was almost embarrassing. They were an old married couple. It wasn't right. Dina approached their table and glanced at Casey with a sympathetic look on her face.

"I hate to be the bearer of bad news, Casey," Dina announced timidly, "but Deputy Holt is issuing you a parking ticket."

Casey quickly turned to look out the window, appeared shocked, and forced her mother out of the booth so she could get up. "He is unbelievable!"

"Be nice, Casey!" her father scolded even though he didn't bother to stand and stop her.

"Oh, I will," she announced while turning toward her father. "I'll smile while I give him the verbal lashing of his life." Casey hurried away from the table.

Catherine eyed Brandon while sitting back in her seat. "Yep, she's your daughter."

"Are you kidding? That girl has Catherine written all over her," Brandon replied.

"Oh, please," Catherine snapped. "I *never* acted that way."

Brandon stared at her with a surprised look as his mouth hung open. "Have you met you?"

Catherine glared sharply at him. He smiled and chuckled at her look. She hid her smile and looked away. Casey hurried from the diner and crossed the street toward the parking spot where her gray horse was tied. A ruggedly handsome, dark-haired deputy in his late twenties, Deputy Vaughn Holt, stood next to the parking meter with Casey's horse tied to it and wrote on his pad. Casey approached him and her horse, stood near the horse's head, and glared at Vaughn. He didn't bother acknowledging her.

"Deputy--"

He briefly eyed her with little emotion and continued to write the ticket. "Casey--"

"What do you think you're doing?" she calmly asked despite her obvious raging temper.

Vaughn casually pointed at the invalid meter with his pen and gave her an innocent look with those dark eyes of his. "Issuing you a parking ticket."

"To a horse?"

He returned his attention to his ticket pad and showed little reaction. "Nope, to the owner of the horse."

As she stared at his handsome profile, she wondered what she ever found appealing about him. Vaughn ripped off the ticket, folded it, and casually stuck it between the horse's bridle and its ear. Casey pulled the ticket out and allowed her hostility to boil over.

"You can't ticket a horse for a parking violation," she suddenly growled.

"I believe I just did."

Casey waved the ticket with annoyance while glaring at him. "*This* is harassment."

"No, *that* is a ticket." Vaughn indicated the meter with a cleverly raised brow. "And *that* is an expired meter."

Casey indicated Vaughn while sneering. "And *that* is an arrogant asshole."

He didn't appear the least bit affected by her insult and almost welcomed the challenge. "You may be the town darling, but that won't get anywhere with me."

Casey was stunned and moderately offended by his comment as she stared at him. "Town darling? Since when?"

The sheriff's blazer pulled up to the curb near them. A plump, older man in a policeman's uniform, Sheriff Wiley, got out of the car and approached them. Wiley was a small-town sheriff stereotype. He'd obviously had too many doughnuts, indicated by the tautness of his shirt buttons over his mid-section, and spent too much time sleeping in his cruiser over the years. The sheriff looked at both and appeared curious.

"What's going on here?" Sheriff Wiley asked.

"Your deputy gave me a parking ticket for *my horse.*"

Wiley looked at Vaughn and appeared almost stunned. "Seriously, Vaughn?"

The deputy immediately became defensive. "The meter is expired, there's horse excrement all over, and she knows she's not supposed to ride her horse in town," Vaughn reminded him.

The sheriff shook his head with shame. "I know you're fairly new here, Deputy, but she's been riding her horses into town since she was in kindergarten." Wiley took the ticket from Casey, tore it, and placed it in Vaughn's hand. "I'm sure you have more important things to do than write parking tickets to the pretty girls of Darwood Falls."

Vaughn stared at him and appeared stunned. Wiley turned toward Casey and offered a pleasant smile while placing his hand on her shoulder. He'd always been overly friendly toward her growing up, and his friendliness had only increased as she got older. She was never sure what to make of him.

"Don't let Deputy Holt intimidate you, Casey," Wiley announced. "New deputies are always a little John Wayne until they're properly broken in. But don't you worry; I'm looking out for you."

Casey stared at him with an odd look. He smiled warmly at her and returned to his blazer. She stared after him as he drove away, appearing dumbfounded. She then turned to Vaughn, who shut his ticket book with disgust and possible embarrassment.

"What just happened?" she asked more to herself.

"What do you think?" Vaughn scoffed while avoiding looking and her then walked away.

Could it be true? Was she the town darling?

Chapter Three

The sheriff's blazer pulled up to the police station less than two blocks from the diner. Sheriff Wiley got out of his blazer with his usual lunch-to-go from the diner while attempting to juggle his take-out coffee and the newspaper. Abby approached him and nearly cut off his path to the police station. He attempted to keep from losing his lunch or coffee from his sudden stop. Despite the scowl on Abby's face, Wiley attempted to be polite.

"Good afternoon, Abby," he announced cheerfully. "If you're here about added security for the fair, everything is under--"

"No, that's no why I'm here," she remarked with the annoyance evident in her voice. "I saw Deputy Holt giving Casey Remington a ticket half an hour ago."

"Yeah, it was just a misunderstanding," Wiley announced. "Deputy Holt is still following the police handbook like it's gospel. I took care of it."

"So I saw," she huffed. "That's why I wanted to speak to you."

Wiley appeared puzzled.

"That girl has been granted special privileges since the day she was born," Abby said matter-of-fact. "Deputy Holt is the first one with enough courage to stand up to her and that whole family, for that matter."

Sheriff Wiley stared at Abby with a look of surprise. "I don't think Casey or her family has received any special privileges from anyone in the police department. She's a good kid."

"She's disrespectful toward me," Abby launched back while glaring at him through narrow, hateful eyes.

"I'm sorry you feel that way, Abby, but I don't have jurisdiction over interactions between citizens."

"Perhaps you'd prefer to have this conversation with my husband," Abby scoffed while folding her arms across her chest and gave him a demanding look.

Wiley suddenly frowned while staring at the smug look on her face. "Just exactly what is it you expect me to do?"

Abby smiled with all the sweetness of a mafia kingpin. "That's more like it," she replied. "I expect you to use a firm hand while dealing with that manipulative little twit, Casey. Put an end to her riding that horse through town." She appeared pleased with herself. "Yes, that should do for starters. And no more special treatment toward her. If she breaks the law, I want you to come down on her *hard*."

Sheriff Wiley frowned and nodded. "Good day, *Mrs. Ridgeway*."

Wiley was usually informal, except when someone pulled rank on him, and Abby was pulling rank. He continued past her and into the police station. Abby stroked her fur shawl, grinned proudly, and turned toward Town Square.

†

Casey leaned against the back wall of the diner's main building with Dina, who sat on an old crate and massaged her feet. Casey was distracted by what happened with Sheriff Wiley earlier. It still bothered her, and she wasn't sure why.

"Why couldn't I be a secretary instead of a waitress?" Dina groaned softly.

"Because the thought of being a secretary makes you violently ill," Casey replied.

She eyed Casey sharply. "It's not the idea of *being* a secretary that makes me ill; just the thought of *certain* secretaries." Dina rested her head against the wall and sighed. "I don't want to be a waitress all my life."

"I told you before," Casey announced. "You can have my job at the antique store. I hate antiques. I hate the way they smell; I hate the dust they attract." She grimaced. "God, I hate dusting. You should let me talk to my parents."

"You're not going to get out of it, Casey," Dina informed her. "Your parents want you and Grey to take over one day. I'm not part of that equation."

"You're practically their daughter," Casey insisted matter-of-fact. "I'll ask them tonight."

"No, don't," Dina protested and slipped back into her shoes. "I sponge off you and your family enough."

"You're being ridiculous."

There was a long silence. Casey once again sank into thought about the earlier Deputy Holt and Sheriff Wiley incident. Dina studied Casey and appeared curious.

"What's really bothering you?" Dina finally asked. "You hate this alley."

"That's because it smells."

"That's probably my feet," Dina teased and stood. She stared at Casey a long moment and appeared sympathetic. "I know something's bothering you. Was it Deputy Holt?"

Casey shrugged but didn't look at her. "Something he said."

Dina appeared surprised with her eyes wide and something resembling a grin on her face. "Did he hit on you?" The thought obviously pleased her.

"What? No!"

Dina groaned and rolled her eyes. "I swear he's gay."

"You need a boyfriend bad," Casey scoffed. Her look turned serious and she tensed. "He called me the town darling."

She stared at Casey with an odd look on her face and absolutely no understanding. "Okay--?"

"That's derogatory, Dina," she announced.

"I wish men would offend me like that," Dina replied dryly.

"He thinks I get special treatment," she insisted. "He practically called me Melanie."

"Okay, that would be an insult," Dina remarked. "I don't get why you're so bothered over one little comment. You never cared about anything he said before."

"Yes, but then Sheriff Wiley came along and ripped up the ticket," Casey informed her. "He proved Deputy Holt right. Is that how people see me? Am I the cute and fuzzy bunny that can do no wrong?"

"The only time you're cute and fuzzy is when you've had too much to drink," Dina teased with a grin. "You're making something out of nothing. Everyone knows Sheriff Wiley has an old man crush on you."

Casey groaned and rolled her eyes. "I'm going to be ill."

"You do realize that you don't have to picture men naked when I tell you they have a crush on you," Dina remarked.

"Yet I always do."

"Seriously, you're the one who needs a boyfriend."

✝

Ernest Harford's home was located on the further edge of town and set back on a hill with a long driveway leading up to it. Considering the town's moderate means and casual appearance, the Harford Estate set itself apart with its glitz and glamour. The only other home in town that remotely compared to the elegant estate was the mayor's home only a few blocks away. Despite Ernest's perceived wealth, his was new money. He lacked the style and grace his sister, Abby, somehow managed. Ernest, along with his sister, came into their wealth nearly twenty years ago when a distant relative died and left them several hundred acres of worthless land. The worthless land turned into a gold mine, when they literally discovered gold beneath the property. They sold the land for millions and overnight became the wealthiest families in Darwood Falls. Shortly thereafter, Abby's husband was elected mayor, and Ernest helped run the town from behind the scenes.

Despite the beauty and grandeur of the mansion and estate from the outside, the interior left something to be desired. The elegance of the grand hallway had faded from years of neglect. Personal belongings were carelessly lying about, and it was easy to assume it had been a long time since the place had been cleaned. Ernest's wife had died nearly ten years earlier and the condition of the home showed it. The doorbell rang. Ernest hurried through the hall for the foyer. He opened the door to reveal Mayor Lance. Neither man appeared very enthusiastic in the company of the other.

"What is it this time?" Ernest muttered and walked away from the door.

Lance entered, looked around, and showed his distaste for the condition of the home. He immediately followed Ernest into one of the nearby rooms. The study was even less attractive than the grand hallway. Papers were scattered along the floor, the garbage can was overflowing, cigar ashes from the ashtray were piled high, and there were at least four empty whiskey glasses on the cluttered desktop. Ernest took a seat behind the desk and pushed the whiskey bottle toward Lance. Lance declined and removed some old books from the chair in front of the desk. He sat in the chair and appeared less than

19

enthusiastic. A small, gray cat jumped on Ernest's lap and purred affectionately. He pushed the cat off while making a face of disgust for the animal. Ernest puffed on his cigar and blew smoke toward the ceiling. The ceiling was coated with a thick, brownish yellow film from years of cigar smoke.

"So what's the catastrophe this time?" Ernest teased.

"I think Brandon Remington intends to run against me in this year's election," Lance said while frowning.

"He said he wasn't," Ernest casually announced with little interest. "Brandon has a business to run. There's no perk for him to be mayor. He's too much of a 'good old boy'. He'd be bored out of his mind."

"Of course he denied his intent to run," Lance announced firmly, "but I think that's just a story. That whole family has been acting strange lately." He suddenly sat forward in his chair and glared at Ernest. "If he becomes mayor, we're both screwed. It's party over for you too."

"I can't believe you're actually worried about this," Ernest said with a chuckle. He leaned forward and grinned. "You have the law on your side, Lance. Use it. Get Sheriff Wiley to dig up some dirt on Brandon. He was in the military, for God's sake. There has to be some dirt on him somewhere."

"Sheriff Wiley is going to retire soon," Lance said. "He's been difficult to persuade lately."

Ernest groaned softly. "No imagination," he scoffed. "You control Wiley now more than ever. You can use his retirement against him. Besides, you have three ambitious, young deputies eager to make a name for themselves. Surely, you can persuade any one of them to do your bidding. Isn't Deputy Tucker dating your daughter?"

"Yeah, they're pretty serious," Lance said with a defeated sigh.

"Rumor has it Deputy Holt has it out for Casey too."

"I see you've been talking to Abby," Lance muttered.

Ernest grinned and took another puff from his cigar. "I'm sure I can persuade my boys to pay special attention to Brandon's brood. Grey bartends at the tavern; and Casey spends a lot of evenings hanging out there."

"Persuade," Lance reiterated sternly. "I don't want them hurting that girl."

"Jesus, Lance," Ernest bellowed. "You too? What's this hold Casey Remington has over the men in this town?"

"No hold," Lance snapped. "I just don't condone hurting innocent girls."

"Fine," Ernest scoffed. "I'll tell the boys to use the kid gloves on her sweet ass."

†

*T*he Remington's large, remodeled farmhouse was nestled in a beautifully landscaped setting. There was a large barn fifty yards from the house with acres of pastures contained within wooden fencing. Several horses grazed within the lush pastures in the afternoon sunshine. Casey stood in the paddock while lunging Storm in a circle around her. Her well-trained horse required limited guidance. With verbal commands, she sent him into a canter. Storm cantered in a circle around her then tossed his head and kicked up his heels.

"Whoa," Casey called to him and hid her smile.

The large horse stopped on command and turned to look at her. She knew he knew what he did. There were times he was like a little kid trying to get away with something. He snickered softly as if laughing at her.

"Yeah, real funny," she remarked then shook her head. "You're bored; I get it."

She approached the horse and removed the lunge line from his halter. She motioned with her hand for him to stay as she slowly backed several feet from him. He tossed his head.

"You're such a brat."

Casey stood several feet away while facing him and raised her hands in the air. Storm threw his head and reared up on command. She lowered her hands and he came back down on all four hooves. Casey laughed softly. She was pleased with his training. He was a smart horse, although sometimes he was a little too smart for his own good. Storm tossed his head and rocked slightly as if wanting to rear again. His ears perked forward with anticipation.

"Okay," she sighed. "One more, but then that's it."

Casey raised her hands again. Storm reared up and thrashed out with his hooves while towering high above her. Seeing his underbelly just a few feet away from her face was almost sobering. She lowered her hands. Storm didn't come back down. He thrashed his hooves and maintained his balance on his hind legs.

"Now you're just showing off," she scoffed.

He finally landed and snickered at her, arching his head and awaiting his treat. Casey approached and gave him a treat then firmly patted his thick neck.

"We'll need to practice a little more before we try that with me on top."

21

"You're kidding, right?" came a male voice from behind her.

Casey turned toward the gate where her brother, Grey, stood and leaned on the top railing. Grey was a lean, tall man only a few years older than Casey was. He didn't have their father's rugged good looks. He actually looked more like their mother. It wasn't necessarily a bad thing. Not to say he was girly; he just had more of a sweet boy look. He was never going to have their father's muscular build. If he was lucky, he'd end up more athletic, but for now, he was just gangly.

"That was a private conversation between me and my man," Casey informed him.

She looked at Storm and shooed him away. He took off across the paddock and stuck his head over the fence to converse with the pretty mares one pasture over. Casey approached Grey by the gate and leaned on the top rail near him.

"Tell Dad and you're toast," she said firmly.

"And then when you end up on your ass with a broken leg or a concussion, they're going to yell at me," he replied. "I wish they'd gotten me that puppy instead of a sister."

"You're no prize yourself," she said teasingly while flashing a smile.

"Things were nicer around here when you were off at college during the week," he scoffed and straightened. "I don't know how they could stand you at college."

"Why do you come out here? Just to torment me?"

Grey appeared surprised while staring at her with his most serious look. "Of course, why else?"

Casey hid her smile and shook her head. "I'm wishing I'd gotten a puppy instead too."

"You'd miss me," Grey informed her.

She appeared to consider the comment then smiled and shook her head. "No, I don't think so."

†

$\mathcal{J}$t was later that evening. Casey finished saddling her gray horse, which was tied to the hitching post just outside the barn. Her father approached and placed his arm across the horse's rump. Casey glanced at him and knew immediately what was on his mind before he even spoke. He smiled pleasantly, as was his usual warm-up for one of his 'talks' with her. She just smiled and continued tightening the saddle's girth.

"I know you hate when I lecture--" he began.

Casey smiled teasingly. "Then don't."

"We've been over this before," he announced with a defeated sigh. "You're twenty-one and have every right to go to the tavern, but I don't like the element that hangs out there. It's a breeding ground for ill-mannered young men."

"You mean the Harford boys?"

"Of course I mean the Harford boys," he said with a groan. "I've heard and *seen* things that bother me, Casey. They're bad news."

Casey wondered why her father felt compelled to state the obvious. No one needed to be reminded of the Harford boys' reputation. They were bad news since kindergarten. She smiled as she placed her hand on the saddle horn above her while facing him.

"You don't have to worry, Dad," she assured him. "They aren't going to bother us with Grey tending bar. Besides, you taught me to defend myself."

"That doesn't make me feel any better," he remarked. "There are four of them. Wild dogs always travel in packs. Besides, I'm still allowed to worry. You're my little girl. If something happened to you--"

"Nothing's going to happen to me."

"Yes, you're a know-it-all twenty-something," he remarked with a defeated sigh. "I'm sure your invincibility button will protect you from harm."

Casey laughed at him, kissed his cheek, and offered a warm smile. "That's right, so stop worrying. I'll be home by midnight as usual."

He attempted to mask his smile with a frown. "Why'd you have to turn out so much like your mother?"

Casey laughed softly. "Why does she always say I'm too much like you?"

"Well, you know your mother," he replied. "She likes to believe she's a lady. There's a side of her no one would believe if I told them."

"Wow," Casey teased. "Between you and Mom, it's amazing Grey and I turned out so normal."

"Real funny, young lady."

Casey mounted her horse, saluted him, and rode away. Brandon stared after her, smiled, and shook his head.

Chapter Four

The two-story tavern was located in a clearing along a back road just outside town. It resembled an old farmhouse that had been converted into a bar and was often mistaken for a bed and breakfast. It was around nine o'clock that night, and the tavern appeared alive with activity. The dirt parking lot was already filled with mainly pick-up trucks. There was a long, sturdy hitching post alongside the building with several horses tied to it. Casey's gray horse was among them. The town was small enough and rural enough that horses were a common mode of transportation, particularly among drunk patrons. Most times, the horses would get their intoxicated riders home safely. On some occasions, the horses would make the journey back alone and some poor drunken cowboy wannabe would wake up in a field somewhere. Country music was heard pulsating through the walls from within the tavern. The rustic interior reflected the farming lifestyle of the town. The old, hardwood dance floor was crowded with men and women line dancing to the country music.

The tavern was a multi-purpose entertainment complex. There were those who came to dance the night away, while others came to drink, socialize, and pick up overnight companionship, and still others who came to play pool, darts, and make a few side bets. Waitresses dressed in jeans and low-cut tops hustled pitchers of beer to the filled tables within the smoky rooms. There were several pool tables in the back that seemed to remain filled throughout the night. The crowd varied in age from early twenties to late sixties. There was always something for everyone at the tavern. Grey busily tended bar and seemed to enjoy the excitement of it. Grey, like Casey, had attended college, but lost interest in his major after his second year. He took time off from college to reconsider his major and lacked enthusiasm to return. With their father's intent to run for mayor, Grey assumed he'd take over at the antique store to help his mother. Casey unenthusiastically put in her time just to appease their parents. Someone had to take over, so Grey appointed himself.

A moderately attractive waitress in her twenties, Melanie Ridgeway, waited for Grey to refill her pitchers of beer. Melanie, the mayor's daughter, seemed out of place as a waitress in the smoke-filled tavern. With the sort of money her family had, it didn't seem as if she needed to work. Abby certainly couldn't approve of her daughter waiting tables in a bar, so her reason for working there remained a mystery to most. A handsome deputy in his late twenties, Deputy Tucker Kennedy, approached Melanie from behind, spun her in his arms, and kissed her quickly on the lips. Tucker had been labeled the town stud the last five years running, so it was no surprise that he dated Melanie, being from what was considered one of the most prestigious families in Darwood Falls. She pulled away while smiling and smoothed his deputy's uniform.

"Hey, handsome," Melanie announced while grinning. "What brings you here? I thought you were working tonight."

"I just thought I'd pop in quick and say hello," he announced then smiled with a lustful grin. "I'm off at six A.M. Leave the back door open for me?"

Melanie appeared to consider playfully then grinned. "I'll be off at two." She pressed against him and ran her hands along his uniform. "Maybe you could slip away for half an hour or so."

He grinned and was obviously pleased with the idea. "Vaughn's working tonight," Tucker offered. "He's not much for radio chatter and probably won't miss me."

"Hmm, then I'll leave the light on for you," she cooed. "Just don't let my mother catch you sneaking in."

"Are you kidding?" he announced cheerfully. "Your mother loves me. It's your father I worry about."

"Then you have nothing to worry about, because he loves you too," she remarked while grinning.

"I can't wait," he replied to her enthusiasm. "I'll see you later."

They kissed passionately and with a little too much aggression. Casey and Dina sat at the bar and watched the exchange. Casey rolled her eyes. Tucker finally pulled away from Melanie, grinned, and left the crowded tavern. Dina watched Tucker leave while staring dreamily.

"What I wouldn't give for one night with that man--" Dina said to Casey with a soft sigh.

"I can't believe you're in love with the town stud," Casey scoffed while shaking her head.

Dina looked at her and appeared insulted. "I can't believe you're not."

It wasn't that there was anything wrong with Tucker; Casey just didn't care for men who spread the joy of themselves with every attractive woman in town. Most of the men in town were farm boys looking for just one woman to settle down with and raise a family. It was a bit old-fashioned, but she preferred that to the alternative. Casey wasn't actually sure how she felt about the whole marriage and motherhood gig. Maybe she needed the right man to come into her life. Melanie collected her filled tray from Grey and hurried away from the bar. Grey approached his sister and Dina, leaned on the bar near them, and grinned deviously.

"Is Dina drooling over Deputy Tucker again?" Grey asked.

Dina smirked her disapproval to his teasing. "You're just jealous because half the women in town want him."

"Damned right," Grey replied and straightened. "There should be a law against one man having that many women chasing him."

"I think I left something in my car," Dina announced.

"Sure you did," Casey said with a laugh.

Dina hurried across the tavern and nearly ran out the door after Tucker. Casey disapproved of Dina's current secret crush. If it wasn't bad enough that she wanted anything to do with a man Melanie was involved with, it was almost sinful for her best friend to be in love with the town stud. He'd been passed around so many times; it was almost disgusting.

Grey again leaned on the bar, looked at Casey, and grinned lustfully. "So, is Dina spending the night?"

"She does most Friday nights," Casey replied then suddenly looked at him suspiciously. "Why? Are you wondering what time you need to get up to see her running around in her tank top and panties?"

Grey's sudden and perverse interest in Dina was borderline annoying. Neither of them was very good with relationships, and the last thing she needed or wanted was her best friend dating her brother. When they broke up, which would eventually happen, it would make things awkward for everyone.

"She wants me to look," Grey informed her.

Casey stared at him and appeared stunned by the comment. "You're sick. She thinks of you as her brother."

"Yeah, her very horny brother."

"She doesn't do it to turn you on," Casey protested. "Her parents are non-existent. She sees us as her family."

Grey straightened and frowned at his sister. "You're no fun." He then appeared more serious. "You realize you have about two hours before the Harford boys show up and start their reign of terror."

"Yeah, but they're not usually drunk until midnight. That's why we always leave by then."

"I'm glad that fancy college degree is good for something."

Dina entered the tavern, approached them at the bar, and appeared depressed. "Missed him."

Casey refrained from commenting. "I see a pool table opening up," she announced. "Let's snag it before someone else does."

She groaned and shook her head. "What's with you and playing pool? There are other things to do here."

"Yeah, we could get drunk," Casey announced. "Unfortunately, neither of us drinks."

"I have good reason," Dina muttered and looked across the bar to a corner table.

Casey didn't bother looking and refrained from comment. A woman roughly in her forties, although much older in appearance, sat with her back to the wall while huddled over her usual scotch on the rocks on the table before her. She appeared so drunk that she was nearly comatose. Her once gorgeous, long blonde hair was rumpled, and her dark make-up screamed 'rent by the hour'. When Dina finally looked away with disgust, Casey cast a glance at the pitiful woman and frowned. The pitiful woman was Dina's mother, Olivia. A once beautiful woman, Olivia was driven to the brink by her cheating husband. Undeniably a tragedy, Olivia made her own choice to give up on life and her daughter. Perhaps a more caring person would feel sorry for her, but Casey couldn't. She nearly destroyed Dina with her own misery. Now she just drank herself into oblivion and occasionally traded her body for a few drinks. Most nights she passed out at her table and remained there until morning.

"So I guess that leaves playing pool," Casey remarked to Dina while brushing off the image of her best friend's pathetic shell of a mother.

"We could always dance," Dina commented and already seemed to forget about her mother.

"Okay, first, it's country music," Casey informed her. "Ewe. Second, I don't dance and certainly not in front of other people."

"I've seen you dance," Grey commented from behind the bar.

He received a sharp look from Casey. "No one asked you."

"You know, I remember putting on a show once for some of your father's military--"

Casey glared at Dina. "I don't dance."

Dina made a face while looking at Grey and pointed at Casey, as if to say 'how about this one?'

Grey grinned enthusiastically. "I dance," he announced and did a little dance behind the bar. It was actually quite awful.

Dina's grimace told her feelings. "Hmm, I wouldn't exactly call that dancing."

Grey rolled his eyes and extended his hand to Casey for her usual comment.

She immediately took her cue and responded with, "Like a cat coughing up a hairball."

He shook his head. "Why did I have to have a sister?"

Chapter Five

It was a little after ten o'clock that night. Casey and Dina played pool in the back along with a few other patrons. The mood was genuinely upbeat and friendly. Casey and Dina appeared to be having a good time joking with each other while playing their game. Four men ranging from their early to late twenties entered the pool area in a bustle of commotion, causing the mood of the entire room to change drastically. The four men were the infamous Harford boys, Wayne, Ryan, Blain, and Fred. They laughed loudly, talked dirty, and joked around inappropriately with the other patrons. The few other women who were in the backroom made a hasty departure almost immediately. Several men appeared disgusted shortly thereafter and left rather than confront the four. It was almost sinful how no one in town was willing to stand up to them. They were even above the law. Wayne and Ryan took the recently vacated pool table that had mysteriously opened. Casey and Dina glanced at the terror train that was the Harford boys. Both women exchanged looks and appeared disgusted.

"Ten o'clock. They're early," Casey muttered.

"They're also bombed," Dina added while casting a stray glare at the four repulsive men. "Do you want to leave?"

"No, we're going to finish our game," she replied. "We can't let them intimidate us, or they've already won."

"More words of wisdom from your father?"

"Actually, from his mildly psychotic military buddy," Casey replied. She appeared to consider. "I suppose that doesn't help my case much, huh?"

"No, but you're absolutely right," Dina replied. "Someone has to stand up to them." She sighed softly. "I just wish it didn't have to be us."

Ernest's four sons were tall and built like college linebackers. None were overly muscular nor excessively round. Ryan would probably be considered the 'pretty boy' of the group. He was reasonably attractive with shorter hair that he'd actually taken time to comb. He was also the only one who had taken time to shave that day. The others appeared unshaven for days or longer. Although none dressed to impress, Ryan made an attempt with moderately clean jeans free from holes and a shirt with few wrinkles and stains. Wayne was the undisputed leader. He was the loudest and had the foulest mouth. His hair was unkempt and nearly to his shoulders. Although sometimes the style of young men, his hair was long out of laziness. He had a day or more growth of stubble on his moderately creepy face. Casey wasn't sure if it was his beady, little eyes or his twisted smile that created the creepy effect. His slightly tattered, moderately stained jeans and wrinkled, torn shirt screamed hillbilly. The only thing missing from his ensemble was the bib overalls and a banjo strumming "Dueling Banjos" in the background.

Blain and Fred were bottom feeders. Void of their own personalities, they fed off their two dominant brother's insolence and reacted accordingly. If separated from the pack, they would almost be considered tolerable. An odd odor wafted from the four men. At times, there were often strange odors from the good old boys hanging out in the tavern, but it was usually a farming smell. With the Harford boys, it was an unidentified cross between body odor, cheap cigars, and what could only be described as fungal stench. It was a repulsive combination, and in confined quarters, the fumes could potentially be lethal.

Within twenty minutes, the four boys managed to clear the entire backroom without trying. Casey and Dina were all that remained in the room, which being alone with those boys was never in any woman's best interest. Wayne and Ryan stared at the two women and grinned most sinister. Neither woman gave them a second look. It was a repulsive feeling of being mentally undressed by the most loathsome of creatures. One of the young waitresses, Jeannie, entered the back with their pitcher of beer. They taunted and flirted with her as if she was their personal plaything. It was nearly impossible for her to avoid their groping hands. She obviously wanted nothing to do with them and managed to pull away, which infuriated them even more. Casey had heard stories from Grey about their treatment of the waitresses, Melanie being the exception, since she was related to them. It seemed surprising that their taunting and groping never led to something worse. Casey wondered if they just never took it that far or if they did and it just went unreported. Others who had complained about the Harford boys were met with protest when it came to actually pressing charges. That's where the law fell short. Sheriff Wiley was at the top of that corruption chain. It was a pick your poison sort of deal. Even if charges were pressed, Ernest would somehow pull strings to get them off and then the victim would be made to suffer.

"See if you get a tip, bitch," Ryan scoffed at poor Jeannie, who'd already had most of her body fondled by each of the four at that point.

Jeannie hurried from the pool area without a word. It seemed obvious she didn't care about getting a tip from them. Dealing with human debris such as the Harford boys couldn't be easy for the young, moderately attractive woman. Casey glared at Ryan and his cheap, perverse grin. She couldn't get over her feeling of detest for him and his brothers. She never knew it was possible to loathe another human being that much. And what was that damned smell? Wayne caught her disapproving glare, stared back at her, and appeared humored by her look.

"I'm sorry about my brother's language," Wayne said with a chuckle. "He didn't know there was a virgin present."

Dina immediately tensed. She no longer wanted to be there. Casey glared at Wayne with a cold stare and didn't take her eyes off him. She knew she was inviting trouble and that her father would be disappointed that she didn't steer clear of the infamous boys, but something inside her wouldn't allow her to back down. Wayne appeared to tense from the strange way she stared at him then laughed and returned to his game. Oddly enough, she had intimidated him! Her small victory empowered her. Casey finally dismissed the four mad dogs and focused her attention on her game with her friend. They briefly exchanged looks. Dina's concerned look told her she was ready to leave.

"Last game," Casey informed her softly, having read her thoughts.

Dina appeared grateful and moved between the two pool tables to line up her next shot. Wayne studied her buttocks as she was bent over. He slid the thick end of his pool stick between her legs, grazed her crotch, and moaned mockingly. Dina jumped with a startled gasp and spun toward them with a look of surprise and anger. All four snickered and smirked.

"Knock it off!" Dina cried out.

Casey glared at the four loathsome men then shook her head with disgust. It wasn't the first time Dina had been groped by one of the Harford boys. For a woman, turning your back on any of them was a serious mistake. The four seemed to be on their worst behavior tonight. The fact that they were mostly drunk didn't help their charming dispositions any. Casey and Dina attempted to finish their game without giving the appearance of rushing it along. They played for a few more minutes before the four men start making dirty comments and suggestive remarks while jokingly grabbing their own crotches. Dina became increasingly tense while Casey became more agitated. It was a bad situation brewing. Casey eyed an easy shot from the far end of the pool table. She hesitated and reconsidered. Something at that moment snapped inside her head. She wasn't sure if it was her mother or her father in her coming out, but she opted for the more aggressive move. Casey went for the shot between the two tables closest to the Harford boys, placing her back to them, which was something she never did, and leaned over to make her shot. She wasn't just setting up one shot but two. Wayne moved behind her, grabbed her hips, and grinded against her with a groan. Casey suddenly thrust the butt of her pool stick back and into Wayne's groin, dropping him to his knees. Two ball corner pocket. She'd succeeded on making her first shot. She turned toward them with the pool stick aggressively clutched in her hands and glared at the three standing men. She was well aware of the repercussion that was certainly about to follow.

"You bitch!" Ryan shouted and leapt for her.

Casey swung the pool stick for his head with intent to drop him. Ryan caught the pool stick just short of his head and backhanded her across the face. He slammed her backwards against the pool table. Dina appeared alarmed and ran for the opening to the bar area. Blain caught her around the waist and held her against him from behind while laughing. Dina fought Blain's hold and attempted to keep his hands from grasping her breasts as he grinded his hips against her backside.

"Grey!" Dina cried out across the noisy bar.

While pinning Casey against the pool table, Ryan grinned lustfully, grabbed her hair, and roughly kissed her on the mouth. He suddenly tensed and broke off the kiss with a gasp. Casey stared at him through narrow eyes as her hand clamped with a vice-like grip on his crotch. She stared into his horrified eyes with a cold and almost psychotic look and straightened as he began to sink. Fred bolted toward them as Ryan was halfway to the floor. Casey released Ryan as Fred swung his pool stick at her. She dodged the stick, causing it to strike the pool table with a loud clatter behind her. In the distance, Grey was seen leaping over the bar and pushed through the crowd.

"Get your hands off them!" Grey shouted as he ran for them, alerting the entire bar.

A crowd quickly followed Grey. Casey darted away from the table as Fred leapt for her. She turned and karate kicked him in the ribs, knocking him backward. He tumbled over Ryan and crashed to the floor. Wayne finally returned to his feet and grabbed Casey from behind, partially subduing her. Grey repeatedly punched Blain in the back, kidney area until he finally released Dina. Dina jumped away from Blain and kicked him in the shin. Blain jumped in pain and turned toward Grey, who was about to hit him again. Blain punched him in the abdomen then across the face, sending him into the gathering crowd. Within seconds, half the tavern was throwing punches, chairs, and beer bottles. Glass was heard shattering, women screamed, and chairs broke. Casey continued her struggle to break free from Wayne's bear hug from behind. She aggressively threw herself to one knee and catapulted him over her shoulder. Wayne harshly struck the floor and gasped with agony. As Casey moved to her feet, Ryan suddenly appeared before her and backhanded her across the face. She fell backwards and onto the pool table. He attempted to jump on top of her with intent to harm. Casey used her leverage from the pool table to kick him in the chest and threw him backwards into several fighting men, knocking several to the floor. Sirens were heard in the near distance.

"Cops are coming!" someone yelled.

The few people who heard the sirens scattered. People screamed as the three deputies and Sheriff Wiley entered. Few of the fighting patrons in the back saw them arrive. Grey leapt onto Blain's back and punched him on the back on the head. Blain slung Grey from his back, turned toward him, and punched him in the mouth. Grey was thrown roughly into a nearby chair. Dina saw the deputies in the next room. Grey was about to leap to his feet to rejoin the fight when Dina jumped on his lap, knocking him back into the chair, and kissed him. Grey appeared surprised but returned the kiss regardless. Wayne lunged for Casey. Casey kicked for his groin. He deflected the kick, and she struck his thigh instead, nearly knocking him over from the force. Fred appeared alarmed and pulled Wayne away.

Someone grabbed Casey's arm from behind. She turned and punched Vaughn in the mouth. Vaughn appeared momentarily dazed then glared at her. Those still remaining within the tavern appeared to fall suspiciously silent. Casey gasped and covered her mouth. She couldn't believe she'd hit Deputy Holt!

"I am so sorry--"

Vaughn grabbed Casey's wrist, spun it behind her back, and tossed her across the pool table while handcuffing her. His aggressiveness surprised her. She honestly didn't think he had that much fight in him.

"That's striking a police officer."

"Come on," Casey protested from her forward position across the pool table as he placed the cuffs on her behind her back. "I barely even hit you."

She knew that was a lie. She'd given him a good shot. She was actually surprised he was still standing. If he hadn't been handcuffing her, she'd almost be impressed. Vaughn pulled Casey up from the pool table and spun her to face him. She stared at the wildly unpredictable look in his eyes and his bleeding mouth. She felt both concerned and bad at the same time. Tucker and Mitchell were already taking others out in handcuffs. Most of the bar had cleared out in only a few minutes. Sheriff Wiley approached Vaughn and Casey with a look of surprise. Dina remained on Grey's lap as both watched in silence. There was no way this was ending well.

"What's going on here?" Wiley demanded in a gruff tone.

"She struck a police officer," Vaughn informed him and dabbed the bleeding cut on the corner of his mouth.

"By accident," Dina chimed in. "Wayne started it."

Wiley glanced around the backroom with a curious look. "Where's Wayne?" he asked.

"He slipped out the back while Deputy Holt was handcuffing Casey," Grey retorted with hostility.

Dina firmly squeezed his arm to silence him. He didn't need to get himself arrested as well. It would serve no purpose.

Wiley suddenly glared at Vaughn with surprise. "You let Wayne get away so you could arrest a little girl?"

Vaughn appeared stunned by Sheriff Wiley's comment then turned defensive. "She's not a little girl, and she's the one who threw the punch."

"It was an accident. I said I was sorry," Casey announced. It was true; she actually felt bad about it. "You hurt me worse when you threw me on the pool table to cuff me." She knew she deserved it, but she didn't need to be arrested tonight. Her parents' lecturing her echoed through her thoughts.

"You threw her on the pool table?" Wiley suddenly demanded while glaring at Vaughn.

"I was handcuffing her--"

Wiley eyed the bruises on Casey's face and immediately appeared sympathetic. He shook his head with disgust. "Looks like she's been roughed up enough for one night. Take those cuffs off, give her a ride home, and get out on that road and catch some drunk drivers." Apparently, Wiley didn't take Abby's threat seriously.

Vaughn appeared disgusted and removed the handcuffs as Wiley walked away to patrol the tavern. Casey rubbed her wrists and avoided looking at Vaughn. She felt bad, but she didn't want him to know just how bad. Vaughn smirked with contempt and extended his hand in the direction of the door.

"After you, princess," Vaughn scoffed with a sneer on his handsome face.

"What about my horse?"

Vaughn obviously wasn't in the mood to deal with her now. "Your brother can take your horse home," he growled.

"I can?" Grey suddenly questioned from his chair with a look of horror on his face.

"Move it," Vaughn snapped at Casey.

Chapter Six

*T*he police blazer drove along a dark, isolated stretch of road leading away from town. Darwood Falls was usually a fairly quiet, conservative town. Being mostly farmers, a lot of residents were in bed by the time the sun went down. Most speeders on the back road were usually non-locals just passing through. The isolated back roads encouraged aggressive drivers to joyride at frightening speeds. The woods and sudden curves often caused navigational problems for those unfamiliar with the roads and usually left cars in ditches, head on into trees, or a mangled mess of metal and fiberglass at the bottom of the infamous ravine. Three or more times a year, a car would fail to negotiate the curve, plow through the guardrail, and plummet into the ravine below. One out of three times, the car turned into a fireball, but in all cases, the driver never survived. Patrolling the road late at night saved lives and brought in massive amounts in fines to their town. Vaughn drove his police cruiser while Casey pouted in the back behind the mesh partition. She painfully flexed her hand then shook it.

"I think I broke my hand," she remarked simply to no one in particular.

"Good."

She glared at the back of his head with annoyance. He was very infuriating for someone so handsome. "Wayne started it," she retorted with irritation.

"And what did Wayne do?" he suddenly demanded to know while glaring back at her through the mirror.

Casey frowned while sulking. "Forget it."

The Harford boys were above the law. Everyone knew that. Ernest Harford was Mrs. Mayor's brother. Anything they did was swiftly swept under the carpet. Corruption ran rampant in their otherwise friendly little town. The last thing she wanted or needed was to recount Wayne and Ryan's sexual advances toward her and Dina to Deputy Holt. Casey collapsed against the seat with disgust and stared out the window. She suddenly appeared concerned and sat up straight.

"This isn't the way to my house."

"The sheriff said to take you home and patrol the road," Vaughn announced. "He didn't say in what order."

It was just a little before eleven when Vaughn pulled the blazer into a small cove alongside the road within the woods and placed it in park. Casey stared at the back of his head with a shocked look. For a brief moment, she wondered if Vaughn intended to murder her and ditch her body in the woods. He seemed a little moodier than usual tonight. Maybe that was her fault. When he didn't make a motion to draw his weapon or get out of the car, she realized she'd seen one too many horror films.

"You're seriously going to keep me locked up in here while you patrol your speed trap?" she lashed out.

"Yep."

"Sheriff Wiley is going to hear about this," she scoffed.

"I'm just a dumb, hick cop following orders," he informed her. "How about some music?" Vaughn turned on the radio that played country music.

Casey appeared horrified to the music coming from the radio. "Oh, come on. Not country music," she suddenly protested. "This is cruel and unusual punishment." She collapsed against the backseat and groaned with disgust.

Vaughn strummed the steering wheel in rhythm with the drumming in the song. Casey rolled her eyes. At least he wasn't singing. He then sang the refrain purposely out of tune. She cast a glare at the back of his head. For a moment, she swore he was smiling at her in the rearview mirror.

✝

*I*t was 11:30 P.M., and it had been half an hour since the tavern was cleared out by Darwood Falls' finest. The four Harford boys hung out in the dark woods not far from the tavern. Fred kept watch on the road barely visible through the woods while Ryan, Wayne, and Blain rubbed various body parts in response to the pain Casey had inflicted upon them. In Blain's case, it was pain Grey had inflicted.

"I'm going to kill that bitch," Wayne scoffed and cast his back against a nearby tree. He immediately regretted the action and rubbed his back.

Ryan gingerly rubbed his crotch several times and remained uncomfortable. "Stand in line," he groused without taking his hand from his crotch. "Damn it, I can't feel my balls. That bitch dug her claws into them and almost ripped them off."

"I guess daddy's been teaching them a thing or two from his military days," Blain scoffed and rubbed his head. "That prick, Grey, didn't hit that hard, but he knew *where* to hit."

"She's not getting away with it," Wayne growled and straightened with discomfort. "I'll get even with that bitch."

"Better make sure she doesn't see you coming," Ryan remarked and again tugged at his crotch. "Son-of-a-bitch! I think she did rip them off!"

"I think we're clear," Fred said from his position overlooking the road. He'd somehow managed to avoid taking a beating like his brothers. He was either smarter than he looked or less aggressive than he pretended. "Sheriff Wiley just left."

"We'll wait a few more minutes then go back for the truck," Wayne muttered.

†

*O*t was now close to midnight, and it had been an hour since Vaughn parked in his speed trap with Casey locked in the back of the police blazer. Casey was now slouched in the backseat while staring at the ceiling with boredom. She couldn't believe he was holding firm on his ridiculous punishment. She knew he had it out for her, but she swore he was getting some sort of perverse pleasure out of detaining her like this. She wanted to say something, but she couldn't think of anything that would help her situation--only make things worse. She had a few choice names she was just dying to call him at that moment. She bit her tongue and attempted to play it cool. She couldn't let him know he was winning. Vaughn held a crossword puzzle book in his hand and thoughtfully tapped his pen to his lips.

"What's a seven letter word for fried batter? Begins with an 'f'," Vaughn asked while deep in thought.

"Fucker--" Casey muttered.

Vaughn casually consulted his crossword puzzle with a serious look. "Hmm? No, that's six letters."

Casey screamed in her mind. She couldn't believe she actually thought he was cute when he was first hired. She sneered while staring at his profile in the front seat. He actually was cute, and it irritated her to no end. She was almost glad she hit him now. She refrained from expressing those feelings as well. In her current situation, pissing him off could still result in him killing her, dismembering her body, and scattering body parts throughout the woods. Casey grimaced at her own morbid thoughts. She sort of doubted Deputy Holt was the serial killer type. She again glanced at his profile. Vaughn was too much of a Boy Scout for that. She was quickly running out of ways to entertain herself mentally.

✝

*T*he empty tavern was filled with broken bottles, overturned tables, broken chairs, and food carelessly scattered about the floor. It was just a little after midnight. Grey evaluated the scattered chairs and replaced those that weren't broken. Melanie and Jeannie cleaned up the broken glass.

"Well this sucks," Melanie scoffed.

"At least we get to go home early," Jeannie replied with little enthusiasm.

"Yeah, after doing twice the clean-up and zero tips," she huffed.

Melanie glared at Grey's back several times and sneered with disgust at their situation. Jeannie dumped glass from her dustpan into the bag near Melanie, who still glared at Grey.

"It's all his fault," Melanie snapped lowly, catching Jeannie's attention.

Jeannie uncertainly glanced at Grey, who replaced one of the tables then looked back at Melanie. "How is it his fault?" she asked. "He was just defending his sister."

Melanie rolled her eyes, groaned softly, and glared at Jeannie, who now collected unbroken bottles from the floor. "Casey obviously did something to provoke them."

Jeannie straightened and glared at Melanie, who appeared almost clueless. "Stop defending your cousins, Mel," she snapped. "Thanks to those illegitimate perverts, I have bruises on my ass and my boobs."

She gave Jeannie a quick once over and sneered in response. "With the way you dress, of course they're going to make passes at you," Melanie remarked. "Men want to see cleavage. It gets us better tips. You have to expect some harmless flirting."

"Harmless flirting?" Jeannie nearly exploded. "Copping a feel is not harmless flirting, and this goes way beyond just copping a feel!"

"You're such a drama queen," Melanie scoffed lowly and walked away.

Jeannie stared after her with surprise.

†

*W*ayne and his brothers emerged from the woods near the tavern just moments later and crossed the parking lot. Ryan suddenly stopped and stared at the gray horse tied to the hitching post by itself. A devious grin crossed Ryan's face.

"Wayne," he called up ahead.

The three brothers turned and looked back at Ryan. He deviously indicated the tied horse. All three approached and stared at Storm, who appeared to be lazily dozing.

"That's Casey's horse, right?" Ryan announced.

Wayne suddenly grinned and slapped Ryan on the arm. He grimaced with discomfort. Obviously, that was sore as well. Blain and Fred were a little slow catching on to the conversation.

"What's the plan?" Blain asked.

"I think a bucket of anti-freeze," Wayne replied with a sinister grin.

"That'll kill the horse," Fred protested.

The three boys looked at their brother and raised their brows while grinning.

"No shit," Ryan replied.

"That's going a little too far," Fred remarked. "We're not killing the horse."

"Yeah, and where would we get anti-freeze this time of night?" Blain replied with a defeated sigh.

"Fine," Wayne scoffed, "we won't kill the horse. We'll untie it and chase it off."

"That's better," Fred said.

Ryan approached the horse, which now woke up and watched him. He untied the reins from the hitching post and threw them over the horse's neck. Storm looked back at the wall before him and propped his back foot without a care. All four stared at the horse.

"How do we make him move?" Blain asked.

"Don't they yell 'yah' or some shit?" Ryan asked.

"Ah, hell," Wayne snorted. "You just hit them on the ass."

Wayne smacked Storm on the rump. The horse snorted and tossed his head. His ears pinned in response.

"Well, that really worked," Ryan remarked.

"We need to hit it with something," Wayne announced then looked around.

He grabbed a thick branch and approached the horse from behind. As he raised the branch, Storm snorted and kicked Wayne in the abdomen. Wayne was thrown to the ground, clutching his abdomen, and writhing in agony.

"Stupid horse!" Ryan cried out and swung his fist for the horse's nose.

Storm's ears suddenly pinned back as he lunged for Ryan's arm. The horse bit his forearm. Ryan cried out, jumped away from the horse, and clutched his arm.

"Shit!" Ryan cried out. "The fucking horse bit me!"

Without warning, Storm lunged for the four men with his teeth bared and his hooves thrashing. As his large head swung wildly, all four boys scattered. They ran for their truck with the horse in pursuit. All four jumped inside the truck. The truck started. Storm spun around and kicked the passenger side door with his back hooves, causing a large dent. The truck burned out in reverse, turned, and sped away. Storm snorted then returned to the hitching post at a leisurely walk.

†

Another hour had passed, now a little after 1:00 A.M., and it was nearly two hours Vaughn had kept Casey locked in the back of his patrol blazer. Casey sat on the backseat floor with her head against the mesh divider and her bare feet propped against the backseat. Vaughn appeared to be sleeping while slumped in his seat. From her position on the floor, she could see his profile. He was only a few inches from her where he slept. For a moment, she actually thought he looked almost innocent while asleep. She couldn't help but wonder what it was that her mother liked so much about him. Did her mother think Deputy Holt was good looking? Is that why she secretly hoped he'd become sheriff when Wiley retired?

That was a creepy thought. The radio continued to play soft country music. Casey sang softly to the romantic song on the radio. Vaughn opened his eyes and listened as she sang. A tiny smile crossed his face, although she couldn't see it.

"I thought you hated country music?"

Casey suddenly silenced. "I thought you were asleep," she muttered softly. She didn't exactly hate Deputy Holt, but it seemed as if they were always at each other's throats. Casey was sure her mother couldn't be right. She had been nice to him in the past, but it didn't alter the way he treated her. Perhaps she should use her confinement to ask the question finally. "Why do you have it out for me?"

"I don't have it out for you," he announced simply. "You're a spoiled little girl who gets coddled when what she really needs is a good spanking."

His words floored her, causing her to turn slightly on her hip and stare at his profile. His face was only inches from hers through the partition. Since when was she a spoiled, little girl? Melanie was spoiled. She found his comment insulting but quickly masked her hostility.

"Huh? Okay," she remarked gently. "You wanting to spank me is a little disturbing."

Vaughn glared his disapproval at her through the partition. She stared into his eyes a moment and suddenly felt uncomfortable being that close to him. She'd never actually looked into his eyes before. She'd never seen such dark eyes. Casey looked away, moved to the seat, and faced forward. Vaughn sat up as well. She was getting tired, and playing games with Deputy Holt was unsatisfying.

"What time is it?" she asked with a weary sigh.

"Almost one."

Casey groaned softly and rolled her eyes. It was ridiculous that he had kept her there so long. There were laws against kidnapping, although she wasn't sure if they applied to Darwood Falls' finest. Deputy Holt seemed to enjoy making up his own rules. She remained uncomfortable and still felt his eyes upon her. She glanced at him. He was staring at her through the rearview mirror with those dark eyes. She felt her entire body tense and shifted with discomfort.

"Grey will be home a little after two. If he gets home and I'm not there, he's going to call Sheriff Wiley."

"I don't care what you tell Sheriff Wiley."

Casey placed her bare feet against the mesh divider, played with the grates with her toes, and frowned while staring out the side window into the darkness. Vaughn continued to study her through the mirror. She was feeling particularly self-conscious now. She wished he'd stop staring at her.

"I don't intend to tell him anything. I wouldn't want to get you fired," Casey said gently. "You're probably the only honest cop in this messed up town. I hit you, and you had every right to be mad. Sheriff Wiley shouldn't berate you for doing your job."

There was an odd silence. Vaughn straightened in his seat and started the blazer.

"I should get you home."

Casey quickly sat up with renewed enthusiasm. She was surprised by his sudden change of mind. Had he waited all that time for an apology? She had said she was sorry right after she hit him. It didn't make sense. She decided not to overthink it. It was late, and she was tired.

"Can you take me back for my horse?"

"Your brother was told to take your horse home," he informed her.

"He doesn't ride in the dark. There was that whole bat incident--"

Vaughn groaned with disgust. "Fine, but I'm driving by your place to make sure you went directly home," he remarked sternly and again looked at her through the mirror with his dark eyes.

"If I'm not there, you have my permission to spank me," she teased.

Vaughn appeared stunned while staring at her through the mirror. She caught his look and chuckled softly. She was proud of herself; she'd rendered the Boy Scout speechless.

†

*I*t was almost 1:30 A.M. when Grey's car pulled up to the Remington farmhouse. He was almost an hour earlier than usual, since the barroom brawl shut them down early. There was a light on at the house and one above the barn. Grey got out of his car looking nearly exhausted and slightly battered from his impromptu bout with Blain Harford. He glanced at the barn as he headed for the house and suddenly stopped. Casey's horse wasn't in the pasture with the others. If her horse had been outside the tavern, he hadn't seen it. If he was honest with himself, he hadn't actually looked. He appeared curious as he stared then frowned and shook his head.

"You'd better believe Sheriff Wiley's going to hear about this," Grey scoffed then headed for the house.

He unlocked the door and entered with disgust. The kitchen was dimly lit by the light above the stove, which his mother usually left on for him upon returning late at night. He heard his parents' moving around in their room upstairs. It seemed odd that they would be up so late. They were used to his late hours at the tavern and never waited up anymore. Perhaps his father realized Casey never made it home. As long as his father was up, there was no reason not to share another story of corrupt law enforcement with him. His father would also cause more of a commotion with Deputy Holt not returning Casey immediately following Sheriff Wiley's orders. A thought suddenly occurred to Grey. What if Deputy Holt did something to Casey? Vaughn Holt had always been the quiet one. It was those quiet ones who often caused the most trouble. Grey was suddenly concerned for Casey. He needed to alert his father more now than ever. He needed to make sure his sister was okay. He was about to head up the back, kitchen stairs, when he heard his father coming down the living room stairs. Grey hurried across the kitchen for the living room.

Chapter Seven

*I*t was almost 1:45 A.M. by the time Casey rode her horse up the long, gravel driveway to the farmhouse. She had been on autopilot nearly the entire ride home. Storm knew the way to the farm. Horses could always find their way home. She dismounted near the barn, wearily unsaddled her horse, and turned him loose into the paddock. After returning her saddle to the tack room within the barn, she headed toward the house. She couldn't believe how exhausted she was from doing nothing all night. Grey's car was parked out front. She was a little surprised he was home early, but it probably had something to do with the brawl. Thankfully, Grey had left the light on for her. She didn't doubt he was sitting up waiting for her. Despite their differences, Grey could be a little protective over her. With corruption in their town, his protectiveness wasn't surprising. Casey entered the dimly lit kitchen and found it odd that there were no other lights on. Maybe Grey hadn't waited up for her after all. It actually didn't bother her; she was too tired to get into the entire Deputy Holt debate with him tonight anyway.

She had been heading for the backstairs, when she heard a faint thump from the living room. Casey paused by the kitchen steps, looked to the living room archway, and appeared bewildered. Maybe Grey had waited up for her after all. She debated just heading to bed to avoid the long debate that was sure to follow, but thought better of it. He would undoubtedly enter her room, once again without permission, and just disturb her sleep anyway. It was best just to get it out of the way now. She headed across the kitchen and entered the dimly lit living room. Casey suddenly stopped. Grey lie on the floor and was covered in blood. She gasped with horror and ran toward him. He weakly lifted his head and saw her as she approached.

"Casey," he suddenly gasped. "Run!"

Casey slid to a stop halfway to him, spun around, and came face-to-face with a masked intruder holding a large hunting knife. As the intruder raised the knife, Casey screamed and impulsively thrust her palms into his chest, shoving him away from her. The knife slashed her forearm as he stumbled backwards. Casey felt the sting but was almost unaware of her injury as she darted past him. She ran across the kitchen and up the backstairs rather than out the front door. The intruder chased after her and was only a few feet behind. She grabbed a photo from the wall, spun, and struck him with it. The glass shattered against his elbow as he shielded his head. She then planted her foot into his shoulder from her elevated position on the stairs above him, and shoved him down the stairs. He stumbled down a few steps but caught his balance. Casey continued up the stairs with a greater head start now. She bolted into the dark master bedroom, slammed the door, and locked it. She turned while out of breath toward her parents' bed.

"Dad! Someone's in the house!"

There was no response. Fear swept over her as she flipped the light switch on the wall next to the door. Her mother and father were lying partially beneath the blood-soaked covers. Her father appeared to have been stabbed in his sleep with a single stab wound to his neck. Her mother had obviously tried to defend herself, indicated by the cuts to her hands and arms, and was half off the bed. Casey stared at her butchered parents while frozen with fear. For a moment, it didn't seem real. There was a thump against the door, jolting her out of her daze. She ran toward the bed and grabbed the bedside phone near her slain father. There was no dial tone. She cried out while tossing the phone aside then hesitated only a moment before removing a key from the bedside drawer. She ran for the nearby gun cabinet. The door vibrated again. Casey fumbled with the key in trembling hands and unlocked the cabinet as the bedroom doorframe suddenly splintered. She removed a double-barrel shotgun as the door flew open, turned toward the door, and without hesitation, pulled the trigger.

The intruder saw the shotgun and dove out of the room as buckshot from both barrels exploded the door. Casey tossed the shotgun aside and grabbed the .357 Magnum revolver. Her mind had momentarily shut down and she intended to shoot the first thing that moved. When nothing moved, she uncertainly approached the shattered door and steadied the massive gun as it trembled in her hands. There was no one there. She could barely control her heavy breathing as she stepped into the dimly lit hallway. She looked both directions while steadying the gun then hurried along the hall with her back to the wall. She only paused once before her darkened, open bedroom door to peer inside. The sheer curtains fluttered inward from a breeze blowing through the open window. Nothing else moved within the darkened room. She hurried past her bedroom and for the back, kitchen stairs while attempting to make as little sound as possible.

Casey appeared on the backstairs with the gun leveled and her back to the wall. The dimly lit kitchen was empty and nothing moved. She looked at the closed kitchen door with the fear evident on her face. She considered her options only once and darted to the cupboard beneath the sink. She removed a first aid kit and hurried for the living room. She paused within the archway to the living room, looked around for signs of the intruder, and then hurried to Grey's side. She set down the large gun and fumbled through the medical kit.

"I'm here. It's okay," she said softly to him.

Grey's eyes were shut and he didn't move. Casey stared at him with alarm as panic swept over her.

"Grey?"

He didn't respond. Unbeknownst to her, the intruder crept down the main stairs behind her. He made his way quietly down the steps and approached her from behind with the bloody knife clutched in his hand. Although barely noticeable, the faint sound of his leather gloves gripping the knife sounded like a freight train to Casey. Casey suddenly grabbed the gun from the floor alongside her, spun on her hip, and fired wildly at the stairs. The startled intruder leapt behind her father's lounge chair for shelter. Casey stood up, showed no emotion, and fired several shots into the chair. The .357 shells exploded through the chair and one or two shattered the window behind it. The gun clicked empty several times as she continued to squeeze the trigger. She finally gasped and returned from her rage-induced trance. Casey stared at the shredded chair with multiple bullet holes through it. There was no sound or movement. She had gotten him! She took a step toward the torn chair. The intruder suddenly leapt out from behind the chair and tackled her to the floor just past Grey's motionless body. Casey screamed and held back the knife. He grabbed her throat to subdue her. She rammed her knee into his inner thigh, narrowly missing her intended target, and jolted him enough to loosen his grip on her throat. Having momentarily stunned him, she scrambled to her feet and ran into the kitchen.

Casey ran from the house, leaping the four steps from the porch, and raced for the barn with the intruder only a few yards behind her. All the horses were immediately alerted and watched from the pasture. Casey reached the gate and attempted to unlatch it as Storm snorted loudly in panic from several feet away. The intruder roughly tackled Casey to the ground, and they rolled several times. She ended up on top and punched him in his masked face. As she attempted to leap off him, he grabbed her foot and pulled her to her hands and knees. Storm snorted, pinned his ears, and reared up in the paddock. Casey looked at the intruder on the ground behind her holding her ankle and kicked him in the shoulder. She jumped to her feet and again ran for the gate. Storm bolted back and forth before the gate with his head high while snorting loudly. The intruder tackled her roughly into the gate, vibrating it with a loud clatter. Storm's ears were pinned back and his nostrils wrinkled as his teeth bared. Her horse had never shown such aggression before. As the horse lunged forward, the intruder slung Casey roughly to the ground and narrowly avoided the horse's teeth. Casey rolled several times across the ground. She appeared disoriented as she slowly moved to her hands and knees. The man dressed entirely in black approached and kicked her in her side. Casey gasped, clutched her ribs, and nearly fell the rest of the way to the ground.

Storm continued to snort loudly and bolted past the fence. The intruder grabbed Casey's hair and pulled her to her knees. She gasped painfully and looked at the man now standing over her. The sound of thundering hoof beats was all Casey heard. As she looked at the fence, the massive gray horse majestically jumped the tall gate and charged for them. The intruder saw the charging horse, gasped, and released Casey. Storm sideswiped the man with his shoulder and knocked him to the ground while sliding to a skidding stop. The horse pivoted on his hindquarters to face the man on the ground, pinned his ears, squealed loudly, and reared up over the fallen man. The alarmed intruder rolled out of the path of the thrashing hooves as they violently and repeatedly struck the ground in a purposeful attempt to crush him. Her horse had come to her defense, something Casey never would have imagined if she hadn't seen if for herself.

Casey ran for Storm, steadied him as he danced in place, and easily swung onto him bareback. The intruder sprang to his feet as Casey sent the horse into a gallop. The intruder slashed his knife as they passed, slicing Casey's leg and the horse's hindquarters. Storm popped into a buck, thrashed his hind leg in response to the pain, and suddenly reared up, causing Casey to topple off his back. Storm raced down the driveway as blood ran down his leg from the gash. Casey appeared dazed while slowly moving to her hands and knees and watched the horse disappear down the driveway. Her attacker punched her on the side of the head. Casey collapsed to the ground and appeared to be out cold. He slung her over his shoulder and carried her back to the house.

†

It was a little after two o'clock in the morning. The police blazer drove along the dark back road past thick woods and large fields. It was a peaceful, quiet night with just enough humidity to bring about a storm closer to morning. The massive gray horse suddenly galloped onto the paved road in front of the blazer. The police blazer slammed on its brakes and skidded with a loud squeal. The horse reared up in the middle of the road directly in front of the vehicle with blood streaking its hind leg then bolted across the road and continued into the nearby field.

†

The masked attacker carried the motionless Casey into the kitchen and tossed her onto the table. She slowly woke with a look of disorientation. He placed the knife to her throat and grabbed for her jeans. Casey suddenly became alert, gasped with horror, and kicked him in the thigh. She once again missed her intended target. He was thrown backwards all the same, allowing her to leap off the table, and run for the backstairs. The killer knocked her forward into the island counter, spun her to face him, and grabbed her throat. Casey clutched his wrist while she gasped for air. He moved the knife to her pants and attempted to cut off her jeans. With every ounce of strength she had, she punched him in the face. He suddenly thrust the knife into her lower abdomen. Casey gasped from the sharp, excruciating pain of the knife piercing her body and stared into the killer's eyes. The front door suddenly burst open to reveal Deputy Holt with his gun aimed.

"Police! Freeze!"

The intruder turned toward Vaughn with the knife dripping blood still in his hand. He slowly raised his hands preparing to surrender. Casey's knees buckled and she sank while clutching the counter and her bleeding abdomen. Vaughn saw Casey clinging to the counter with her blood-soaked hands and appeared horrified. His look suddenly hardened. He straightened, turned toward the killer, and, without flinching, shot him three times in the chest. The intruder flew backwards through the archway and into the dining room. Vaughn appeared alarmed and ran for Casey. She looked at him with an almost blank expression, gasped painfully, and sank. Vaughn caught her while staring into her eyes with horror, lowered her to the floor, and immediately applied pressure to her lower abdomen while holding her. Casey clutched his neck with her bloodied hands and sobbed.

"He killed them! They're all dead!"

Vaughn stared into her eyes with his mouth hanging open in apparent shock. He fumbled for his words. "An ambulance is coming," he finally gasped. "Just stay with me, okay?"

Casey clung to him, buried her face into his neck, and fell silent. Her blood-covered hand slowly fell down his chest. Vaughn tensed with horror while staring at the motionless woman in his arms.

"Casey? Don't you dare die!" he gasped. Tears streaked his face. "Don't do this to me! Please, Casey, stay with me!"

She didn't respond; just remained limp in his arms. Vaughn held Casey's head to his neck and sobbed softly.

†

Less than thirty minutes had passed, although it seemed longer, before the paramedics raced Casey out of the kitchen on a stretcher. She was completely white and appeared lifeless, although the actions of the paramedics suggested she was still clinging to life. Sheriff Wiley stood alongside Vaughn, who leaned his back against the bloody island counter and stared blankly at the large amount of blood on the floor. His arms, neck, shirt, and pants were also covered in Casey's blood. Vaughn uncertainly looked at the blood on his hands and started to tremble. Wiley placed his hand on Vaughn's shoulder. Vaughn didn't even seem to realize he was standing alongside him.

"You okay?"

For a moment, Vaughn appeared unable to respond. He finally managed a weak, "Yeah, I'm--I'm fine."

Wiley firmly massaged Vaughn's shoulder and weakly smiled. "Let's have a look at our bad guy."

Vaughn uncertainly walked alongside Sheriff Wiley to the dining room archway. The intruder was gone without a trace of blood! Both appeared alarmed as they stared at the emptiness of the dining room.

Vaughn vigorously shook his head and stared through wide, horror-filled eyes. "He went down right there!"

"Are you sure you hit him?" the sheriff asked and seemed reluctant to look at his deputy.

Vaughn suddenly spun to face the sheriff with a frightening look of rage in his eyes. "Three times in the chest--dead center!"

Wiley looked at him from his sudden outburst then appeared to consider. "No blood. Bulletproof vest?"

Vaughn vigorously shook his head and remained unpredictably hostile. "This was no random home invasion," he exploded. "He knew the Remington's were armed!"

"He couldn't have gotten far. We'll find him," Wiley assured him then turned fatherly and sympathetic. "You should go home and rest."

"No, damn it, I want that bastard!"

†

*I*t was a little after four in the morning. Casey's gray horse grazed in a lush field not far from an old, abandoned barn. The house had been torn down years earlier. The barn wasn't in great shape and had seen better days. Blood from the gash saturated the horse's hindquarters and ran down its leg. Storm stomped his hind leg several times while grazing. A police blazer pulled up the overgrown dirt lane and stopped several yards away from the horse. As Vaughn got out of the blazer, Storm lifted his head and looked at the deputy. Vaughn removed a halter and lead rope from the blazer then approached the horse. Storm snorted while watching him. As he got closer, Storm took off across the field. Vaughn, still in his bloodstained uniform, appeared defeated, shook his head, and returned to his blazer.

†

*O*t was five in the morning and the approaching sunrise was overshadowed by storm clouds rolling in. Thunder cracked and lightning flashed. The large gray horse galloped across the field toward the back of the fairgrounds. The faint whinnying of another horse was heard calling out. Storm suddenly slowed while turning toward the distant woods. A horse and rider emerged from the woods. Storm snorted with his head high in the air and pranced a few steps before galloping toward them. The large gray horse slowed before the horse and rider and snickered a long, loud greeting to the other horse, who returned the snickers. They touched noses and snorted their greetings. Vaughn dismounted the mare from the Remington farm and approached Storm with the halter and lead rope. He easily slipped the halter over the horse's head as the two horses continued to snicker and snort to each other. It started raining as he led both horses across the fairgrounds toward the distant arena barn. Moments later, Vaughn approached the large barn with both horses as the rain poured down upon them. A pick-up truck arrived at the barn as he was about to enter. The local veterinarian, Dr. Stein, got out of the truck and hurried toward them and the barn with his medical bag.

Moments later, Vaughn held the gray horse in the barn aisle while Dr. Stein cleaned the gash on its hindquarters. Storm snorted and thrashed his leg in response to the pain. He nearly clipped the vet with his hoof. Vaughn held onto the lead rope and attempted to keep the horse from bolting. Storm reared slightly and nearly pulled Vaughn off his feet. Dr. Stein jumped out of the way while Vaughn attempted to control the panicking horse.

"Whoa, easy, boy," Vaughn said in a soothing tone to the large horse. The horse snorted and tossed his head. Vaughn gently caressed the horse's nose. "It's okay. It's going to be okay."

Dr. Stein watched Vaughn clinging to the horse's head as his forehead touched the horse's forehead. The horse snorted softly in response. The vet patted the horse's neck while producing a syringe. He gently slapped the horse's neck then stuck it with the syringe. The horse barely flinched.

"What was that?" Vaughn asked.

"A horsey Valium," Dr. Stein replied. He drew solution into another syringe, waited a few minutes, and then approached the horse's neck. "Once I give him this, he's going to be heavily sedated. It should last long enough for me to stitch the cut."

The vet inserted the needle into the horse's neck vein and dispensed the contents directly into the horse's bloodstream. Storm's head almost immediately lowered and his large body sagged. Vaughn appeared surprised by the sudden sedation. Dr. Stein cleaned the gash on the horse's hindquarters and shook his head with disgust.

"I'm beyond shocked," Dr. Stein remarked softly. "Who would go after the Remington's like that? Are they really dead?"

Vaughn clung to the horse's lowered head and stroked its forehead. He stared off and didn't answer at first. "There's still no word on Casey's condition," he replied softly. "Last I heard; she was still in emergency surgery." He trembled slightly and drew a shallow breath. "There was so much blood--"

Dr. Stein glanced at the distant look in Vaughn's eyes and the pink stains on his uniform then returned to stitching the gash on the horse's hindquarters. "Do me a favor, Deputy?"

Vaughn gently cleared his throat and came back to life. He sniffed and wiped his tears. "Yeah, sure. What do you want me to do?"

The vet focused on suturing the gash and responded without emotion, "Kill the bastard who murdered the Remington's."

"I thought I did," he replied softly.

Chapter Eight

*T*he rain poured down in the early morning hour, drenching the cemetery grounds. A sea of large, black umbrellas surrounded the three caskets awaiting burial. Casey stood in the pouring rain, her black, leather jacket and jeans soaking wet, as she stared blankly at the three caskets. The reverend was speaking, but his words were inaudible to her. She could hear the voices of others talking over her, but she couldn't make out their words. She heard Dina's voice as she repeatedly said the same thing over and over. Her voice seemed so garbled--so far away. Casey just stared at the caskets and kept thinking this was just some cruel joke being played on her. She had no family; there was no one left. The voices seemed much louder now. She wished everyone would stop talking over her. She just wanted to be left alone with her grief. Images from that godforsaken night kept repeating in her mind--playing out in an endless loop of terror, pain, and tremendous sorrow. She subconsciously rubbed her lower abdomen and felt the gut-wrenching pain as the killer stabbed her. It was over, but it felt so real. She uncertainly looked at her hand. Blood seeped between her fingers as she clutched herself. Casey suddenly gasped and removed her trembling hand from her bleeding abdomen. There was so much blood!

"Don't do this to me!" Deputy Vaughn's voice called out. "Please, Casey, stay with me!"

She lowered her bloodied hand and looked around the cemetery. It was still raining, but everyone was gone. She was now standing alone before the three caskets. She heard Dina's muffled voice still speaking over her. Her voice was louder now and the words were become clearer.

"I'm here for you, Casey," Dina was heard softly speaking over her.

Casey looked around the cemetery as the rain continued to drench her. She could hear Dina, but she couldn't see her. Where was she? She was all alone! She allowed her face to fall into her bloodied hands and sobbed softly. A hand touched hers. She sniffed and looked up. The rain had suddenly stopped. She stared into her father's eyes. He stood before her while holding her hand and smiled reassuringly.

"You're not alone, Casey," he said gently. "I'm here for you. I'll always be here for you."

Casey held back her sobs and squeezed his hand in response. He warmly touched her face then kissed her forehead. Her father pulled back and looked into her eyes.

"You must go with him," he said gently.

She stared into his eyes with bewilderment. "Go with him? Who?"

There was a blinding light. Voices were shouting over her, but she couldn't understand what they were saying. Casey shielded her eyes and watched her father vanish into the light. The light was warm and inviting. Her mother's voice was heard from the other side. Casey smiled and headed toward the light. She wanted to see her mother again; she wanted to hold her and tell her how much she loved her.

"I'm coming, Mom," she cried out while holding back her tears. "I'm here!"

She felt someone grab her hand. She looked behind her to a shadowy figure just outside the light as he clung to her blood covered hand.

"Casey, come back," the male voice cried out.

She stared at the man's outline a long moment and attempted to see his face. She was sure he wasn't her father, but she couldn't make out the voice. There were too many voices shouting over her now. She held his hand but remained confused. The way he held her hand was so comforting, she didn't want to let go.

"Stay with me, Casey," he sobbed softly while clinging to her hand. He sounded so frightened. She squeezed his hand and moved closer to him. "That's it; stay with me."

His voice was now soft and comforting. She listened to his voice while straining to see who he was. It was no use. She couldn't see him. When she looked back, the light had vanished. Her mother and father were gone. She'd lost them again. As she turned, the man holding her hand had also vanished. Dina was now speaking over her. She wanted that man back. She felt so cold and frightened now. She looked around, but she was alone in the cemetery. Dina's voice was now louder and clearer. She was somewhere close by, but she didn't see her.

"I'm here for you, Casey," Dina said gently.

Casey looked around the empty cemetery for her friend. All three caskets were now gone. She was completely alone except for the sound of Dina's voice speaking over her. A strange, repetitive beeping sound caught her attention. What was that sound? Where was it coming from? She again turned. A brilliant bright light shined in her face. She shielded her eyes and blinked almost painfully from the light. Casey slowly opened her eyes and saw Dina hunched over her where she lie. Dina held back her sobs and clung to Casey's hand. Casey uncertainly looked around and realized she was in a bed. It was morning, and the sun was shining on her from the open blinds. Had it all been a dream? Was her family still alive? As she painfully looked around, she could see several lines attached to her and monitors steadily beeped, indicating she was still alive.

"Hey--" Dina said softly with a warm smile although she struggled to keep from crying.

Casey stared at Dina and realized it hadn't been a dream. It was true! Her family was dead! She shut her eyes and sobbed softly. Dina quickly moved onto the bed and gently held her.

"I know. I'm here, Casey," Dina said softly. "It's going to be okay."

She clung to Dina despite the tremendous amount of pain involved. Everything hurt, but she could only think of what had happened to her family. "They're dead, Dina," Casey gasped while sobbing. "My parents and Grey--"

"I'm not dead yet--" Grey gasped softly from nearby.

Casey managed to look past Dina to where Grey lie in the next bed. His eyes were closed and his breathing was shallow, but he was alive! Casey smiled and sobbed tears of joy.

✝

*I*t was a little after seven that morning. There was an urgent pounding on Ernest's front door. Ernest wearily walked down the stairs dressed in his finest, satin pajamas and approached the front door to the unrelenting pounding. The little gray cat rubbed against his legs. He shoved the cat aside with his foot then proceeded for the door, looking exhausted and irritated.

"Yeah, yeah, I'm coming!"

Ernest unlocked and opened the heavy front door to reveal the mayor. Lance stormed into the foyer in a state somewhere between panic and rage.

"What the hell did you do?" Lance exploded while repeatedly running his fingers through his hair as he paced the foyer.

Ernest stared at him with surprise and finally appeared awake. "What are you talking about?"

"What am I talking about? Where the hell have you been all morning?"

"It's barely even morning," Ernest retorted while looking annoyed. "I was sleeping until you started pounding on my door. What happened?"

"What happened? What the hell do you mean by 'what happened'? I didn't want Brandon running for mayor, but I didn't expect you to have him killed!"

"Killed?" Ernest suddenly cried out with astonishment. "Brandon Remington is dead?"

"Brandon and Catherine! And don't act all surprised!" Lance stopped pacing and pointed a warning finger at Ernest. "I have half a mind to call Sheriff Wiley and tell him what you did! Casey and Grey are clinging to life in ICU! I told you not to let them hurt her! How could you do something like that? I--I should shoot you where you stand!"

Ernest stared at Lance with surprise and possible horror to the news. He vigorously shook his head. "I don't know what happened last night, Lance, but I had nothing to do with it."

"No, you had my half-witted nephews do your dirty work!"

"Lance, you need to calm down."

"Calm down? I'm an accessory to murder--double homicide, to be specific!" Lance cried out and again returned to his paranoid state. He once again paced and shook his head. "I won't be a party to this. I have to tell Sheriff Wiley before he calls in a homicide detective. This was not what I meant when I asked for your help!"

"Damn it, Lance, relax!" Ernest shouted.

Lance stopped pacing and turned to face Ernest with a strange look in his eyes. His hostility was quickly replacing his paranoia once again. Ernest took a deep breath and looked into Lance's eyes with a serious expression.

"I had nothing to do with what happened to the Remington's last night," Ernest said firmly. "I swear to you, my boys had nothing to do with killing anyone either. There was a fight at the tavern, the police showed up, and they came home. I swear, Lance, they didn't leave the house after that."

Lance appeared surprised while staring at the sincere look on Ernest's face. "My God, you're telling the truth, aren't you? Neither you nor my nephews had anything to do with what happened at the Remington farm."

"That's what I've been trying to tell you," Ernest announced and appeared to relax, although he was clearly shaken. "My boys aren't killers. You, of all people, should know that."

†

*I*t was later that same afternoon following the night of the brutal slayings at the Remington farm. Casey was partially elevated in bed and stared at her unconscious brother as the nurse checked on him. She'd been watching him nearly all morning, and he hadn't said much since he proclaimed he still lived. She was concerned he wouldn't pull through. The nurses seemed reluctant to tell her his condition. 'He's fine' seemed to be the only answer she got. Since she hadn't seen this nurse earlier, perhaps she'd surrender more information.

"Is he okay," she asked the nurse.

"He's fine," the nurse replied.

Casey wondered if there was something they weren't telling her. Was he really *fine*? Or were they just humoring her because of her fragile state?

"He's on a lot of pain killers," the nurse continued. "He's going to be in and out. Give him a day or two."

At least her answer was a little better than the answer the others had given. Sheriff Wiley and Deputy Holt entered the room looking almost like she felt. The nurse looked to the doorway, saw them, and appeared cheerful while looking back at Casey.

"Oh," the nurse said. "You have company."

As the nurse left the room, Wiley and Vaughn approached her between the two beds. Wiley gently touched her hand and smiled with an odd tenderness she'd never seen before. His look was almost fatherly.

"How are you feeling?" Wiley asked.

"I look better than I feel."

Vaughn glanced at Grey and appeared concerned about his condition. He gave a nod toward her brother. "How's Grey?"

"He feels better than he looks," she said while attempting a smile. "He's loaded up on the good painkillers."

"I'm glad you're finally awake and alert," Wiley announced. "Dina said you were clinically dead."

Casey smiled matter-of-fact. "Supposedly I went to the light-- twice."

"That's pretty scary," he remarked gently then hesitated and cleared his throat. "What do you remember about last night?"

She considered the question and drifted out a moment as if reliving some dark trauma. "Three gunshots and then a feeling of peace," she said softly. She snapped out of her trance and looked at Sheriff Wiley. "Who was he?"

Wiley and Vaughn tensed simultaneously. Vaughn looked away. It was hard to tell if he was ashamed or enraged.

Wiley fidgeted, clung to Casey's hand, and looked into her eyes with sincerity. "We don't know. He got away."

Casey's expression suddenly shattered. She felt her entire body tremble, which was undoubtedly a spike in her already frail blood pressure. Her attention immediately focused on Vaughn, who kept his head down.

"I thought you shot him?" she suddenly cried out.

Her sudden outburst caused him to look up and meet her glare. "I did," he announced defensively. "Three times."

Casey's mind was racing and her entire body was twitching with her spiking blood pressure. The monitors attached to her started reacting with a series of loud beeps.

"Why didn't you make sure he was dead? How did he get away?" she suddenly demanded. Her look turned hateful and her eyes cut through him. "You were right there!"

Vaughn stared at her and appeared momentarily traumatized by her tone and the unpredictably wild stare. "I assumed he was dead. He should have been dead. I needed to keep you from bleeding out."

Sheriff Wiley attempted to comfort Casey and calm her with a soothing tone. "Casey, Vaughn did the right thing," he assured her. "If he'd released pressure on your wound, you would have bled to death. You can't blame him for saving you."

"He should have left me die!"

Both men stared at her with surprise. Casey was almost surprised by her own outburst. She'd meant it too. Grey's eyes slowly rolled open to his sister's shouts.

"What's happening?" Grey asked in a groggy tone from his nearby bed.

"Did you hear that, Grey?" Casey demanded while gripping the bedrails.

"The part where the killer got away?" Grey said softly. "Yeah, I heard that."

Casey shot up straight in bed despite the pain it caused her and glared at Vaughn with a vengeful look in her eyes. "This is all your fault! If you hadn't kept me in the back of your cruiser the whole night, I would have been there," she lashed out. "I could have stopped it!

Vaughn stared at her with a look of guilt. He appeared unable to respond. He knew he had screwed up and nothing he could say would fix it. Wiley again attempted to calm her.

"If he would have taken you home when he should have, you'd be dead, Casey," Wiley gently informed her. "The killer entered through your bedroom window. Deputy Holt saved you and your brother."

Casey didn't care. She just wanted to jump out of her bed and hurt Vaughn. The pain in her abdomen was finally getting the better of her. She clutched her lower abdomen and cringed with pain while maintaining her venomous glare.

"Get him out of here!" she shouted.

Grey was already out again. The nurse and doctor hurried into the room, looked at Casey, and appeared alarmed. Blood seeped through the sheets and between Casey's fingers from her abdomen. She'd almost certainly torn her stitches.

"I'm sorry, you have to leave," the furious doctor informed them.

Vaughn stared at the blood and appeared momentarily traumatized. He turned and left the room without another word. Vaughn hurried into the hallway and leaned against the wall just outside the door. Wiley appeared from Casey's room, paused before him, and patted his shoulder while giving him a reassuring look.

"You did the right thing, Vaughn," he announced firmly. "You're a hero. She'll eventually see that."

Vaughn stared up at the ceiling tiles and groaned softly while shaking his head with disgust. "I did everything wrong last night," he remarked softly with the hurt evident in his voice. "I should have shot him in the leg, but I went for the kill shot. If I hadn't let my emotions take over, he'd be in custody."

"The man had just stabbed Casey," Wiley informed him with an odd look of mayhem in his eyes. "He was holding a knife. Anyone would have done the same thing. I want a piece of that bastard, and I wasn't even there to see what he'd done."

Vaughn rolled his eyes shut and allowed his head to fall into his hands with a groan. "I'll never get over the sight of her bleeding like that." He lifted his head and looked at his trembling hands. "I had her blood all over me." He groaned softly and allowed his head to hit the wall behind him as his eyes closed. "I don't even remember pulling the trigger."

Wiley gently rubbed Vaughn's shoulders. "Go home, Vaughn," he said gently. "You were up all night chasing her horse. You need some sleep."

Vaughn's eyes suddenly opened and he glared at Sheriff Wiley. His look was vengeful. "I'll sleep after I catch the killer."

Chapter Nine

Vaughn slept restlessly in the chair behind his desk within the police station bullpen. He twitched in his sleep, gasped, and suddenly woke. He looked around the nearly silent, mostly empty bullpen. He groaned softly, placed his feet on the floor, and half collapsed on his desk while rubbing his eyes. He was obviously exhausted, despite his freshly showered appearance. As he looked across the bullpen, he saw the Harford boys leaving the station. Tucker and Mitchell stood in the interrogation room doorway and silently watched the four leave. Vaughn quickly stood and had to catch himself from falling back down. He caught his balance and hurried to his fellow deputies.

"What's going on?" Vaughn demanded to know. "Why are the Harford boys leaving?"

"We finished questioning them," Tucker replied while looking over Vaughn's appearance with concern. "Shouldn't you be at home getting some rest?"

"I wanted to be there when you questioned them," Vaughn said firmly. "Wiley told you that."

"All four have airtight alibis," Tucker replied. "There was no reason to wake you."

"Vouching for one another isn't airtight," Vaughn snarled in protest.

"All four boys returned home an hour after the tavern brawl a little after midnight," Tucker announced. "Wayne's girlfriend showed up a few minutes later and spent the entire night with him. Both she and Ernest swore none of them left all night."

"As if they couldn't have slipped out unnoticed," Vaughn remarked. "And a girlfriend and father aren't exactly credible alibis either."

"Yes, they could have slipped out unnoticed," Tucker agreed. "But her car blocked theirs in the driveway, and she insists none of the cars were moved the next morning. I went by that way myself around two in the morning." He fidgeted at his own comment and gently cleared his throat. "Their cars were there just like she said."

"You were out that way around two?" Vaughn asked.

Tucker remained tense then timidly smiled. "Mel got off work at the tavern around two," he announced. "I just stopped by her place to make sure she got home okay, that's all."

Mitchell snorted a devious laugh. Tucker glared at him, causing him to flinch. Vaughn frowned with disgust. It wouldn't be the first time Tucker saw a little *action* during the line of duty.

"I get it," Vaughn muttered, not needing to hear the intimate details of his rendezvous with Melanie. "Did you happen to notice if their cars were still there when you left Melanie's house?"

Tucker frowned, having been caught slipping out to sneak one in with his girlfriend, and nodded. "Yeah, they were still there when I left around three."

"It couldn't have been them," Mitchell informed Vaughn. "Why are you so convinced it wasn't just some drifter or a random home invasion?"

"Because the killer wore a bulletproof vest," Vaughn remarked sternly to Mitchell. "He wore a vest, because he knew Brandon Remington was armed. Our killer broke into that house with the sole intent to kill everyone inside. That means it was personal and premeditated."

"And I'm telling you," Tucker assured him, "it couldn't have been any of the Harford boys."

Vaughn frowned and returned to his desk. He collapsed behind it with disgust.

†

*I*t was later that evening when Dina entered Casey's hospital room with some fresh flowers in a vase. Casey sat up in bed while holding her lower abdomen. She stared blankly at the sheets and didn't acknowledge Dina. Grey was now awake and alert. He played with the remote for the bed and simulated sounds while raising and lowering his head. He was obviously still on the good painkillers, and they worked, because he certainly wasn't feeling any pain. He immediately noticed Dina entering the room and appeared a little too enthusiastic.

"Hey! It's Dina! Hi, Dina!" Grey announced excitedly and waved at her.

Dina eyed him and appeared surprised by his jovial condition. "Looks like someone's on the good stuff," she replied.

"Oh, yeah. I'm loving this spaceship," Grey informed her then patted the bed alongside him while grinning. "Come fly with me."

"Maybe later," Dina informed him while returning the smile then approached Casey, who hadn't even looked up when she entered. "Hey, how are you feeling?"

Casey finally looked up with a hardened expression. "Like someone ripped my insides out with a butcher knife." She wasn't inaccurate with her description either.

Dina immediately frowned and became tense as if harboring some terrible secret from her friend. "I guess they told you," she said softly.

"Yeah," she grumbled under her breath. "They told me about the hysterectomy."

Dina sat on the edge of the bed and hugged Casey while fighting her emotions. "I'm so sorry, Casey."

"It's okay," Casey said with a sniff and wiped her tears. "I wasn't sure if I wanted children anyway, so that's one less thing to worry about."

Dina frowned while holding her and rubbed her back. For some reason, Dina's coddling wasn't making her feel any better. Casey just wanted to be left alone in her misery, but everyone kept trying to cheer her up. Dina pulled back far enough to look at Casey and attempted a more cheerful conversation to get her friend's mind off the hysterectomy.

"The doctor said if I get a visiting nurse, I can take you home in a couple of days," Dina announced. "I have a company cleaning the house--"

Casey felt alarm sweep through her. She pulled away from Dina and stared at her with horror. "I can't go back there!" She couldn't believe her friend was even suggesting it.

"My apartment is too small," Dina gently replied. "Staying at your house is the only way I can take care of you and Grey."

Grey grinned and chuckled from his own bed across the room. "Oh, yeah. Dina running around in her *lacy* panties--"

Casey appeared defeated and once again looked down at her covers. She was stranded in her own, personal hell. She didn't know how to free herself from the haunting memories of her parents' murder, and her and Grey's near death experience. Her mind was filled with every conceivable emotion all of which were playing tug-o-war with her sanity. She wanted to lash out at someone. She wanted to *hurt* someone. She wanted someone to be accountable, but she didn't know whom to blame. It seemed a long time had passed since either of them had spoken. Dina was content to just sit with her and be comforting. Casey didn't want comforting. She wanted revenge. She knew she couldn't say those feelings aloud. They had to be suppressed. She had to bury those emotions. She finally allowed sorrow to fill the void.

"I heard the rumors around town," Casey said softly.

"Small people with small minds," Dina assured her without even knowing to which rumors she referred.

"I heard everything from them blaming the murders on my father's boldness; my mother being too pretty; to me being a tease."

"And *none* of them are true," Dina firmly announced. "Most people around here know that. You know how people like to gossip."

Casey continued to stare at the covers while her mind again raced. Feelings of revenge once again filled her head. Although her voice was soft, her tone was harsh. "I heard it going around that the killer sexually assaulted me."

Dina suddenly tensed and uncertainly looked at Casey. She seemed surprised at what she was hearing. "That's not true," she firmly insisted then appeared concerned and sought reassurance. "Right?"

Casey snorted a laugh, glanced at Dina, and now wore a twisted smile. "No, I wasn't worth the effort." She hesitated only a moment. "I didn't tell anyone about it, since nothing actually happened. Deputy Holt must have witnessed the attempt and put it in his report. I guess the story grew into something far worse as it spread around." She shook her head with disgust. "Why the hell would he report that? I mean, if I didn't feel the need to mention it, why would he?"

"Maybe we should stay off the subject of certain deputies," Dina suggested.

Casey's disgust quickly turned hostile. She could feel herself slipping into a dark place. Her anger was becoming harder to control with each passing hour, but she feared admitting it to anyone. She feared mind-altering medications and the dreaded psychological evaluations. If she could just hit something or break something, she was sure she'd feel much better.

"I just can't believe this town actually thinks we somehow brought this heinous act down upon ourselves," she lashed out with bitterness in her tone. "That we stirred the pot and got burnt because of it."

"No one thinks that," Dina quickly interjected in a quick attempt to keep Casey's anger from rising.

Casey eyed her friend and raised a cocky brow in response. "I hear them at the nurse's station, Dina. All day I've heard things from around town coming out of that nurse's station," she hissed. "I know what's being said."

"Well, I haven't heard anyone blaming any of this on you or your family, and I work in gossip central," Dina said firmly. "Sure, people are talking about it. Nothing like this ever happened around here before. They're going to talk, but no one's blaming your family that I've heard."

"These people were supposed to be my parents' friends. It's very disrespectful to them and their memory," Casey said lowly while staring into Dina's eyes.

Dina saw the look in Casey's eyes and tensed. There was something frightening and unfamiliar about Casey. She brushed it off. "Those are just words from the small-minded people; not the ones who really matter. In fact, the town is having a memorial for your parents on opening day of the fair," she announced, managing to swiftly change the subject. "Any relatives you want me to contact?"

Casey felt her body once again sag with exhaustion. There were too many drugs coursing through her system. She speculated the nurses were giving her more than the standard painkillers that she had requested. Despite the sore subject of relatives, Casey maintained a more sedate state.

"No, my uncle is a lush and hasn't been around since I was born," Casey replied and once again felt defeated. The anger was gone and depression was quickly taking its place. It was a vicious, never-ending circle.

"Oh--" Dina continued to maintain the lighter mood. "You and Grey will attend, right?"

Casey drifted out a moment. Her mind was everywhere but on the current conversation. She snapped out of her trance and realized Dina was still waiting for a response.

"When Grey comes down from his high, we'll discuss it," Casey replied without enthusiasm.

✝

It was two days later. The town was going about business as usual while preparing for the upcoming town fair. Dina stood outside the antique shop with a stack of memorial fliers clutched in her hands. She stared at the building with a look of confusion. Boards covered the door and windows. They hadn't been there yesterday, and how they got there so fast was a mystery. Mayor Lance approached Dina on the sidewalk, appeared bewildered, and stared as well.

"Are Grey and Casey selling the shop?" Mayor Lance asked with a look of surprise on his face.

Dina uncertainly shook her head and appeared unable to take her eyes off the boarded up antique shop. "I don't know," she replied. "I went by their house to inspect it after the cleaning crew had been through. The house is boarded up too." She remained stunned and continued to stare at the building. "Casey called me last night and said something about her uncle visiting them in the hospital. She said they were moving in with him."

"And he had the house and shop boarded up that fast?" Lance asked with surprise.

"I assume so," she replied softly. "Her horses are gone and the barn's been cleaned out."

"That's strange."

"Yeah, especially since she'd never met this uncle of hers," she informed him. Dina slowly shook her head and fought her tears. "I just get this bad feeling that I'm never going to see her again."

"Casey and Grey were put through hell only a few days ago," Lance said to Dina. "She's dealing with a lot right now. She probably just needs time to sort through it. Maybe a few weeks away from here is what she needs."

"Maybe," Dina muttered then looked at the memorial fliers in her hand. "I just wish she'd confided in me, that's all. She didn't even leave a forwarding number or address. She just said she'd let me know when she was settled."

"I know you're worried about her," Lance said gently. "You just work on posting those memorial fliers. She'll attend; you'll see."

Dina stared at the building and frowned. She obviously wasn't convinced of it.

Chapter Ten

*T*wo years later. The once beautiful Remington farm was overgrown with tall weeds. The wooden fence was falling down, the landscaping was overgrown, and the boarded up house was in desperate need of paint. The sheriff's blazer drove up the overgrown driveway and parked in front of the house. Vaughn got out of the blazer and approached the house. He walked up the porch steps, and instead of approaching the door, he comfortably sat on the railing with his back to the support beam. He rested his head against the beam, shut his eyes, and appeared to escape into another world. His uniform proudly displayed the sheriff's badge on the breast pocket. The months that followed the double homicide of Casey's parents were the roller coaster ride that changed the town's perspective in many ways. Although the murders remained unsolved, Sheriff Wiley recommended Deputy Vaughn Holt to become his successor as sheriff. The town unanimously agreed. Somehow, he was deemed a hero. He had saved the lives of Casey and Grey while thwarting the first murderer the town had seen in its history. Despite his skepticism for the reason behind his promotion, Vaughn accepted the sheriff's position. Now, two years later, he still sat at the scene of crime while no closer to solving the murders than he had been the days that followed.

A thump within the house caught his attention. Vaughn leapt from the porch railing and approached the front door. He uncertainly placed his hand to the doorknob. As he turned the knob, the door opened! It was supposed to be locked. Vaughn removed his revolver from its holster, carefully pushed open the door, and slowly entered the house. As Vaughn entered the kitchen, it was obvious the occupants had left in a hurry. Everything remained within the house, although now with a thick, dusty layer covering it. His eyes immediately strayed to the island counter, but the blood had been painstakingly cleaned two years earlier by the crew Dina had hired. As Vaughn stared at the dusty area before the island counter, the echoing of three gunshots from that chilling night could be heard. Vaughn tensed and took a deep breath. The boarded windows allowed little light to enter, but through the light of the open door, Vaughn saw footprints in the dust across the floor. They headed into the dark living room. Vaughn removed a small flashlight and shined it toward the living room archway. A floorboard creaked within the living room. Vaughn leveled his gun at the archway and firmly gripped the trigger. The flashlight shined in the face of a man in his early fifties. Rory, the real estate agent, gasped with alarm and immediately raised his hands.

"Don't shoot, Sheriff," he announced defensively and allowed a tense laugh to escape. "It's just me."

Vaughn groaned and replaced his weapon with disgust. Rory lowered his hands and attempted to relax. The rumor had spread rapidly through town of how Deputy Vaughn Holt supposedly shot the killer three times in the chest after witnessing Casey's stabbing. The cowboy mentality of the town rejoiced the deputy's quick reflexes and swift actions. They didn't want a sheriff who was unwilling to pull the trigger when faced with life and death. On the flip side, a large portion of the town suddenly feared the man they most respected. Although he'd only drawn his weapon on a few occasions since that night, most were chilled when they saw Sheriff Holt holding his gun.

"What are you doing here, Rory?" Vaughn asked with the bewilderment clearly on his authoritative face. "How did you even get here?"

"The wife dropped me off. I'm waiting for the electrician," Rory explained.

Vaughn appeared immediately curious while staring at the realtor. "Electrician? For what?"

"Didn't you hear? I guess some guy is renting the old place," Rory said proudly.

The sheriff appeared surprised then said eagerly, "You spoke to Casey or Grey?"

"No, their uncle called and asked us to get the power turned back on and hire someone to clean and cut the weeds around the house," he replied. "Usually that means they're looking to rent or sell. He didn't ask for a sign, so I'm guessing they have an interested renter. Guess those kids went through their inheritance and need to recoup some losses. I expect the place to go up for sale in the near future. Be nice to get someone into that old antique shop too. I'm tired of looking at the place all boarded up." Rory made a face and appeared squeamish. "Such a grim reminder of what happened, you know."

"It's been two years," Vaughn said with a gentle sigh. "No one expects them to ever come back." He casually looked around and seemed to have trouble looking past the island counter. Vaughn was almost certainly off reliving bad memories. He finally looked back at Rory and appeared casual. "Looks like they left almost everything behind."

"Pretty much," Rory replied. "Although they did empty out the gun cabinet." He fidgeted but managed a weak smile. "I'll admit I was concerned about what I might find. I'd heard Dina had the place cleaned after, you know, but I still wasn't sure what I'd find. I can honestly say I didn't want to see any grisly reminders of what happened here. I heard it was pretty gruesome."

"Yeah," Vaughn said under his breath.

Rory immediately fidgeted with a strange realization. "Oh, I'm sorry, Sheriff," he said gently. "I almost forgot you were here that night."

"I never have," Vaughn scoffed and uncertainly ran his fingers through his hair. He again looked at the island counter, subconsciously wiped his hands on his pants, then looked at his clean hands and frowned.

†

One week later. The fairgrounds appeared deserted in the early evening setting. Storm clouds had rolled in and thunder rumbled in the distance as flashes of lightning lit up the clouds. The annual fair was growing near and would soon be flooded with locals and visitors alike. On the opposite end of the fairgrounds from the horse barn and arena was the stage used for the talent show and bachelor auction. The faint sounds of hammering and shouting voices were heard from near the stage. Mayor Lance and his wife, Abby, rode in a stylish golf cart toward the distant stage. Lance was dressed casual for his fairgrounds inspection, but Abby was dressed to impress, even though there would be few to impress. As Lance stopped the golf cart near the stage, Ernest appeared on stage with former sheriff Wiley. Although a little older and a little rounder, Wiley appeared more relaxed now in his retirement.

"I thought we'd add a few more lights to the stage this year," Wiley informed Ernest and casually indicated their locations. "Last year it was getting close to dark before we finished."

"I know an electrician who will give us a deal," Ernest informed him.

Lance and Abby disembarked their luxury golf cart and approached the large stage. Both walked up the steps leading up to the stage. Abby's high heels clunked across the stage. She paused and looked around with an approving smile.

"I like the new surface on the stage," Abby boasted to no one in particular. "Melanie is going to be pleased. She got a splinter in her foot last year."

"Nothing's too good for my darling niece," Ernest announced cheerfully to his sister then grinned. "I paid for the upgrades myself. When Melanie wins this year, it'll be--what? Four years in a row?"

"Five, Ernest," Abby playfully scoffed then smirked and shook her head. "Honestly, how can you forget these things? She's your only niece."

Wiley tensed and looked around while pretending not to listen to the conversation. There was being proud of your child and then there was stacking the deck in your child's favor. There was a fine line between the two, and it was difficult to say whether Melanie actually won on her own talents. Most of the judges were supporters of both the mayor and Ernest. Abby suddenly glared at Wiley in an almost scolding manner.

"You're suddenly very quiet," Abby remarked and raised a cocky brow. "Something on your mind, Wiley?"

"No, nothing," Wiley replied. His carefully hidden look revealed there actually may have been, but he wasn't about to speak his mind.

Lance inspected the stage while grinning proudly. "This year's fair is going to blow our town away. One hundred years," he announced cheerfully. "The entire town is psyched for it. It's going to be spectacular. Our expected attendance is nearly double. We have vendors coming from all over the country to participate." He then looked at Ernest with a serious expression. "I don't want *anything* ruining it."

"Relax," Ernest grumbled and apparently took some offense. "My boys have been perfect angels. Now that Wayne's married, they've all settled a bit."

Abby rolled her eyes. The term 'settled' was apparently subjective. Wiley frowned and looked away, possibly in fear of saying something he shouldn't.

Ernest obviously felt the mood shift, appeared humored by it, and shook his head. "Trust me," he announced boldly. "*Nothing* is going to ruin this fair."

The shrill sound of a horse neighing in the distance caught their attention. All four looked across the fairgrounds toward the distant hillside. There was a clap of thunder. A large, gray horse reared up with a sharp squeal as lightning flashed behind it. The horse's hooves pawed the air then harshly struck the ground. The gray horse snorted loudly then galloped across the field toward the woods with a loud neigh that almost resembled a war cry. All four watched the running horse as if they'd seen a ghost. Wiley walked to the edge of the stage with his mouth hanging open and watched the horse disappear into the woods.

"Was that--?" Lance gasped softly.

"It certainly was," Wiley replied while staring in disbelief.

✝

*O*t was later that same evening. The storm had passed through quickly, although the roads remained wet. Despite the early hour, there were several trucks already parked in the tavern's parking lot. Even though it was only Thursday, there would be a good crowd since a live band would be playing later. The tavern appeared nearly empty, with the hard-core drinkers hanging out at the bar. A weary looking Dina carried a pitcher of beer to the pool area. It was early, and she was already exhausted. She appeared unhappy and lacked enthusiasm. As she approached the pool area, it was easy to see why. The Harford boys played pool at one of the back tables and joked around. Apart from the four men, the back was empty. Dina appeared reluctant to approach them and, instead, set the pitcher on the nearby table. She attempted to slip away unnoticed. Wayne must have slipped around the front and cut her off before she could escape. The cheap grin on his face was enough to cause her to cringe.

"Where are you going so fast?" Wayne asked in a devious tone. "Don't you want your tip?"

Wayne flashed a dollar bill and attempted to slip it down her shirt. Dina took a quick step back to avoid his hand near her cleavage. The last two years took their toll on her, and she appeared to have little fight left within her.

"Leave me alone," Dina muttered and attempted to go around him.

Wayne again stepped in front of her and grinned cheaply while playing with the dollar bill in his grease-stained fingers. Someone suddenly bumped into Wayne from behind. His attention sharply fixated on the man who had run into him. A meek looking man in his late forties, who stood no more than 5'8", gave Wayne an apologetic look.

"Pardon me," Ruger announced politely and attempted to walk past.

Wayne gave Ruger a jolting shove to his shoulder, preventing him from passing. "You have a problem?" Wayne snarled and stared down upon the meek man.

Dina watched the exchange with concern and uncertainly slipped out of the pool area. Ruger stared at Wayne, who towered over him by several inches, and appeared completely innocent of any wrongdoing.

"No, I don't have a problem," he replied casually.

"Well, you're about to have one," Wayne growled and grabbed Ruger by his shirt.

Ruger didn't flinch nor show emotion to Wayne's hands on him. A tall, muscular man appeared behind Ruger and glared at Wayne over top of Ruger's head. The stranger stood two inches above Wayne at an impressive 6'4". He folded his muscular arms across his chest and raised his brow in question. His green eyes pierced through Wayne's with a look that would chill most men. He oddly resembled a science experiment gone astray.

"Is there a problem?" the large man gruffly asked while staring down Wayne.

Wayne stared at the thirty-something year old, muscle-bound man with a look of surprise and quickly released Ruger. He chuckled softly and shook his head almost meekly.

"No, no problem," Wayne replied while taking a quick step back with his hands in the air.

The tall, muscular man, Diesel, nodded his approval and smirked most sinister. "Glad to hear," he replied then nodded Ruger to the nearby pool table.

Ruger grinned slyly, almost taunting Wayne, and joined Diesel at the free table. It would appear as if Ruger enjoyed his rather large trumping card. If it hadn't been for the impressiveness of his friend, the Harford boys would almost certainly have mopped the floor with the meek man. As the men began their pool game, Dina slipped into the backroom and offered the two newcomers drinks. She appeared relieved to have reinforcements as a buffer for the Harford boys. They weren't easily intimidated, but this was one battle they seemed unwilling to fight.

Chapter Eleven

A little while later, the sheriff's blazer drove past the tavern, as was Sheriff Holt's usual practice on busy nights. The blazer suddenly slowed to the point of skidding and sharply turned into the parking lot at the last second. Vaughn jumped out of the blazer with a shocked look on his face and uncertainly approached the hitching post alongside the building. Casey's large, gray horse, in full western tack, was tied to the rail on the very end. Vaughn slowly approached the horse, ran his hands along the horse's shoulder, and walked to its left hindquarter. Vaughn ran his hand along the massive scar on the horse's hindquarters. As he stared at the horse, an image from that night of him attempting to control the soaking wet and bleeding horse in the arena barn sudden flashed through his mind. Vaughn studied the horse then returned to its head. Storm snickered softly and pushed his large nose into Vaughn's chest nearly knocking him off his feet. He petted the horse's nose, appeared curious, and headed toward the tavern entrance.

Vaughn entered the tavern and looked around. There were very few patrons at the bar and only one or two were women. He studied each one from his position in the doorway, squinted, and appeared bewildered. He uncertainly approached the bar where Dina awaited her drink order. She seemed to be in a better mood now than she had been earlier.

"How's it going this evening?" Vaughn asked casually.

Dina looked at him, offered a tiny smile, and shrugged. "More of the usual," she replied. "Why?"

Vaughn appeared deep in thought then snapped out of his daze, smiled, and shook his head. "No particular reason."

The bartender, Mack, handed Dina a scotch on the rocks and a highball. Vaughn eyed the drinks and immediately became curious.

"Some hardcore drinkers tonight?" he asked.

Dina flashed a smile and freely gossiped. "Non-locals," she replied cheerfully. "I may actually make descent tips tonight for a change."

"Are they worth checking out?"

She eyed him and snorted a laugh to his casual interrogation. "No, they're not biker dudes or gang bangers," she replied in a mocking tone.

Vaughn grinned and snorted a laugh to her comment. As Dina walked away, he turned to the bored looking bartender. "Mack, can I get a coffee to go?"

"Sure thing, Sheriff," Mack replied cheerfully.

Vaughn leaned against the bar and glanced around with more than a passing interest. He carefully studied each woman, but they were the usual bar flowers. Dina's mother sat at the end of the bar and flirted with a disinterested local. The end of the month was coming fast, and she probably needed rent money. Vaughn helped himself to some free pretzels and turned Mack's newspaper toward him to read the headlines. Dina entered the pool area in the back with her tray containing the two drinks. She set the drinks on a nearby pub table for Ruger and Diesel. Ruger politely smiled and paid her double the tab. Dina grinned with renewed life and headed back toward the main bar area. Ryan was suddenly alongside her, as if innocently passing. She saw him too late to avoid him. His hand groped her breast through her tank top. She jumped with surprise then immediately turned angry. Ryan laughed at her. He obviously knew she wasn't going to do anything about it. Dina appeared to consider an appropriate reaction, but she was reduced to sneering at him instead. She was about to push past him when a woman was heard from nearby.

"Some things never change--"

Dina and the four men looked toward the opening to the main bar area. Casey leaned casually against the doorframe just inside the pool area with her arms folded across her chest and a strange smile on her face. Dina stared at Casey and appeared stunned. It was like seeing a ghost.

"Casey?" Dina gasped with surprise.

Dina carelessly shoved Ryan out of the way, hurried for Casey, and threw her arms around her. Casey briefly returned the embrace, although something seemed oddly different about her. Dina didn't appear to notice or simply didn't care. She stepped back and stared at her best friend with tear-filled eyes.

"I can't believe it's you. You haven't written or called," Dina gasped. "Where have you been?"

"Finding my way," she replied with the same, strange smile still on her face.

Dina appeared excited possibly for the first time in two years and bounced around happily. "I'll tell Mack I'm taking the night off," she announced. "We'll hang out and catch up."

"Tonight may not be good," Casey's casually replied.

Dina appeared confused and almost stunned as she stared at her friend. Casey grinned slyly while looking into the pool area, walked past Dina, and approached Ruger at the second pool table. Casey smiled and indicated the pool stick.

"May I?" Casey asked.

Ruger smiled charmingly, apparently taken by the beautiful woman, and handed her the pool stick. Casey casually twirled the stick skillfully between her fingers and approached the Harford boys at the next table. They were watching her closely as well. She was a ghost of the past; they couldn't help but stare.

"Fifty dollars a game," she said firmly while wearing a cheap grin. "Who am I playing?"

All four boys suddenly seemed to come to life. Wayne grinned while looking lustfully over her. It didn't take long for the shock to wear off and their true personalities to quickly surface.

"The prodigal child returns," Wayne said with a chuckle. "Did you miss me?"

Casey stared at him and smiled slyly. "I've done nothing but think about you the last two years, Wayne," she informed him. She glanced at Dina and showed little reaction. "Scotch on the rocks."

Dina appeared surprised by the request or possibly by Casey's actions. She uncertainly turned toward the bar area and nearly ran into Vaughn, who stared at the pool table with the same look of surprise.

"Is that Casey?" he asked without taking his eyes off the familiar yet somehow unfamiliar woman.

Dina appeared tense and uncertainly shook her head. "I'm not sure."

Casey barely resembled the innocent, young girl either had remembered. Dina stared a moment longer then turned toward the bar area. Grey stood directly in front of her with a strange smile on his face.

"Dina--"

Dina appeared surprised to see him then smiled with delight. "Oh, my God, Grey!" she cried out excitedly and threw her arms around him.

Grey tensed as she clung to him, appeared reluctant to return the embrace, and quickly released her. Dina pulled away and stared at him. Her look conveyed her confusion and possible concern. He oddly resembled a human taken over by an alien lifeform. He lacked emotion in light of their reunion, much like Casey.

Grey stared past her at Vaughn with a strange, tiny smile. "Deputy Holt--or is it Sheriff?"

Vaughn approached him and appeared curious while studying him. He, too, apparently noticed the strange behavior. "It's sheriff," he replied. "When did you return?"

Grey turned and headed toward the bar forcing Vaughn to follow him. "We're just visiting," he announced casually. "Buy you a drink?"

Vaughn followed a few feet behind while studying him and remained suspicious. Back within the pool area, Casey shot ball after ball into each pocket while watching Wayne and Ryan circle her like hungry wolves. Their eyes remained on her with each shot. She showed no reaction to their behavior, although she watched them from the corner of her eyes.

"Hmm. I've missed that ass," Wayne announced with a throaty chuckle.

"Looks even better than I remember," Ryan said with a lustful grin.

"And still completely off limits," Casey casually informed them with little emotion.

All four boys laughed. Ryan rubbed against Casey's buttocks as he passed her. Casey rammed the stick behind her, narrowly missing Ryan's groin. He jumped and laughed.

"She's twice as feisty too," Ryan teased.

"Probably not getting it enough," Wayne laughed.

Casey lined up her next shot while ignoring them as Wayne paused behind her. She watched him out of the corner of her eye. Wayne grabbed her hips and grinded against her from behind. Casey kicked back and struck him in the shin. He released her with surprise. She spun with the pool stick in both hands and hit him square in the chest, shoving him back.

"Don't touch me again," Casey growled while glaring into his eyes. "That's your only warning."

Wayne appeared surprised by her sudden reaction and even more to her tone. Fred and Blain moved in closer while Ryan laughed at his brother.

"Yeah, Wayne," Ryan announced. "She only likes it from men in masks."

All four men snickered. Casey's cold expression didn't change as she casually took a step closer to Ryan.

"Is that supposed to be funny?" Casey growled.

"Nah, just stating a fact."

Blain suddenly grabbed Casey from behind and attempted to hold her as Wayne approached with a grin.

"Someone needs to teach you a little respect," Wayne said with a lustful look in his eyes.

Wayne moved closer to her while Blain held her then ran his finger along her neckline and toward her cleavage. Ruger and Diesel were now watching from across the room. Diesel took a step toward them in an attempt to intervene.

Ruger stopped him with a raised hand and casually responded, "That's not our fight."

Casey grabbed Blain's arm and used him as leverage to kick Wayne with both feet. Wayne was thrown across the room. Ruger watched him fall to the floor near him. Casey tossed Blain backwards and onto the pool table while he still clung to her. Casey rolled over Blain and stood on the pool table. Blain sprung to his feet. Casey flipped the pool stick with her foot and into her hands. She twirled the stick and moved into a fighting stance. Blain and Wayne lunged for her. Casey somersaulted over them and landed on the floor behind them. She swung the pool stick and struck Wayne and Blain. Ryan lunged for her. She spun into a backwards roundhouse kick and knocked him backwards. He crashed into a nearby table. The beer pitcher and glasses fell to the floor with a crash. Vaughn entered the pool area with Dina behind him. Casey spun, kicked, and struck each man with the stick and her feet. Grey casually entered the pool area with his drink, took a seat, and watched the fight with little reaction. As the last man hit the floor, Casey remained in her attack position with the stick and watched them. All four writhed around the floor while clutching various body parts. Vaughn and Dina stared at Casey with shocked expressions. Ruger and Diesel chuckled. Casey casually straightened, tossed her stick to Ruger, and looked at Vaughn with a devious, twisted smile.

"Sheriff--"

Casey casually turned and placed her hands behind her back. Vaughn removed his handcuffs, shook his head, and cuffed her wrists behind her back. Wayne slowly moved to his knees.

"I'm going to kill that bitch!" Wayne shouted as blood seeped from his mouth. "You'd better lock her up!"

Vaughn led Casey past Wayne. Casey kicked behind her, unobserved by Vaughn, and struck Wayne in the face. Vaughn looked back. Wayne lie motionless on the floor. Vaughn appeared puzzled. Casey flashed a smile at Dina as they passed.

"Yeah, I'm kind of busy tonight."

Deputy Tucker hurried into the tavern as Vaughn escorted Casey toward the door.

Vaughn indicated the Harford boys to Tucker. "See that those boys go home."

Tucker looked into the pool area, where all four Harford boys writhed in pain, and appeared stunned.

Chapter Twelve

Casey sat quietly in the backseat with her hands cuffed behind her and appeared peaceful and oddly content. Being trapped in the back of Vaughn's police blazer wasn't nearly as confining as she thought it would be. The cuffs were a bit dramatic though. Vaughn glanced at her through the rearview mirror several times. She caught a glimpse of his dark eyes staring back at her. Oddly enough, he wasn't nearly as intimidating as she'd remembered.

"Is this new?" she finally asked, breaking the silence.

Vaughn pulled over to the side of the road, threw the blazer into park, and stared at her through the mirror. His dark eyes were now demanding.

"Why, Casey?" he suddenly demanded to know. "You're back one day and you take on all four of them."

"One-on-one hardly seemed fair," she casually replied.

"You deliberately went out of your way to piss them off," he scoffed.

"Yes, I know their father is tight with the mayor and will be up your ass about it," she replied. "I've heard this story before, and I have to say the ending really sucks."

"We'll stay here all night until you answer my question."

The way he looked at her through the mirror with those dark eyes conveyed his seriousness. She could probably play this game with him for a few more hours, but she really didn't feel like wasting the time.

"Why?" she asked innocently. Her eyes suddenly narrowed. "Because they're like a pack of wild dogs and the law won't do anything because of who they are." Her emotions took over for a moment as her voice lowered considerably. "They get a free pass to sexually harass and assault every woman within groping distance." Casey took a deep breath, pulled her anger back inside, and her calmness again returned. "I gave them fair warning before defending myself."

Casey casually relaxed and stared out the window with little expression. Vaughn continued to watch her through the mirror. She didn't acknowledge him.

"This is my town now, Casey," he informed her firmly. "If you came back for revenge, I'll lock you up. If they did something to you, you need to press charges. It'll look better in case they press charges against you."

She finally looked at him in the front. His comment humored her. "Are you kidding? They don't want it getting around that they were beaten up by a girl." She took a deep breath and sighed. "No, they'll probably break into my house late one night, kill everyone I care about, and brutalize me," Casey announced then considered the comment. "Oh, wait. That already happened."

There was an odd silence between them. Casey now stared back at him through the mirror. Although not nearly as intimidating as she remembered, staring into his eyes even through the mirror wasn't easy.

"There's nothing connecting them to the murders," he informed her. "I've been over it a thousand times, and I'm no closer to a suspect than I was two years ago."

"Perhaps if you made sure he was dead--" Casey muttered and stopped herself from saying anything more. That subject was a hot button issue and now wasn't the proper time to get into that particular debate.

"Don't start with that," he retorted. "Not a day goes by that I don't think about that night."

Vaughn rested his elbow on the door and held his temple with disgust. It was obvious he didn't know what to do. He quickly straightened and composed himself. He once again looked at her through the mirror.

"If you're going to stay in my town, you're going to play by my rules," he announced firmly. "If you have a problem, you come to me. You will not take justice into your own hands. Do you understand?"

There was a strange silence. Casey stared back at him through the mirror. "Yes, I understand."

Vaughn put the blazer into gear and drove back onto the road. The sheriff's blazer pulled into the tavern parking lot and up to Grey, who casually leaned against the hitching post with a strange smirk on his face. Vaughn got out, eyed Grey's smirk, and opened the back door for Casey. She casually got out and handed Vaughn the handcuffs.

"I believe these belong to you."

Vaughn took the handcuffs and gave her a look of surprise. Casey and Grey mounted their horses and rode away. Vaughn stared after them with a concerned look.

†

Country General Hospital was located nearly twenty miles from town. It was situated in what some might consider a city, although not much of a city, but it was certainly large in comparison with Darwood Falls. For a Thursday night, the hospital appeared busier than usual but not nearly as busy as late night on weekends. Country General Hospital was where Casey and Grey had been airlifted to on the night of their brutal attack. The emergency room had few patients waiting to be seen, but the hospital was loud with commotion. Fred Harford leaned against a nearby wall and watched his three brothers writhing in agony within the waiting room. The few remaining patients watched them and kept their distance from the unruly, angry men.

"What the hell is taking them so long?" Wayne demanded while holding the bloody cloth to his still bleeding mouth and showed general discomfort to nearly every part of his body.

Blain was unusually silent as he sat in a chair while holding his jaw and kept his eyes closed. Ryan writhed in agony while clutching his foot and ribs. Ryan glared at Fred, who watched in silence and appeared mostly unscathed. Ryan obviously wasn't pleased that his youngest brother wasn't suffering alongside them.

"Go get a doctor, you idiot!" Ryan shouted at Fred.

"If you actually stopped to think about it," Fred began then grinned slightly, "it's kind of funny."

All three suddenly glared at him. He tensed slightly and tried not to grin.

"I'm going to kick your ass in three seconds," Wayne growled lowly. "Did you even try to stop her?"

"Sure I did," Fred protested. "She punched me in the gut and knocked me on my ass with some sort of karate leg sweeping thing. Face it, Wayne; she's not a girl we want to piss off."

"Really?" Wayne scoffed with the hostility in his eyes as he sprayed blood while he talked. "Well, I'm going to bring that bitch to her knees."

"Before or after she takes your head off?" he asked with a cocky tilt of his head.

Wayne sneered at Fred. The hospital doors were thrown open to reveal Ernest. He stormed across the emergency waiting room and approached his sons. He stopped short of them and stared with surprise.

"What the hell happened?" Ernest demanded. "Were you messing with those biker guys again?"

"No, it was Casey fucking Remington," Ryan lashed out and immediately doubled over while clutching his ribs.

Ernest stared at his injured sons with his mouth hanging open. "Casey's back?" He suddenly shook his head in disbelief. "Wait, are you telling me Casey did this to you?" He instantly became enraged. "One woman beat the crap out of all four of you?" he suddenly demanded.

"She pulled some martial arts bullshit on us," Ryan groaned while attempting to find a comfortable position.

Ernest stared at the three writhing in agony then looked at Blain, who barely moved and refused to speak. "You've got anything to say?" he demanded.

"She broke his jaw," Fred said flatly from the wall behind his father.

Ernest spun and looked at Fred. He appeared surprised he wasn't writhing in agony with them. "Sat this one out?" he scoffed. He obviously knew Fred wasn't much of a fighter.

"I took a few hits," he replied while casually straightening. "I was the only one smart enough to admit defeat." Fred appeared reflective. "You know, I get the feeling when she said 'no' she actually meant it."

Ernest glared at Fred. He stared back at his father and tried hard not to smile.

"I'm going to get some coffee," Fred announced casually. "You want anything?"

"Yeah, a son with a backbone," Ernest scoffed. "You stand up for your brothers."

"They were wrong," Fred simply informed him.

"That doesn't matter," he snapped with hostility. "Family comes first! Right or wrong, we take care of our own. You remember that."

Fred frowned and walked away. Ernest rolled his eyes and shook his head with disgust. "He's getting to be like his mother," he scoffed.

"What are we going to do about Casey Remington?" Wayne gasped and then spit blood onto the floor.

"You leave that to me," Ernest informed him. "The law will protect us. Remember who you are."

Chapter Thirteen

*I*t was early the following morning. The Remington farm was neatly groomed, the fences were mended, and several horses grazed in the pasture. The house appeared almost pristine with fresh landscaping and paint. The sheriff's blazer pulled up to the house. Vaughn got out of the blazer and looked at the jeep and car parked in the driveway as he walked toward the house. The garage door was partially open to reveal a black, vintage sports car, which briefly caught his attention. He walked onto the porch, approached the front door, and promptly knocked on it. A moment passed before the door opened to reveal Diesel in only a pair of floppy shorts. His muscles had muscles, and his mere presence was overpowering with testosterone. Vaughn stared at the large man who towered over him by several inches and seemed surprised by the barely dressed stranger who answered the door.

"Yeah?" Diesel snorted with little interest.

"Sheriff Holt," Vaughn announced casually. "I'm here to speak to Casey about an incident at the tavern."

Diesel stared at him only a moment without emotion. "She's in the shower. Come back later." He shut the door.

Vaughn stood before the door with a shocked and dumbfounded look. The door once again opened to reveal Ruger, who smiled timidly.

"Sheriff Holt? I'm sorry about Diesel," Ruger announced. "He's not really a people person. Please, come in. Casey will be along soon."

Vaughn eyed Ruger and uncertainly entered. He followed Ruger across the kitchen. Diesel sat at the island counter and read the sports section of the newspaper.

"Could I offer you some coffee and doughnuts while you wait?" Ruger announced pleasantly.

"Uh, yes, thank you."

Vaughn eyed Diesel and leaned against the nearby counter. Ruger opened the doughnut box and appeared surprised when he discovered it was empty.

"Huh? Fresh out of doughnuts."

"Coffee will do," Vaughn replied simply and kept an eye on both men.

Ruger poured some coffee into a mug and handed it to Vaughn. Grey entered the kitchen, glared at Diesel, and rolled his eyes with disgust.

"God, Diesel. Put some clothes on," Grey scoffed. "It's too early in the morning for all that testosterone."

Diesel didn't react or bother looking up from his newspaper. "Fuck off."

Grey approached the doughnut box, opened it, and groaned with disgust. "What happened to all the doughnuts I bought this morning?" he demanded then glared at Diesel, who didn't bother to look back. "A dozen doughnuts--?"

Diesel glared at Grey. Grey grabbed his car keys with disgust and left without acknowledging Vaughn. Ruger casually prepared two mugs of tea. Vaughn observed the scene in the kitchen and remained curious.

"I'm sorry; I didn't catch your name," Vaughn finally initiated an introduction with Ruger.

Ruger glanced at him and maintained his cheerful mood. "I'm Ruger Quinn and that's Diesel Mann."

Diesel didn't bother looking up or even acknowledging the introduction. Vaughn focused his attention on the seemingly approachable man.

"Are you the uncle we'd heard about?" Vaughn asked while leaning on the island counter.

Ruger grinned and appeared humored. "I'm an unofficial uncle. It's an honorary title. Friend of the family."

Diesel snorted a laugh. Ruger glared his disapproval at Diesel, who still didn't look up, and then looked back at Sheriff Holt with a charming smile.

"Just ignore Diesel," Ruger announced. "His manners are the only thing worse than his attitude."

Casey entered the kitchen in a worn tank top and a pair of old shorts. She saw Vaughn standing by the island counter, immediately stopped, and groaned lowly with disgust.

"Oh, God. What now?" she muttered.

It was too early in the morning to deal with Sheriff Holt. Mornings were particularly difficult for her. She was never quite herself until early afternoon. Her emotions usually ran rampant in the morning. She was liable to say anything. Ruger noticed her and smiled warmly. She'd been seen. There was no chance to retreat to her room and avoid the hellish morning awaiting her. Casey forced a smile and approached Ruger by the counter. He smiled and handed her a cup of tea. She kissed him on the cheek, took the tea, and eyed Vaughn.

"Good morning, Sheriff," she announced while attempting to hide her sneer. "To what do I owe the pleasure?"

Vaughn removed a carefully folded paper from his jacket and tossed it onto the island counter. "The Harford boys are pressing assault charges against you."

Ruger casually picked up the paper, glanced over it, and appeared curious. "Assault? You mean self-defense."

"Broken fingers, sprained wrist, broken jaw, cracked scapula, three cracked ribs, fractured cheekbone, and a dislocated shoulder," Vaughn informed him.

Casey appeared stunned and uncertainly shook her head. "That can't be," she protested then smiled slyly. "I distinctly remember breaking someone's foot."

"This is serious, Casey. I have to arrest you," Vaughn informed her.

"Yes, I'm sure you're very excited about cuffing me again but hold that thought," Casey announced while grinning.

Ruger removed a laptop from the counter behind him, placed it on the island counter, and opened a file. A video of the entire incident played on the screen taken from a spy cam. Vaughn watched the entire incident with astonishment. Once it ended, he looked at Casey.

"You knew they'd do that, didn't you?"

"I knew they'd do something," she casually replied. "I just needed to walk into the room. This is what they do to women. Someone had to do something about it."

"If that's the case, why hasn't anyone ever reported it?" he asked with a curious look.

"Because nothing ever happens," she growled, quickly losing patients. "It just gets swept away. My mother pressed charges against Wayne once. A week later, the report vanished." Casey folded her arms across her chest and glared at Vaughn. "I read it in her journal."

The accusation surprised him. "I never heard about that."

Casey smirked knowingly.

Vaughn appeared tense and quickly considered his next move. "I'm going to need a copy of that video to get the charges against you dropped," he informed her. "I'd also like to see your mother's journal."

"You don't need a copy of the video," Casey informed him. "Grey sent it to Judge Burke, Mayor Ridgeway, Wayne's wife, and a dozen or so guys from the tavern." Her look hardened. "As far as my mother's journal--that's private."

"It could help solve the murders," he informed her and appeared surprised at her reluctance to share it. "Why would you withhold it?"

"Because there's nothing in there that implicates anyone. I've read through it dozens of times," she informed him bluntly. "Besides, it's my mother's private thoughts."

Vaughn placed his hands on his gun belt and stared at her while shaking his head with disbelief. "I can't believe you're this uncooperative. You know I'm trying to help," he announced then appeared disgusted. "And I hope you realize that by sending that video around town, those boys will just want a bigger piece of you next time."

"The feeling's mutual."

Vaughn stared at Casey and appeared more defeated then surprised. "You're digging yourself a grave, Casey," he announced firmly, "and your pleasure over it scares me." His look softened. "Why won't you trust me?"

There was an odd silence as she stared at him. Her look caused him to tense almost as if he already knew her response.

"It's difficult trusting the law when they follow a corrupt mayor," she finally replied.

"I take the law very seriously," he informed her with sincerity in his tone. "Things are different since I became sheriff of Darwood Falls."

Casey cleverly raised her brows and tilted her head. "Weren't you dating the mayor's daughter?"

Vaughn stared at Casey in silence or was it surprise. Ruger stared at his tea while hiding his smile. Apparently, he was enjoying the sheriff roast. Diesel finally looked up and grinned his humor. If Vaughn was disturbed, he hid it well.

"Briefly, but that had no influence on the law," he replied with some reluctance.

"Never underestimate the value of a good blowjob," Diesel retorted then chuckled.

All three glared at Diesel. He smirked and looked back at the sports page without further comment. Vaughn set down his coffee and appeared disgusted.

"Obviously, I'm not getting through to anyone here, so I'll be in touch."

Vaughn left the kitchen and headed from the house. Dina appeared in the doorway as Vaughn left, stared after him, and then looked at Casey.

"Is this a bad time?" Dina asked.

"When Sheriff Holt stops by, it's always a bad time," Casey muttered.

Dina approached her near the island counter, eyed Diesel without his shirt, and appeared amazed. "Oh, wow--" she said softly to Casey. "Thanks, but I didn't get you anything."

Casey snorted a laugh. That was the standard reaction to Diesel without his shirt on. At least he wore shorts. His willingness to strut around in his brief underwear was quickly shutdown by Ruger a long time ago. There were just some things no man wanted to see first thing in the morning. A muscle-bound man in briefs sporting morning wood was high on that list.

Dina's look turned more serious. "Can we talk?"

Casey nodded to the kitchen door. Dina left the kitchen with Casey, only briefly glancing back at Diesel on the way out. They walked onto the porch and sat on the recently restored rocking chairs. Casey glared past the porch to the sheriff's blazer that remained parked out front. Vaughn was standing alongside his blazer in the driveway while talking to Grey with his box of doughnuts. Dina noted Casey's cold stare at the sheriff. Dina tensed and shifted in her chair.

"Why didn't you call or write?" Dina finally asked, breaking Casey out of her death stare at the sheriff. "I thought I was your best friend."

As Casey stared at Dina, her expression softened, and she lowered her head. Things were more complicated than she could possibly explain. "I was in a very bad place for quite some time," she said softly and drifted into her own thoughts.

An image of Casey and Grey arguing flashed through her mind, although their words were inaudible. Casey suddenly punched Grey in the mouth. He clutched his bleeding mouth and looked at her with the horror evident in his eyes. Casey snapped out of her daze, avoided looking at Dina, and fidgeted.

"When I finally sorted out my life, it just seemed like too much time had passed," Casey replied gently.

"I wanted to help you. I was here for you," Dina said sternly. She suddenly appeared defeated, looked down, and spoke more softly. "They were like parents to me too."

Casey could only stare at Dina. It pained her to know she caused such turmoil for her longtime best friend. She finally shifted in her chair and avoided looking at her friend.

"I'm really sorry, Dina. I was just *angry*."

Angry was an understatement. She was insane with anger and consumed with grief. Only one thing kept her focused, and that's what brought her back to Darwood Falls. Dina again spoke, snapping Casey back to reality.

"I would have taken anger over nothing," Dina replied then inhaled deeply and attempted a tiny smile. "Well, I'm glad you're back, even if I am still mad at you." She then appeared curious and attempted to hide her smile. "So what's the deal with the living god in there? Are you and he--?" She lustfully raised her brows in suggestion. "--you know."

Casey suddenly laughed. "No, he's a free agent," she replied then appeared to give it some thought and added, "and he's kind of a whore."

"Yeah, but--who cares," Dina said while grinning. "With a guy like that, one night is more than enough."

Casey rolled her eyes and hid her smile. She wasn't about to agree with her friend on that, but Dina always did like the popular guys. Loosely translated--town studs. A thought then occurred to Casey.

"What happened with Tucker?" Casey asked. "You were so hot for him. I know Melanie dumped him. Did you ever pursue that?"

Dina snorted a laugh and shifted uncomfortably in her chair. "To be honest," she announced, "I had my chance with him, and I just couldn't do it."

"Really?"

"It's stupid, but I just kept hearing this voice in the back of my head saying, 'he's Melanie's leftovers'." Dina rolled her eyes. "I just couldn't bring myself to sleep with the same man as that girl. The thought sickened me."

"But you were so head over heels for him," Casey reminded her. "Should that really matter?"

Dina glared at Casey and cleverly raised her brows. "Remember how handsome you thought Vaughn was when you first laid eyes on him in his uniform?"

Casey's expression twisted into a sneer. "That's different," she remarked. "I was fifteen at the time. At that age, romantic was a guy with a cool car."

"Who did you like that had a cool car?" Dina remarked with a humored look.

"You're missing the point," Casey replied.

"No, I think I've made one."

Casey groaned and shook her head. Dina was insufferable at times. Her friend needed to mind her manners, because she wasn't above subjecting her to sheer torture. An afternoon cleaning with Ruger would wear the fight out of her.

"I hope you're not spreading those rumors around about my teenage crush on Sheriff Holt," Casey remarked. "That was a long time ago."

"Relax," Dina groaned. "I've kept that secret for years. I wouldn't betray your confidence."

"You told my mother," Casey reminded.

"That didn't count," she insisted. "She already knew."

Casey rolled her eyes. Several yards away, Vaughn stood next to his police blazer and stared at Grey while shaking his head.

"You don't seem to understand the seriousness of the situation, Grey," he firmly insisted. "Your sister is going out of her way to enrage some very unsavory characters."

Grey appeared understanding and approachable. "I appreciate your concern, Sheriff, and I do understand the seriousness of her actions," he insisted. "I promise I'll talk to her." Grey's look turned serious. "I know it's been two years, but she's still dealing with what happened. If it wasn't for Ruger and Diesel, she never would have gotten through this."

"Family friends, huh?" Vaughn asked while appearing deep in thought.

"Well, one was a little more than friends with Casey," he said with a sly grin. "If you get my drift."

"Yeah, I'm pretty sure I do," Vaughn muttered.

"But, hey, at least getting it nightly made her tolerable," Grey said while deviously raising his brows in a perverse manner.

"Uh, huh," Vaughn said and tensed. "This conversation is starting to make me uncomfortable."

"Oh, because she's my sister. I understand."

"Yeah, that too," Vaughn muttered.

"Don't worry about Casey," he announced and added a reassuring nod. "I'll make sure she plays nice."

"That would be--" Vaughn hesitated, considered his words, and sighed deeply. "--quite an achievement."

"Lighten up, Sheriff. You're going to go prematurely gray for nothing." Grey suddenly grinned and opened the box of doughnuts. "Doughnut?"

Vaughn smiled and declined with a slight shake of his head. Grey maintained his grin and waved the box of freshly baked, colorful doughnuts before him.

"Come on," he teased, "you know you want one. Everyone knows cops love their doughnuts."

Vaughn snorted a laugh and took a pink doughnut with sprinkles. "Thanks."

Grey shut the box and nodded. "Thanks for stopping by, Sheriff."

Sheriff Holt got into his blazer, backed up to the barn, and then drove down the driveway. Grey watched him drive away then sneered. He turned and headed for the porch where Dina sat with Casey. His relatively charming smile again returned as if on cue. He walked onto the porch and set down his doughnuts on the table next to Casey.

"Guard those while I get my coffee," Grey said firmly.

Dina suddenly jumped up from her chair with a little too much enthusiasm. "I'll get you some coffee."

"That's not--"

Dina hurried past him and into the house. He watched her hasty retreat, collapsed into the vacant chair with a disgusted moan, and smirked.

"She saw Diesel without his shirt, didn't she?"

Casey grinned. "Yep."

"Great," he groaned. "Now I get to hear Diesel banging her all night long."

Grey opened his box of doughnuts, snatched one, and ate it with disgust.

"What did our illustrious sheriff have to say?" Casey asked while raising a curious brow. "I assume it was about me."

Grey casually nodded. "He said you've got a great ass and asked if he could throw you over the hood of his cruiser and bang the shit out of you," Grey casually replied. "I said, 'sure, why not'. He seemed pleased. I don't think we'll need to worry about him after you close that deal."

Casey sneered at Grey and folded her arms over her chest. "If I thought you were serious, I'd probably have to kill you."

Grey chuckled. "He suggested you play nice."

"With him?" She snorted a laugh. "Yeah, right," she scoffed. "Like that's going to ever happen. For me, playing nice with Sheriff Holt would be kicking him everywhere except in his boys. What did you tell him?"

Grey shrugged, again without looking at her, and took another bite from his doughnut. "I told him I'd make sure you played nice." He glared at her with his brows raised. "And you're going to play nice."

She glared back at him and smirked. "You're dreaming."

Grey smiled deviously at her. "Oh, we'll see about that, my darling sister."

Chapter Fourteen

*L*ater that morning, Vaughn walked across the small bullpen toward his office. There appeared to be no one around, which was good, since he appeared to be in a foul mood as he entered his office. He stopped just inside the doorway. Ernest sat in the chair before his desk and flipped through a folder that had been lying on top. Vaughn approached, snatched the folder from Ernest, and walked behind his desk. He tossed the folder down as he collapsed into his chair and looked at the man across from him.

"Come in, Ernest," Vaughn scoffed lowly. "Won't you have a seat?"

Vaughn leaned back in his chair, folded his hands across his abdomen, and stared at Ernest with little expression. Ernest grinned and leaned forward.

"And I thought Wiley lacked manners," Ernest remarked. "You really should work on your disposition."

"What do you want?" Vaughn now demanded with limited patience.

"Casey Remington behind bars would be nice for a start," he snapped.

"Sorry, Ernest," Vaughn announced. "It was self-defense. I saw the video myself."

"Along with half the town," Ernest scoffed. "That girl is a menace and needs to be put in her place."

"You're absolutely right," Vaughn replied. "These damned women today think they have the right to keep men from pawing their bodies. What the hell kind of world are we living in? Next they'll be speaking their minds and then the whole world will just go to hell."

Ernest sneered at Vaughn.

"God," Vaughn continued with a sigh, "I miss the good old days when we could just club them over the head and drag them into our caves."

"You're a real prick, you know that?"

"So I've been told," Vaughn scoffed. He leaned across his desk, glared at Ernest, and turned serious. "You tell your boys to stay away from Casey Remington. She and her brother have been through enough."

"She didn't exactly strike me as being traumatized," Ernest remarked. "I don't think she learned anything from what happened to her and her family."

Vaughn straightened without taking his eyes off Ernest. "I'm curious, Ernest. Was that a confession or a threat?"

Ernest appeared annoyed then smirked. "Does this have to do with Melanie?"

Vaughn looked stunned and shook his head while marveling at Ernest's candor. "This has nothing to do with your niece, so stop pretending that is does."

"You're awfully defensive over Casey," Ernest said firmly.

Vaughn suddenly raised his brows and nodded. "You're right; I am," he snorted. "Someone tried to murder her two years ago and nearly succeeded. I'm a little cranky knowing there's a murderer running around my town. And you better believe if he tries to finish what he started two years ago, I'm putting a bullet between his eyes."

Vaughn and Ernest stared at each other a long moment in silence.

"My boys are innocent," Ernest finally scoffed. "We've been through this a thousand times."

"Yeah?" Vaughn sneered. "So let's make it a thousand and one."

Ernest stood with disgust. "Just watch yourself, Sheriff," he snapped. "I helped put you behind that badge, and I can make it all go away."

Vaughn casually stood and placed his hands on his hip and gun handle. He looked at Ernest with no emotion. "No, Ernest," he said flatly. "Shooting a cold-blooded killer three times in the chest put me behind this badge, and nothing short of putting me six feet under is going to remove it from me. Keep your boys away from Casey Remington."

"Or what, Sheriff?" he remarked while sneering.

"Or I'll let her finish what they started in the tavern last night," Vaughn firmly replied.

Ernest glared his annoyance, turned, and left the office. Vaughn watched him leave, sneered with disgust, and shook his head. He flopped back down in his chair and groaned while looking at the ceiling.

"I should probably up my life insurance policy," Vaughn muttered.

✝

*I*t was nearly noon later that day. The town had not changed in two years. The banner across the street appeared almost exactly the same but it now read, "100th Annual Fair". Casey rode her gray horse through town and received several stares followed by smiles and waves. People saw her and began collecting and clucking with one another. Casey wondered if they were happy to see her or surprised she'd returned. She casually glanced at a few of the familiar faces; recognizing her parents' supposed friends. They were the same people who gossiped endlessly about their murders. She wondered which ones betrayed her parents with their callous remarks and finger pointing. The more she thought about it; the less she cared. She loathed them all. Casey rode up to a parking meter just outside the police station. She dismounted the gray horse, tied it to the meter, and placed money in it. As she walked onto the sidewalk, Abby suddenly appeared and approached her. Abby seemed enthusiastic to see her. She really couldn't understand why. Mrs. Mayor had to know how she really felt about her.

"Casey," Abby announced cheerfully while smiling. "I heard you were back. You look great. How have you been?"

As Casey stared at Mrs. Mayor, a thousand thoughts raced through her mind. She wanted to lash out at the loathsome woman but buried her hatred deep inside. A strange, almost disturbing smile crossed Casey's face as she attempted to be polite.

"Mrs. Mayor," she responded almost as cheerfully and wondered if the woman knew how much she wanted to punch her in the face. "Grey and I are doing well. How have you been?"

Abby appeared almost surprised by her politeness and began her usual, long-winded answer to an insincere question. "I can't complain," she replied. "We're getting ready for our 100th annual fair. It's going to be spectacular. The best ever. I hope you and Grey will attend. You missed a lovely memorial service held in your parents' honor two years ago. Perhaps we could do something special in their honor this year now that you're back."

Casey was regretting having been so polite to Mrs. Mayor. She knew she should have started out by punching her in the face. Now, if she did it, it would just seem rude.

"You remember my Melanie?" She suddenly laughed. "Of course you do. It's only been two years. She has this amazing routine for the talent show this year. I do hope you can attend." She suddenly gasped and appeared excited. "You and Grey should participate at the fair. I'm sure we can find something for the two of you to do in order to contribute. Everyone will be thrilled if you participated. You could collect tickets or something."

Casey maintained her smile while screaming in her head. How long did she have to stand here and listen to this woman drone on? Could she punch her in the face? She was suddenly curious if punching Botox would be like punching play dough. The thought of Mrs. Mayor with a fist print permanently embedded in her face was actually quite humorous. As Abby continued to talk with no letup in sight, Casey realized she needed to leave before something unforeseen happened to the woman.

"You know," Casey suddenly announced, interrupting her, "I'll talk to Grey about it and get back to you. If you'll excuse me, I need have words with our sheriff."

Abby nodded and remained enthusiastic. "Yes, of course. Let me know. It was great seeing you again. Stop by the house some time."

"Yeah, I'll do that," Casey replied and silently snickered to herself. As if that would ever happen.

Casey turned and hurried into the police station. She entered the bullpen and looked around. With all her run-ins with Vaughn, she'd never actually been inside the police station before. Surprisingly, she wasn't impressed. Several deputies' desks lined the bullpen and the dispatch desk. Casey sought out the sheriff's office and approached. The door was closed, but Melanie was seen talking to Vaughn beyond the glass. Jeannie sat behind the dispatch desk before Vaughn's office. She looked up, saw Casey, and appeared surprised.

"Oh, my goodness, Casey Remington!" Jeannie announced excitedly.

"Hi, Jeannie."

The former tavern waitress turned police dispatch appeared giddy. "If you're here to rip the sheriff a new one, you'll need to take a number."

"Yes, I see Melanie in there," Casey teased. "The sheriff looks pissed."

"Melanie has that effect on him."

"She has that effect on a lot of people," Tucker announced from across the room

Casey turned to see Deputy Tucker a few feet away. She'd caught a glimpse of him at the tavern last evening, but she'd almost completely forgotten what he'd even looked like. She didn't know how she could forget Dina's fantasy man. Actually, Deputy Tucker was a lot of women's fantasy man. Even Casey couldn't deny he was handsome.

"Good to see you out of those handcuffs for a change. It agrees with you," Tucker remarked while grinning.

"I thought the sheriff might enjoy cuffing me once, you know, for old times' sake," Casey teased.

"Same old Casey," he said with a chuckle. "You really know how to push his buttons. Come to my office. I'll show you around."

Casey walked with Tucker to the next desk over.

He collapsed behind his desk, clasped his hands over his abdomen, and grinned. "Well, what do you think?"

She looked around and nodded. "Very roomy. Nice airflow, but some curtains would probably brighten it up."

He chuckled in response. "What brings you to Darwood Falls' finest?"

"Just wanted to talk to the sheriff," she announced and attempted an embarrassed smile. "We sort of got off to a bad start yesterday." That was a lie. Their bad start didn't bother her in the least.

"You mean you kicking Harford ass?" Tucker teased. "Wiley sent me the video. That was pretty amazing how you handled all four of them. Are you a black belt?"

"Unofficially, I suppose," she replied and appeared disinterested in the subject. "I heard Wiley is tending bar at the tavern. I didn't see him there last night."

"Just Tuesday, Friday, and Saturday nights. He's dying to see you," Tucker said with a grin. "Not that I blame him. You are a sight for sore eyes."

Casey laughed and shook her head. "And you're still as charming as ever." She appeared curious. "What happened with Melanie? You two were quite the couple two years ago."

He shrugged with disinterest. "When Vaughn became sheriff, she jumped ship--and him. What can I say; the girl likes men in power."

"I don't understand how Vaughn became sheriff," she remarked and appeared curious. "I thought you were next in line. What happened?"

"When he saved you, he became a hero," he informed her. "The town wanted him for sheriff, so Wiley appointed him. End of story."

She considered the comment and appeared curious. "So if I had died, he wouldn't be sheriff?" She suddenly laughed. "There's some irony to that."

Tucker chuckled softly. "He's my best friend, so I'm required to be happy for him."

The office door opened, and Vaughn's voice was heard. "Please don't come here anymore, Mel," Vaughn announced from his office doorway.

Casey and Tucker now stared at the sheriff's office. Melanie placed her arms around Vaughn's neck and smiled lustfully while looking into his dark eyes.

"We both know this isn't over," Melanie announced playfully. "You'll come crawling back. They all do."

Vaughn removed Melanie's arms from his neck and showed no emotion. "Stop it."

"Oh, I forgot," she playfully pouted then grinned. "No public displays of affection. Always professional. Last of the true Boy Scouts."

As Casey stared at Melanie, something twitched inside her. There had never been any animosity between them, but her presence somehow bothered Casey. Perhaps it had something to do with Vaughn's cruel reference to Casey being the town darling and needing to be spanked, yet he somehow ended up screwing the mayor's spoiled, little girl. The more she thought about it, all her problems seemed to begin and end with Vaughn. As satisfying as it was kicking all four Harford boys' asses last night, maybe she'd be more satisfied if she struck Vaughn again. Casey dismissed her inappropriate thoughts. Kicking his ass wasn't her reason for calling. She wished it had been. She casually approached Jeannie's desk. Melanie saw Casey and her face lost all expression. She immediately tensed. She attempted a smile and looked at Vaughn while smirking.

"I guess someone's right hand will be getting a workout tonight," Melanie boldly announced.

Vaughn rolled his eyes with disgust.

Melanie turned to Casey and flashed a smile. "He's all yours, kitten." She brushed past Casey, purposely knocking her back a step, and headed for the main entrance.

Vaughn eyed Casey, who watched Melanie leave, and then looked at Tucker. "Can you handle this one? I can't deal with this right now."

Vaughn returned to his office and slammed the door. Casey and Tucker jumped to the sound. Jeannie didn't appear fazed. It was apparently a common response after Melanie's visits.

Jeannie eyed Casey and grinned at her. "The sheriff will see you now."

Casey snorted a laugh to Jeannie's pleasure in Vaughn's torment and entered the office without knocking. Vaughn sat in his chair with his head back and his eyes closed. Casey shut the door behind her and approached the desk.

"I don't know why I bother. No one listens to me," Vaughn remarked mostly to himself then sat forward, looked at Casey, and smirked. "Miss Remington, how may I help you?"

Casey casually sat in the chair before his desk. "Your girlfriend is a real bitch."

"Out."

"Sorry, I shouldn't have--" Casey attempted a weak smile. "Apparently my compassionate hormones were in the parts they took out."

Vaughn appeared to tense from the comment and his expression faded to a less hostile one. He shifted within his chair. "What can I do for you, Casey?"

Casey placed a leather bound journal on the desk before him. Vaughn uncertainly stared at it, opened the journal, and then looked at her with surprise.

"This is your mother's journal."

Casey shrugged. "And you asked to see it."

"I distinctly remember you saying no."

"You want me to trust you?" she demanded and leaned forward. "What's in that journal doesn't leave this office."

"You have my word," he replied and appeared curious. "Why the change of heart?"

"Grey says I have to play nice," she announced while grinning. "This is me playing nice."

He snorted a laugh. "Since when do you listen to your brother?"

"Since he threatened to tell Ruger," she replied then made a face. "It's difficult to explain."

"So Ruger's your kryptonite?" Vaughn asked with a grin. "Good to know."

Casey abruptly stood while smiling. "Grab your holster; I'm taking you to lunch."

Vaughn glared at her and became immediately suspicious. "Okay, now you're up to something."

"I was told to play nice, but that doesn't include begging," she remarked firmly. "Are you coming or not?"

He considered the comment only a moment then smiled and nodded. "Okay, I'll play along."

Vaughn placed the journal in his top desk drawer, locked it, and joined her.

Chapter Fifteen

Casey and Vaughn walked along the sidewalk together while heading for the Boxcar Diner. It was a beautiful, warm afternoon and the smell of residential flowerbeds seemed to linger in the air. Casey inhaled the familiar scent. She didn't realize how much she missed that smell. It reminded her of her frequent rides into town even as a little girl. It almost seemed foreign walking alongside Sheriff Holt. They received several looks and old women were seen gossiping as they watched them. A few elderly women grinned at them as they passed and appeared to give an approving nod. Casey found their behavior strange. Was it that big of a deal to see her on the sidewalk with Sheriff Holt? And about whom were they gossiping? Was it her; or was it Sheriff Holt? She cast a glance at Vaughn as they walked and took in an eyeful of him. He had a commanding presence--that was certain. He was always excessively straight and fairly mature even as a young deputy, but now, he seemed different. He'd reached a level of maturity she couldn't even comprehend.

An image of him busting down the kitchen door two years ago drifted through her thoughts. She didn't remember much about what happened, but she saw the look on his face. She saw how it changed just before he pulled the trigger. Those three seconds defined who he was and forever changed him, and there was no denying he had changed. She felt her heart skip a beat and attempted to concentrate on something else. She needed to push all thoughts of that night out of her mind. She didn't need to lose control of her emotions. No good ever came from allowing her emotions to get in the way. They approached the antique store just ahead of them. It was a welcomed relief. She'd be able to focus on something else. This 'playing nice' with Sheriff Holt wasn't going to end well, and she had Grey to thank for that. He wouldn't think it was such a great idea when she lost control of her emotions and flipped out. Diesel and Grey removed the boards from the door and windows while Ruger casually leaned against a parking meter and supervised. Ruger was an excellent supervisor. He hated getting his hands dirty and loved giving orders.

"What's the deal here?" Vaughn asked Casey.

"The 'Three Stooges' want to open the shop," Casey replied with a hint of humor.

She approached Ruger and affectionately clung to his arm. He smiled in response and patted her hand on his arm. She needed a moment to redirect her emotions. Ruger was her version of a security blanket. He was soft, cuddly, and great to cry on.

"I can't wait to get inside," Ruger announced with boyish anticipation.

"There's quite a collection of antiques," she replied.

"Actually, I just want to clean," Ruger informed her while watching the other men work.

Casey smiled at him and shook her head. "You are so sweet-- and demented."

Ruger hugged her affectionately. Casey absorbed as much of Ruger's positive energy as she could then pulled away as Grey approached them. He was out of breath and smiling as he eyed her and Sheriff Holt.

"What you doing, sister dear?"

"I'm taking the sheriff to lunch."

"Nice," Grey said while grinning. He was obviously pleased that she took his advice to play nice. "When you're finished, you can help with inventory."

"Yeah, sure," she replied simply and smirked. "Not happening." Casey linked onto Vaughn's arm, surprising him, and forced him toward the diner.

"At least bring us some sandwiches!" Grey called after her.

She was obviously ignoring him on purpose. As Grey turned, he nearly collided with Diesel, who wore a serious look on his face.

"Did you say there were sandwiches?"

†

$\mathcal{T}$he Boxcar Diner hadn't changed at all in two years. Even the menus looked exactly the same. Casey sat across from Vaughn in a booth by the window. It was the same booth she and her parents sat within for their last lunch together. She drifted out a moment and once again relived the past. She snapped out of her trance and realized Vaughn was sitting silently across from her. He watched her without comment. For a moment, his stare made her uncomfortable. She saw the fair flier on the table and picked it up. As she studied it, she again appeared distant.

"My father was going to announce his run for mayor at the fair," she said softly without looking up.

"I'm sure he would have won."

She suddenly looked at him and appeared surprised then smiled more naturally. "You think so?"

Vaughn shrugged. "Your father was well respected around town. This town is in desperate need of change," he informed her. "The mayor and I don't exactly see eye to eye."

"Because you and Melanie broke up?"

He immediately shifted and appeared tense. "I'd rather not talk about Melanie."

Melanie was a sore subject, and forcing him to discuss her would only result in another argument. Grey would be displeased if she didn't play nice. She at least needed to make it through lunch without punching Vaughn. Although the prospect of punching Melanie sounded more fulfilling at the moment.

"Fair enough," she replied. "How about we talk about the fair?" Casey casually opened the flier and pretended to be surprised by its contents. "Oh, look at that. Someone's being dunked next Saturday night."

"It's tradition," he announced. "The sheriff and mayor always headline the dunking booth."

Casey offered a devious grin and felt particularly playful. "Hmm, someone is also placing himself on the bachelor auction block."

"That's Jeannie's doing. She hates me," he muttered with disgust. "I'm giving her the money to bid on me. Consider it my contribution."

Casey frowned and glared her disapproval. "You really know how to take the fun out of things."

"I have an image to maintain--and just a little bit of dignity," he added.

Something inside her suddenly snapped. Nice seemed to go out the window. "And Melanie having your baby wasn't part of that image?"

Vaughn appeared surprised and stared at her. "Where did you hear that?"

She casually shrugged. "That was last year's biggest scandal in this one *less* horse town."

"I don't want to talk about it," he snapped with irritation. "It's embarrassing."

Casey felt her claws coming out. She could no longer help herself. "Sort of like the details of my attack?"

He looked at her and seemed puzzled by the hostility. "Those reports are confidential," he informed her.

"Really?" she scoffed. "So how did the entire town find out that the killer tried to rape me?"

Vaughn stared at her and appeared horrified by the comment. "What?" He suddenly shifted in his seat and leaned forward. "You never mentioned that to me."

"I didn't have to, you were there," she snapped hotly.

It was finally time to call him out. The gossip about her attack had enraged her beyond rational thinking, and she was finally bringing it out into the open.

Vaughn shook his head with an odd expression. "All I saw was a man standing over you with a knife," he reported sternly. His look suddenly hardened. "If I had known that, I would have shot him in the balls."

Casey stared at him and was surprised by both his tone and that he hadn't actually known. That night was a blur between the pain and raw emotion, but she vaguely remembered him showing up a split second after the killer stabbed her. He hadn't seen the killer grabbing her pants. She was suddenly ashamed for loathing him for starting such a rumor, but then it dawned on her. She looked at Vaughn with horror.

"Then that means it had to be the killer who started the rumor," she gasped. "I can't believe I didn't think of that."

Vaughn shook his head and sank back in the booth with a defeated look. "There's no way to trace that rumor back to him now."

Casey was once again lost in her own world. She raced to find answers to old questions, but it was possible she'd never learn the truth, and it pissed her off. Abby approached their table looking stunning in her expensive outfit. Vaughn immediately tensed to her presence. Apparently, he wasn't any happier to see Abby than he was to see Melanie. Casey snapped out of her daze long enough to realize that Mrs. Mayor was standing over their table.

She looked at Casey and smiled excitedly. "I can't believe I'm running into you twice in one day!"

Abby scooted into the booth alongside Vaughn. He frowned and reluctantly slid across the bench so she could join them.

"I saw your brother and some other guys opening up the shop," she announced. "That's wonderful that you're doing something with the place." She suddenly hesitated and wore a strange smile. "So, uh, who was that muscly guy at the shop?"

"A close friend, Diesel," Casey replied.

Diesel was good at attracting female attention, which apparently had no age limit.

"Just close friend, huh?" she teased. "Makes me wish I wasn't so happily married." Abby linked playfully onto Vaughn's arm. "And this is the one that got away. I really don't know why my Melanie let this one go."

"Abby--" Vaughn muttered.

"Melanie is the star attraction at the kissing booth," Abby boasted and patted Vaughn's arm. "I'm sure we can count on the sheriff to pay for a few smooches."

"Yeah, I don't think so," Vaughn remarked.

"He's such a Boy Scout. Isn't he adorable?" Abby fussed while playfully patting his shoulder.

Casey cast a glance at Vaughn and grinned. She thought it was adorable that he was so squeamish about Mrs. Mayor clinging to him. She almost felt sorry for him. Almost. The waitress brought their lunch. Abby took her cue and indicated their platters.

"I'll just let you two enjoy your lunch," she announced.

Abby kissed Vaughn on the cheek and left as quickly as she had arrived. Casey eyed the red lipstick print on his cheek and smirked. Vaughn caught her look and immediately wiped the lipstick from his cheek with his napkin.

†

*T*he antique store looked as it had two years ago, except everything was covered in a thick layer of dust. Ruger happily cleaned items in the front room with a dust cloth while Grey and Diesel catalogued the contents of the store. They could be heard arguing as they worked. The antique bell above the front door dinged as the mayor entered. Ruger looked up from his dusty lamp and saw the mayor.

"I'm sorry, we're not open," Ruger announced.

"That's okay, I'm not shopping," Mayor Lance announced as he approached and extended his hand to Ruger. "Mayor Lance Ridgeway."

Ruger accepted his hand and shook it while smiling politely. "Ruger Quinn."

Grey and Diesel took time out from their bickering and approached the front. Grey studied Lance with more than a passing interest.

"Mayor Ridgeway, it's been a while," Grey announced in an almost cheerful tone.

"I'd heard you were back in town," Lance replied.

"From your nephews no doubt," Grey responded under his breath.

"Believe me; they needed to learn some manners," Lance informed him then grinned. "I'm not judging your sister's actions at all." He looked around and appeared pleased. "Are you planning on running the shop?"

"I'd like to at least sell off what's already here," Grey replied. "I haven't actually decided if I want to stay."

"I hope you'll attend the fair next weekend. One hundredth you know," the mayor reminded him.

He was overstating the obvious. The announcements were plastered all over town, and the big, bold banner across the street was hard to miss.

"We plan to attend," Grey replied. "The big guy here has never been to a country fair."

"There's food, right?" Diesel asked gruffly.

"Yes, Diesel, there's plenty of food," Grey replied with an exhausted sigh.

"I like the carnival games," Ruger announced cheerfully. "Will they have those?"

"Certainly," Lance replied and appeared humored. "Spend a small fortune and you might win a cheap stuffed toy for your best girl."

Ruger appeared to consider the comment and nodded with conviction. "Hmm. I'll need one of those too."

"A cheap stuffed toy?" Lance asked with surprise.

"No, a best girl," Ruger teased.

"Those aren't provided," Grey muttered.

"We can always use more bodies for the bachelor auction," Lance announced and grinned at Grey. "All the money goes to charity."

"I'd have to pay someone to buy me," Grey remarked then considered something and grinned lustfully. "Do they still have the kissing booth?"

"As much as the old biddies in town try to get it off the docket, it's back by popular demand," he replied proudly. "My Melanie and Dina are the only volunteers this year. Think you can get Casey to volunteer?"

Grey, Diesel, and Ruger eyed one another then burst out laughing.

"Obviously you've never met Casey," Ruger teased.

"She's not exactly the 'friendly' type," Grey added.

Diesel cleared his throat.

"Except on rare occasions," Grey politely added.

Ruger glared his disapproval at Grey.

"It's kept clean," Lance informed them. "Wiley's in charge of the kissing booth. He keeps an eye on the ladies--and the guy's hands. Maybe you'll get her to reconsider."

"Yeah, and maybe she'll bake a pie too," Grey said while barely holding back his laughter.

All three men again chuckled. Lance smiled and shook his head. They were having a little too much fun at Casey's expense. The bell above the door dinged as Dina entered. Lance glanced at Dina then looked back at the three men.

"You boys have fun," he announced while grinning. "I'll talk to you later."

The mayor nodded to Dina as he passed her to leave. Grey's smile twisted into a sneer as his piercing eyes followed Lance across the shop and out the door. Dina smiled cheerfully as she approached the men with a paper bag in her hand. Grey's attention shifted to Dina, and his charming smile returned as if on cue.

"I saw you guys working and thought you might like some sandwiches," Dina announced.

Diesel practically lunged for the bag and snatched it. "Great. Thanks."

Grey and Ruger watched Diesel walk away with the bag without a care.

"And once again we starve," Grey muttered.

"Do you guys need any help?" she offered.

"Plenty of rags and even more dust," Ruger cheerfully informed her.

Dina took a clean rag from the box and began dusting a nearby chair. She appeared oddly curious about their last visitor. "What did the mayor want?"

"The usual," Grey replied with little reaction. "Attempting to get others to volunteer so he'll look good." He appeared defeated, sank into thought, and sighed softly. "What I really need is for Casey to volunteer."

"I could talk to her," Dina replied without hesitation. "What do you need?"

"Her in the kissing booth."

Dina looked at Grey and appeared almost horrified. "You're kidding? That's asking a lot," she remarked. "Last year, I had to kiss all four Harford boys *twice.*"

Ruger attempted to hide his smirk. "Considering one has a fractured jaw, that's one less," he teased. He seemed a little too proud of the fact.

†

*I*t was nearly one o'clock by the time Casey and Vaughn left the diner together while Casey carried a large take-out bag. As they paused on the sidewalk just outside, Vaughn casually turned to face her and smiled gently.

"Thanks for lunch, Casey," he said. "I appreciate the effort even if you were pressured by your brother." There was a moment of hesitation. "It would be nice if things could be civilized between us for a change."

Casey shrugged. "I give it a week."

He snorted a laugh. "I figured three days, but I appreciate your optimism."

Casey hid her smile and met his gaze. As she stared into his dark eyes, she saw flashes of him holding her as he lowered her to the kitchen floor while she bled and sobbed. Casey suddenly looked away while fidgeting. She had to keep those memories suppressed. If she let her emotions get the best of her, the consequences could cost her dearly.

"I'd, uh, better get food to my guys before Diesel eats the weaker one." As she turned away from him, she wiped a tear from her eye then hurried for the antique shop.

Vaughn watched Casey hurry along town toward the antique store then frowned. Someone was standing over his shoulder. Vaughn glanced behind him and saw Mayor Lance watching Casey as she disappeared into the antique store. Lance shook his head and hid his smile.

"There's just something about that girl," Lance remarked and added a soft groan.

Vaughn rolled his eyes and focused his attention on Lance. "Something I can do for you, Mayor?"

"I heard you had a little disagreement with my brother-in-law this morning," Lance remarked.

"Oh, that," Vaughn snapped. "No, no disagreement. He was in the wrong. Would you like to threaten my badge as well?"

"What?" he suddenly announced then chuckled. "Heavens no! The people of Darwood Falls respect you. If anything, I want you to beef up security for the fair this weekend. I mean, I want everything patrolled." He sighed with defeat. "I'll be honest with you, Sheriff. My nephews are out of control, and I don't want any of those jug heads doing anything to ruin the fair. It's too important. I don't care if you have to knock them on the heads and ship them to Siberia. It's an election year coming up, and I don't want those boys ruining this for me."

"Everything is under control," Vaughn reported while appearing skeptical of the mayor.

"Good, I'm glad to hear," he announced and began walking past Vaughn. He suddenly stopped and gave him a firm look. "And, uh, don't tell my wife we had this discussion."

Vaughn smirked and nodded.

Chapter Sixteen

$\mathcal{R}$uger stood by the front desk in the antique store and ate a sandwich while casually watching Casey and Grey across the room in a heated exchange. Their conversation was loud and clearly heard by everyone. Casey was wild and animated while Grey pursued her persistently.

"Are you out of your mind?" Casey lashed out. "No, absolutely not!"

"You're being unreasonable!"

Diesel approached Ruger at the desk and poked inside the food bag. He removed a sandwich and indicated the exchange with little interest.

"What's with Bonnie and Clyde?" Diesel asked.

Ruger casually shrugged. "Grey just asked Casey to volunteer for the kissing booth."

Diesel glanced across the room and appeared more interested now. "Huh? She's handling it rather well."

"Yeah, I thought so too."

"Come on, Casey," Grey pleaded while dancing around with frustration. "This is so important to me."

She glared at him with her arms folded across her chest. "If it's so damned important then you do it!"

"The guys don't want me in the kissing booth, they want you," he informed her sternly while wildly gesturing then turned more sincere and lay on the puppy dog eyes. "Think of Mom and Dad."

Horror crossed her face, and she immediately became defensive. "Oh, no you don't!" she cried out while pointing a warning finger at him. "I've done everything you've asked up until now. I even made nice with Sheriff Holt, but this is asking too much. Don't hold Mom and Dad over me!"

Grey looked at Ruger across the room and pleaded with his eyes. "A little help here, please."

Ruger appeared innocent and held his hands in the air. "I can't even stand her kissing this one," he said while indicating Diesel. "Why would I condone her smooching half the men in town?"

"You're absolutely no help, you know that?" he snapped. "We need the people in town to see we're one of them." Grey looked back at Casey. "This is why we're here, Casey. I'm making an unbelievable sacrifice." He gave her his best sorrowful eyes. "All I'm asking is to let a few old guys kiss you. You kiss Ruger and Diesel like that all the time."

Ruger looked at Diesel and appeared curious. "Did he just refer to me as old?"

"I think he did."

Dina dusted some trinkets on a shelf and appeared to ignore the conversation, but she was obviously listening with great interest. Grey looked at Dina and practically lunged for her. Dina jumped with surprise.

"Help me out here, Dina," Grey pleaded.

Casey groaned lowly while shaking her head. "Yes, Dina, tell Grey I would not be a good choice for the kissing booth."

Grey looked at Dina and clutched her elbows, forcing her to look into his sorrowful eyes. "Come on, Dina; tell her it's just a quick peck."

Dina uncertainly looked between both, appeared uncomfortable, and fumbled over her words. "That's usually how it works," she said timidly. She hesitated a moment then appeared more confident. "Want me to demonstrate?"

"If you must," Casey groaned while rolling her eyes.

Ruger and Diesel suddenly looked up from the desk with surprise and appeared interested.

"Is she going to kiss Casey?" Diesel suddenly whispered to Ruger.

"Shh--" Ruger hushed him and stared at the women with anticipation.

Both men watched in complete silence and with great interest. Dina turned to Grey and kissed him quickly on the lips then looked back at Casey. Ruger and Diesel both frowned with disappointment. Grey was rendered momentarily speechless.

"Like kissing your grandmother," Dina announced.

Casey wasn't convinced then muttered, "You and your grandmother must have been real close."

Dina frowned and appeared disgusted. "I'm determined to beat that bitch Melanie at something just once," she scoffed. "Apparently, I'm the only women in town brave enough to take her on. I'm sick and tired of her treating me like a second-class citizen just because my father abandoned me and my mother is the town whore."

There was an odd silence around the room. Casey stared at Dina and felt sympathetic. Her best friend had been tortured with her mother's less than respectable reputation from a young age. Casey had been so consumed with her own tortured existence; she couldn't feel her friend's pain.

"You want to take her down? I'll help you," Casey announced firmly then looked at Grey and groaned. "Sign me up."

Grey appeared excited. "Yeah, that's my sister!"

Dina hugged Casey. "Thank you, Casey," she said softly then pulled away and appeared excited. "I'll spread the word at the tavern."

"I'll post it on the fliers in the store window," Grey announced as he hurried across the store.

Ruger rolled his eyes. "And I'll just stand here feeling nauseous," he muttered.

"I think I need to find some extra cash," Diesel remarked. "This fair sounds expensive."

Dina excitedly took Casey's hand and led her to the back of the shop. "We have to decide what you're going to wear. We're going to be so hot."

"Don't I just need a breath mint and lip balm?" Casey protested as Dina pulled her away.

All three watched Dina guide Casey into the back then appeared oddly silent.

"Dina could be a problem," Diesel informed them.

"What if we gave her a job here at the shop?" Ruger suggested with a curious tilt of his head.

"Do we really want to include her?" Diesel asked while poking through the paper bag for another sandwich.

"She's been Casey's best friend since kindergarten, and she loved my parents," Grey informed them. "We can trust her."

"Someone's got a hard on for Casey's friend," Diesel remarked while grinning.

Grey glared at him and wasn't impressed. "That was a long time ago. Things have changed since then," he remarked. "We have more important things to do."

"More important than you doing Dina?" Diesel teased.

Grey sneered at him and appeared to be losing his patience. Ruger rolled his eyes and stepped between the two before Diesel started tossing Grey around like a ragdoll.

"We're obviously losing focus here," Ruger announced firmly then eyed Diesel. "And you need to cool it with the sexual references."

"Says the moral fiber that holds us all together," Diesel snorted while wearing a cheap grin.

Ruger wasn't impressed. His look was cold and serious. "Tread lightly, my friend."

Diesel snorted then walked away.

✝

*I*t was early Saturday morning and just one week before the town fair. All seemed peaceful within the small town of Darwood Falls, but it wouldn't stay that way long. Small pockets of vendors would start filtering into the town to setup for opening weekend. By late week, the town would be a madhouse with vendors attempting to move into the fairgrounds and setup trailers, equipment, rides, and games. Most locals were enjoying the calm before next weekend's storm of visitors. The police station bullpen was quiet and void of life, as it was most Saturday mornings. Jeannie was off on most weekends and the deputies patrolled the town but weren't required to hang around the office. Emergency dispatch would contact them if there were any calls. It was a nice setup, which kept a police presence without unnecessary personnel. Sheriff Holt was the officer on duty this particular weekend, even though next weekend all three officers would be working long hours. Vaughn sat behind his desk with his booted feet propped on top. He leaned casually back in his worn chair and read from Catherine Remington's journal. He had his temple propped against his hand as his brows knitted with concern to what he read.

"No sooner had Brandon left the store," Catherine wrote, *"when Wayne Harford dropped in. I knew he wasn't there to 'look around' as he reported. Ernest would sometimes make purchases, but his sons*

never just stopped in. I kept an eye on him and rightfully so. He approached me at the desk and asked about the settee in the back. He claimed Ernest had sent him to inspect it, but I knew it wasn't true. Ernest never looked twice at that old sofa. I couldn't exactly call him on this, since I prided our shop on being professional. Instead, I went into the back room with him and indicated the antique couch. I knew better than to turn my back on Wayne. It was a mistake many women in town had made, and I'd heard the horror stories. He pointed out a tear in the cushion. There hadn't been one before, so, naturally, I looked. I'd made the mistake and turned my back on the bastard, but I didn't realize what I'd had done until he was already tackling me to the settee. He was like an animal pawing at me, groping my body, and trying to pull off my clothes. I couldn't believe he'd go this far!"

Vaughn stared at the journal in his hand as his mouth hung open. The look of shock on his face was indescribable. He held his breath, turned the page, and continued to read.

"I knew his intentions, and I had to stop him! Being on top of me, he had me at a disadvantage. I had only one action of recourse to stop him, and I took it. I wasn't sure which of us was more surprised by my hand clamped on his testicles through his pants. It wasn't a place on the man I'd wanted to touch, but my hand was there now, and I had every intention to rip them off! He wanted to hit me; he tried to hit me, but I gripped even harder and twisted my hand. I'd never seen a man drop so fast. I made a conscious effort to release him as he fell to the floor. Something inside me screamed to keep ahold of him, but I just wanted my hand off his filthy body. As he clutched himself while writhing around the floor, I considered running out the back door and screaming like a crazy woman, but something snapped inside me. He was a Harford, and there was no justice against a Harford. There was just me. As he writhed on the floor crying like a little boy, I did the unthinkable. I grabbed his arm, twisted it away from him, and I kicked it with all my anger. It snapped with the most hideous sound. He now screamed and begged me to stop. I released his arm and watched him clutch it while crying as he lie on the floor. I still wanted to kill him. From where I stood, I could just as easily snap his neck, but I suppressed those urges. I'd made my point without killing the monster."

Vaughn shut the journal, tossed it on his desk, and ran his fingers through his hair. He uncertainly sat forward and stared at the journal with his brows knitted. He snatched the journal, leaned on the desk, and continued to read.

Chapter Seventeen

The fairground was busy that afternoon. Locals and out-of-towners had volunteered to scrub the buildings and prepare the grounds for the upcoming fair. The parking field was being roped off and signs were pounded into the ground to help direct traffic flow. Former sheriff Wiley played with the sound system at the stage furthest from the main entrance. It made an ear-piercing screech that caused everyone within earshot to grimace and turn. Abby stopped her luxury golf cart and glared at Wiley. He grinned his apologies. Ernest and Mayor Lance stood on stage and shook their heads while pointing at Wiley at the sound system toward the back. Abby drove up to the stage and joined her husband and brother. Wiley continued to fiddle with several switches. When his sound check didn't shatter any eardrums, it was obvious he'd gotten in right. Vaughn approached Wiley and the sound system from across the fairgrounds. Wiley glanced at him, grinned, and returned to his duties.

"What brings you out this way, Vaughn?" Wiley asked. "Pre-bachelor auction jitters?"

"You're a funny man," Vaughn scoffed. "Don't quit your day job."

Wiley looked at him and uncertainly sat on the table. "You look a little distracted. I'm guessing it's something more than putting your butt on the auction block."

"I'm way beyond distracted," Vaughn informed him sternly. "I'm disturbed and possibly sickened by something I'd just read in Catherine Remington's journal."

Wiley stared at Vaughn with a look of surprise. "Catherine Remington's journal? I don't remember anything about a journal."

"Casey gave it to me," he replied and waved his hand. "We're getting off subject." Vaughn tensed while staring at Wiley. "She filed an assault report against Wayne Harford six months before she was killed." He was unusually silent then raised his brows and continued. "I searched every file we have, and I didn't find any report."

Wiley stared at Vaughn and appeared frozen. Vaughn stared back and didn't blink.

Vaughn slowly nodded and appeared to understand the silence. "You know what I'm talking about, don't you? What happened to that report, Wiley?"

Wiley took a deep breath, uncertainly looked around, and then took Vaughn by the arm. "Let's walk."

The two men walked away from the stage area and into a large clearing void of activity. Vaughn continued to cast glares at Wiley, who appeared reluctant to speak as they walked.

"Yes, Catherine filed a complaint against Wayne for attempted sexual assault," he reluctantly remarked. "I took down every word she said, believing every word she said."

Vaughn stopped and forced him to face him. His look was stern and harsh. "What happened to that report, Wiley?"

There was a long silence. Wiley frowned. "Ernest happened."

Vaughn looked up, shook his head with disbelief, and almost laughed. He looked back at Wiley and glared his annoyance. "You let Ernest bully you into burying a sexual assault complaint against his son? The bastard intended to rape Catherine Remington. The only reason he didn't succeed is because *she* stopped him. How could you allow something like this?"

"I didn't allow it, Vaughn," Wiley protested then fell silent and appeared ashamed. "I buried the report to protect her; to protect the Remington's." He took a deep, shaken breath and stared across the fairgrounds at nothing. "There had been a lot of talk going around town that year. Rumor had it Brandon Remington was going to run for mayor. The powers that be didn't like it." He finally looked back at Vaughn. "Ernest came to me with Wayne's side of the story. His version would have caused such a scandal; it would have destroyed any chances Brandon had to win an election." Wiley appeared exhausted. "Yes, Ernest wanted me to bury the complaint, but I didn't do it to keep my job. I buried Catherine's complaint so Brandon would be angry enough to run for mayor."

"That's wrong, Wiley," Vaughn scoffed. "You manipulated the law. That's what we've been trying so hard to put an end to. Brandon was going to run anyway."

Wiley shook his head with a defeated look. "No, he wasn't," he replied softly. "I had to turn him against me, it was the only way."

Vaughn shook his head and looked away with disgust. "That complaint could have made the difference in our search for Catherine and Brandon's killer."

"I know you think Wayne did it, Vaughn, but it couldn't have been him," Wiley announced. "As much as I'd love to pin it on them myself, they didn't do it. Even Casey admitted the man who attacked her couldn't have been Wayne. He's too big."

"Then it was Ryan or Blain," Vaughn interjected.

"We've checked their alibis a hundred times," Wiley replied. "They checked out every time. If you really want to solve the murders, you'll need to come up with a different suspect."

†

Vaughn entered his office with a look of disgust and flopped down in his worn chair behind the desk. He leaned back, clasped his hands over his abdomen, and immediately looked at the ceiling.

"What could have been done differently?" Vaughn asked softly aloud to no one. "If Catherine had reported it to me, would it have made a difference? Or were the Remington's sentenced to death no matter what?"

He shook his head with disgust, leaned forward, and rubbed his already tired eyes.

"The answer's in her journal," Vaughn muttered. "I need to go back further."

Vaughn removed his keys and reached for the upper, right hand drawer. He stared at the drawer and suddenly hesitated. The wood had fresh splinters along the edge. Vaughn tossed his keys aside and pulled open the drawer. The journal was gone!

"No, no!" Vaughn cried out and rummaged through the drawer in vain.

He violently slammed the drawer and pushed his chair away with such force, it struck the wall. Vaughn sprang to his feet and looked around the office while attempting to control his rising temper. His body trembled as he put his hand to his forehead several times while searching for some answer.

"It wasn't Wiley," he insisted softly. "He wouldn't have done this." He remained deep in thought while scratching his brow. Vaughn suddenly looked up and appeared enraged. "Son-of-a-bitch!" He violently kicked the desk, jolting it several inches. He collapsed into his chair, groaned, and covered his eyes. "Casey's going to kill me."

†

It was after two in the morning on Sunday. The tavern's parking lot was nearly empty, with most of the locals finding their way home after a long night of drinking and rowdy adventures. The few trucks remaining out front belonged to those with no place better to be or the few workers attempting to clean up. Wiley counted the register while Dina swept the floor. She was the last waitress remaining, since it was her turn to close-up with Wiley. A few hard-core drinkers remained at the bar and attempted to talk Wiley into one more round. At this time of night, he no longer acknowledged them. It was the only way to get them to leave. Once Dina finished with the floor, she began straightening chairs. Her attention briefly shifted to the corner table. Dina's mother sat slumped in her chair with her elbows on the table and attempted to hold up her head with her hand. She fumbled with her drink, the glass stained with red lipstick prints. Olivia dropped the glass and it shattered on the floor, alerting Wiley and the remaining patrons to the drunken woman's presence. She looked up and appeared unable to focus. For the first time, she stared directly at Dina as her body swayed with intoxication.

"What are you looking at?" Olivia scoffed in a low, slurred voice.

It was possible she didn't even recognize her own daughter these days, not that it mattered, because she didn't acknowledge she had a daughter for many years. Dina frowned with disgust and returned to straightening chairs.

"Go home, Dina," Wiley announced from across the bar.

She looked at him and appeared surprised. "But I still have--"

"I've got it," he replied firmly then offered a tiny smile. "Go on. Get out of here."

Dina smiled gratefully. "Thanks, Wiley."

He gave a slight wave. Dina tossed her apron onto the bar, accepted her purse from Wiley from behind the bar, and hurried for the door. She glanced back only briefly. Olivia was now slumped over the table out cold. Dina headed out the door and showed no

120

emotion to the woman's condition. She walked across the nearly empty parking lot toward her old car parked alongside Wiley's pickup truck beneath the vapor light. As she approached her car, she saw the back tire was flat. Dina groaned with disgust.

"Great," she scoffed.

She'd end up having to wait for Wiley to finish his work in order to give her a ride home. It seemed inconceivable that anyone she knew would be up this time of night. Instead of getting home half an hour early, she was going to be at least an hour later. As she approached her car, she visually assessed the damage to the tire. Her eyes strayed to the front tire. It was flat as well! Dina's eyes widened, and she suddenly appeared horrified. She took two, quick steps backward then turned to run back for the tavern. A man in a mask stood between the two cars, blocking her route to the tavern. Dina gasped and stood frozen while staring at the man. She glanced behind her. Her only option was the nearby woods. They were dark and intimidating. She glanced back at the man as her breathing became heavy. He lunged for her. Dina screamed and ran for the woods beyond her car. Her screams would go unheard. The walls were too thick in the tavern. Her attacker chased after her. Dina ran into the woods without looking back. In the dark, they'd be difficult to navigate, but there was a path somewhere up ahead.

There was the sound of a loud grunt just behind her. Dina uncertainly looked back and suddenly stopped. Her attacker lie on the ground, writhing in agony. She hesitated only a moment then uncertainly headed back for the parking lot and the motionless man. The man in black slowly moved to his feet while clutching his shoulder. Dina jumped with alarm and prepared to turn back for the woods. Her assailant suddenly turned and ran away. Dina watched him run across the parking lot and disappear into the woods across the street. She uncertainly entered the parking lot near her car and scanned the area. Nothing moved. There was no one there, but someone had to be there. Something or someone stopped the man from chasing her. She looked back at the tavern and ran across the parking lot for the door. A police blazer pulled into the parking lot. Dina suddenly stopped and watched the blazer approach. The interior light came on, revealing Deputy Tucker. He looked at Dina through the open window and offered a charming smile.

"Hey, Dina," he announced. "Just making my rounds. Everything under control tonight?"

She just stared at him with her mouth hanging open. Two seconds sooner, and he would have run over her attacker on the road. She appeared relieved and hurried to his open window.

"You just missed him, Deputy," she announced while now panting and holding her chest. "This guy slashed my tires then came after me. He took off into the woods that way," she said while pointing across the street, "just two seconds ago."

Deputy Tucker appeared stunned and quickly grabbed his cell phone. He pressed the walkie-talkie button. "Mitchell, you out there?"

There was a moment of silence. His phone beeped and Deputy Mitchell's voice followed. "Yeah, I'm here, Tucker. What's up?"

"I'm at the tavern," he announced while glancing at Dina. She was looking more flustered now than before. "Some guy slashed Dina's tires then attacked her. He's in the woods north of the tavern. Patrol the area on the other side. I'm having a look-see."

"Roger," came Mitchell's reply. "Should I call the sheriff for backup?"

"Negative," Tucker replied. "I don't want to give him too much of a head start. I'll take Winchester."

"Copy that," came Mitchell's reply.

Tucker jumped out of the truck as Wiley appeared on the tavern porch.

"What's going on?" Wiley suddenly asked.

Tucker nodded Dina to Wiley. "Stay with Wiley until one of us gets back," he informed her.

"You can't go after him alone," Dina cried out.

"I'm not," Tucker announced and removed his rifle from the blazer. "I'm taking Winchester."

Chapter Eighteen

Dina sat at the bar with the few remaining drunks surrounding her with great interest as Wiley slid a glass of whiskey on the bar before her. She accepted the glass in trembling hands and sipped it. Dina made a face and set it back down. She remained visibly shaken as Wiley and the drunks stared at her.

"He started to chase me," she said softly and shook her head, "and, next thing I know, he was down. He was just lying there in agony."

"Think the idiot fell?" Wiley asked.

She shook her head defiantly. "No, he was taken down," Dina announced firmly. "Someone took him down, and they took him down hard."

"But you didn't see anyone?"

"No, no one," she replied. "It was the strangest thing. Who was he, Wiley? What did he want?"

Wiley uncertainly shook his head. "It was obviously an ambush, being your tires were slashed," he informed her, "but no one would have any reason to go after you. You haven't done anything--" He suddenly fell silent.

Dina stared at Wiley as he fidgeted. Her look turned concerned. "You think he came after me because of Casey? Someone wants revenge on her, so they came after me?"

Wiley appeared tense and straightened. "It could be anything, Dina. Let's not go jumping to conclusions."

Dina picked up the glass in her trembling hand and drank the entire contents. It was possibly the first alcoholic drink she'd ever had. The tavern door suddenly opened, startling everyone inside. Grey looked around the bar, saw Dina near Wiley, and hurried for her.

"Are you okay?" Grey asked while placing a hand on her shoulder.

Dina suddenly burst into tears, jumped from her chair, and clung to Grey. He uncertainly held her against him as she sobbed into his neck. Her emotional outburst surprised him. He immediately turned soothing and clung to her.

"It's okay," Grey said softly. "I'll look after you."

Grey looked at Wiley behind the bar. Wiley offered a timid smile and shrugged.

"Thanks for calling the house, Wiley," Grey said gently.

"Sorry to wake you," Wiley replied.

"I wasn't sleeping anyway," he responded. "I'm going to take her back to my house. The boys can wait until morning to talk to her. Give them the message."

Wiley nodded. Grey pried Dina from his body and guided her from the tavern with his arm securely over her shoulder.

†

*G*rey's jeep pulled up to the Remington farmhouse a little before three in the morning. The farm seemed particularly quiet, although several lights were on both in and outside the house. Dina got out the passenger side of the jeep and appeared almost sedate. That shot of whiskey and near exhaustion appeared to take its toll on her. The sound of thundering hoof beats were heard. Both looked across the farm toward the barn. Casey rode her large gray horse across the driveway at a fast gait and slid to a stop several feet before them. Her horse pranced around excitedly while she stared at both with surprise and concern.

"What's going on?" Casey suddenly asked.

Dina stared at Casey on her horse but was too tired to speak. Grey frowned while placing his arm around Dina's shoulder and pulled her to his side.

"Someone attacked Dina as she was leaving the tavern tonight," he replied then gave her an odd, nearly scolding look. "Where the hell were you?"

"Attacked?" Casey suddenly demanded with a shattered look in her eyes that quickly turned to anger. "What do you mean attacked?"

"She's okay," Grey insisted. "She wasn't hurt, but the guy got away."

"Where?" Casey growled as her eyes narrowed and her grip tightened on the reins.

Storm's massive body pranced as he snorted to her rising emotion. The horse was prepared to explode on her command, almost like a racehorse in the starting gate.

"You never mind where," Grey snapped. "Put the horse away and get your ass inside. Let the law handle this."

"Let the law handle this?" Casey suddenly cried out. Storm slung his head in response and reared slightly. "Do you know who you're talking to?"

"Yes," Grey scoffed. "Your friend needs you. Make the right decision for once."

Casey stared at Grey with a wildly unpredictable look then glanced at Dina's sedate condition. She groaned softly and relaxed her grip on the reins. As her body sagged, the gray horse relaxed. She leapt off the horse's back without using the stirrups and headed for the barn, leaving the reins around the horse's neck. Storm turned and followed her without prompting. Grey guided Dina toward the house.

"Casey will draw you a nice, hot bath in the jetted tub," Grey informed her with a soothing tone as they approached the porch. "And I'm going to make you a special hot toddy to settle your nerves."

"Thanks, Grey," she said softly. "I don't know how to repay you."

"You're family, Dina," he replied. "We look out for one another."

✝

Casey was once again alone in the cemetery. Several weeping willow trees were dripping with early morning dew and the ground was wet from the earlier downpour. She uncertainly looked around and her eyes gravitated to the two headstones several feet away. They were overgrown with vegetation. She approached the headstones and removed the plant life covering the name on the first one. She stared helplessly at her parents' names engraved in the whitish gray marble. It was a grim reminder that her mother and father were still dead. She allowed the grief to consume her for only a moment before focusing her attention on the second headstone. Grey was alive. She knew he had survived. Why was there a second headstone? She removed the vegetation to reveal the name engraved on front. Dina Crawford. Casey suddenly gasped and jumped away from the headstone. Her heart pounded roughly in her chest. She suddenly felt a sharp, stabbing pain in her lower abdomen. Casey clutched her abdomen and looked at the blood seeping between her fingers. She lifted her bloodied hand as it trembled and stared at it. She looked around with fright.

"Dina!" she cried out, but there was no one there. No one answered.

A faint, muffled voice could be heard. It sounded like Dina screaming, but it sounded so far away. She looked around and attempted to locate from where her voice was emitting. Casey suddenly tensed and looked at the grave. She uncertainly approached Dina's headstone, knelt down, and listened. Dina was screaming from her casket! Casey cried out with alarm and began ripping through the ground with her fingers.

"I'm coming, Dina!" she cried out as tears streaked her face. "I'll get you out, I swear! I'll save you!"

"She's not in there," came a familiar, soothing male voice.

Casey suddenly looked up from where she knelt before the grave and stared at the shadow of a man standing before her. She stared at him and tried to make out his face. He had come to her once before in a dream she vaguely remembered. She remembered his voice but still didn't know who he was. Dina's screaming from the grave ceased and all was quiet. Casey looked from the grave to the shadowy figure standing over her. She slowly straightened. He extended his hand to her. She eagerly accepted his hand. She remembered the warmth of his touch from before. His touch soothed her and her anguish vanished instantly. She moved into his arms and rested her head on his shoulder. She couldn't believe how good it felt being in his arms.

"I want to take care of you," he whispered softly while holding her against him. "Let me take care of you."

She slowly lifted her head and attempted to look into his eyes. Despite his shadowy appearance, she wanted this man. It didn't matter who he was. She wanted to feel his body against hers as he made love to her. He lowered his head to hers. She strained to meet the lips she couldn't see. A blinding light suddenly hurt her eyes. Casey slowly woke and looked across her bedroom at Ruger standing before the large window as sunshine poured in through the open curtains. He looked at her and grinned. She loved the man, but she felt an overwhelming desire to hit him for ruining her sexually fulfilling dream.

"Good morning, sunshine!" Ruger announced a little too cheerfully.

She groaned and pulled the covers over her head. "Go bother someone else," she scoffed lowly.

She wanted to finish her lustful dream with her mystery man in the cemetery. The covers were suddenly pulled back, causing her to jump. Ruger hovered over her and smiled in an almost sinister manner.

"We have matters to discuss," he informed her.

"Can't they wait until the crack of noon?"

"No, they can't," he replied firmly then suddenly turned serious and commanding. "We need to discuss what we're going to do about your friend."

Casey looked at the clock. It wasn't even seven! She groaned and slowly sat up. She was moderately disheveled from what few hours of sleep she'd actually gotten. There was no point to ignoring Ruger; he wasn't going to go away. He was annoying that way.

"What do you suggest?" Casey muttered. "Stuff her in the wood chipper and press puree?"

"You're disturbingly morbid in the morning," he casually replied while sitting on the edge of the bed near her.

"Fine," she scoffed. "We'll discuss Dina." Casey flopped back down on the bed and groaned softly. "And then I'm installing a lock on my bedroom door."

Chapter Nineteen

$\mathcal{I}$t was 8:00 A.M. Sunday morning and only a few hours since Dina was attacked at the tavern. Despite the early hour and lack of sleep, Dina sat on the porch in a pair of Casey's borrowed shorts and t-shirt. She hugged her knees to her chest while her fixed gaze overlooked the pastures surrounding the Remington farmhouse. She looked exhausted from little to no sleep last night after her close call. The screen door opened. Casey walked onto the porch, eyed her quiet friend, and sat on the porch railing facing her.

"Did you sleep?" Casey asked gently.

"A little," Dina replied without looking at her.

Casey took a deep breath and looked across the farm. It was a difficult conversation to have with her friend. She finally looked back at Dina.

"I wish I could say what happened was just a random event," Casey announced with great seriousness, "but it wasn't. My return made you into a target."

Dina suddenly looked at Casey and appeared stunned. "Do you really believe that?"

"I don't have to believe it," she replied. "I know it. I returned to Darwood Falls with a stick clutched firmly in my hand and poked it at a hornet's nest." She rested her head against the support beam and sighed deeply. "Now they're going to hurt me by going through you."

There was an odd silence as Dina stared at Casey. She finally looked at Dina and appeared curious.

"You don't believe me, do you?" Casey asked.

"Actually, I do," Dina replied softly. "It was the Harford boys, wasn't it?"

Casey shrugged.

"So what do we do?" Dina asked.

"The guys think you should take a little vacation for a few weeks," Casey announced.

"Excuse me?" Dina suddenly remarked.

"Ruger has a nice place a few hours from here," she replied. "You can stay there until this blows over."

Dina stared at Casey a long, silent moment then finally responded. "Until *what* blows over, Casey?" she suddenly asked. "What are you really doing here?"

She didn't respond. She wasn't sure how to respond. Casey stared at her friend and felt responsible for last night's near miss. It was her fault, and she wasn't sure if she could live with herself if she got Dina killed. Last night's dream was enough to convince her that she couldn't handle the guilt.

"You need to go away for a few weeks," Casey informed her firmly.

"No," Dina replied and sat up straight while planting her feet firmly on the porch. "Two years ago, you ran away from your fears. Now you're back to face them. What happened to me last night was nothing compared to what you'd gone through. You need me. No matter what your reason for returning, I intend to stay and fight alongside you. I won't leave you."

Casey stared at Dina with little reaction. She sighed and returned her head to the support beam. "I tried," she announced simply.

The porch door slowly opened on cue. Casey didn't bother looking. Dina uncertainly looked back at the open door.

t

*I*t was Tuesday evening and business at the tavern was starting to pick up despite the early hour. Melanie waited on tables while Wiley tended bar. Melanie hurried from table to table and appeared frazzled. She approached Wiley at the bar and exchange empty pitchers for full ones.

"Where's Dina?" Melanie scoffed. "She's an hour late."

"I don't know," Wiley replied. "I haven't heard from her since that business Saturday night. She didn't call to say she was going to be late."

"She's doing this on purpose," Melanie whined. "She knows we get busy on bowling league nights."

"She'll be here," he assured her.

Vaughn and Tucker sat on the other side of the bar in their street clothing with mugs of beer before them. Vaughn scribbled on a piece of paper. Wiley approached, studied them with interest, and appeared curious.

"What's so interesting on the north side of the bar?" Wiley teased.

"Plotting our attack for the bachelor auction," Vaughn said without looking up from his paper.

Wiley held back his laugh and shook his head. "Are you seriously making Jeannie bid on you?"

Vaughn looked up and appeared serious. "It's the only way my ass goes on stage."

"I think it's a lot of fun," Tucker remarked cheerfully.

"You would," Vaughn scoffed.

Tucker enjoyed making Vaughn squirm. "You're too image conscious, Vaughn."

"It's not my image," he retorted to his best friend. "It's my ego I'm worried about."

"Speaking of the fair," Wiley announced then grinned. "Have you seen the revised fair flier?"

Wiley placed the flier on the bar before them and pointed at the new addition. Both men studied the flier with shared looks of surprise. Tucker suddenly laughed.

Vaughn appeared stunned and looked at Wiley. "This is a joke, right?"

"Nope, no joke."

"I'll believe that when I see it," Vaughn scoffed and pushed the flier away.

Melanie appeared between the two men and clung to both their shoulders while looking at the flier on the bar near them. "Believe what?" she asked cheerfully.

"Casey's working the kissing booth," Tucker said while grinning lustfully.

Melanie's expression suddenly dropped to something resembling a sneer. She snatched the flier, looked at it, and then tossed it down with disgust.

"Someone put that in there as a joke," Melanie scoffed. "She'd never do that."

The front door was thrown open, causing several patrons to turn and look. Dina hurried across the tavern, paused before the bar, and handed Wiley her purse in exchange for an apron.

"I'm late, I know," she announced nearly out of breath while tying the apron around her waist.

"It's okay," Wiley replied with little concern.

Melanie glared her disapproval at Wiley. "Speak for yourself," she huffed then looked at Dina who stood alongside her. "Is Casey seriously working the kissing booth?"

Dina grinned and appeared pleased with herself. "Yeah, I talked her into it. Great, isn't it?"

"Well, bless you, Dina," Tucker said while raising his beer and chuckling.

Melanie turned to Vaughn and sneered at him. "Well, it looks like you might get your chance after all."

"Chance for what?" Dina asked.

Melanie folded her arms across her chest and glared at Dina. "Our sheriff has the hots for Casey," she snapped.

Vaughn groaned and refused to look at her. "I do not," he growled. "Don't start with that."

Tucker, Dina, and Wiley stared at Vaughn with curious looks and awaited an explanation. He avoided looking at them and shifted with discomfort.

"My interest in Casey is and was strictly professional," Vaughn boldly announced.

Dina snorted a laugh then hurried to a nearby table to tend to customers. Tucker suddenly laughed, causing Vaughn to glare at him. Wiley appeared interested.

"Something to add?" Wiley teased.

"Don't do it," Vaughn warned Tucker.

Tucker didn't seem concerned by Vaughn's threatening look. "Back when Vaughn first started as deputy," he announced while chuckling, "he had his eye on this hot, little number."

"Tucker," Vaughn growled while shifting in his chair.

Tucker ignored his friend. "He had his eye on her for weeks before he finally asked me who she was. That girl was Casey Remington."

Wiley and Melanie stared at Tucker with surprise then looked at Vaughn with equal astonishment.

"She couldn't have been more than fifteen!" Wiley suddenly cried out.

"Oh, that's disgusting," Melanie scoffed with a sneer.

"Okay, fine," Vaughn snapped. "I thought she was attractive, but I didn't know she was just a kid."

Wiley and Tucker laughed.

"Come on," Vaughn cried out. "Back me up here, she looked twenty."

"Well," Wiley chuckled, "that is true. It's a good thing Tucker set you straight before you made a fool of yourself."

Vaughn snorted then sneered. "Are you kidding? The bastard let me embarrass myself. It's amazing we're still friends."

Melanie and Wiley suddenly looked at Tucker. He started to laugh.

"Oh, come on," Tucker announced while maintaining his grin. "Initiating the new guy is part of the job."

"You let him ask her out?" Wiley demanded with surprise.

"I didn't ask her out," Vaughn scoffed and shifted in his chair. "I approached her mother in the antique store and asked to see her sister. When she told me that Casey was her daughter, I was able to escape before completely embarrassing myself."

Wiley shook his head and glared at Tucker. "You should be ashamed of yourself."

Melanie suddenly sneered. "And that's why we didn't work out," she announced then glared at Vaughn's profile. "He couldn't get her sweet, little ass out of his head."

Vaughn refused to look at Melanie or even acknowledge her.

"Leave him alone, Mel," Wiley announced then grinned lustfully. "I think Casey has a sweet, little ass too."

Melanie frowned with disgust, grabbed her full pitchers, and walked away as Dina returned with several empty beer bottles.

Vaughn shook his head and groaned as Melanie left. "That night of bad judgment just keeps coming back to bite me."

"At least you have being drunk as an excuse," Tucker scoffed then finished his glass of beer. He pushed the empty glass to Wiley and indicated he needed a refill. "I dated that devil's whore of my own free will."

"Who's the devil's whore?" Casey suddenly asked from behind both men.

Both looked back at her as she appeared seemingly out of nowhere and jumped onto the empty barstool alongside Tucker. He seemed pleased to see her. Vaughn appeared even more uncomfortable possibly wondering how much of their conversation she had overheard.

"Melanie," Dina casually replied while hiding her humor.

Casey was suddenly interested and grinned slyly. "Is this topic officially open for debate?" she teased.

"No, it's closed," Vaughn snapped.

Tucker grinned at Casey, unable to hide his lust, and stared at her longer than he should have. "We just heard the exciting news," he announced.

"Oh? What news?"

"You in the kissing booth," Dina teased while dramatically batting her eyelashes.

Casey rolled her eyes and groaned. The subject was already getting on her nerves, and she still had three more days until the official nightmare began.

"If you're having performance jitters, you can practice on me," Tucker offered slyly.

"Same here," Wiley announced with a grin and leaned on the bar before her.

"Thanks, boys, but I think I'll manage," Casey replied while hiding her embarrassment.

Dina took her filled pitchers and left the bar. Melanie soon returned with a tray of empty glasses. Wiley kept his attention on Casey. He was obviously a little too happy to see her.

"I see you signed up for the talent show," Wiley announced with a pleased look.

Melanie turned to Casey and now appeared stunned. Too much was being thrown at her at one time. "You entered the talent show?" she suddenly squawked.

"Under extreme duress, I assure you," she muttered in response but noted the look on Melanie's face. It was almost entertaining to behold.

The rage was boiling up inside Melanie, but she seemed to pull herself together and made an effort to suppress it. "So, uh, what are you planning to do?"

Casey shrugged carelessly. "I suppose that's up to my brother and Ruger."

The expression on Melanie's face suddenly dropped. "You haven't planned anything?" she cried out with surprise. She managed a tense laugh and shook her head. "Oh, Casey, you're going to bomb. The fair is this Saturday."

"You'll be fantastic," Wiley told Casey while grinning.

Casey thought his devotion to her was almost staggering. He wouldn't believe anything bad about her even if he caught her standing over a dead body with a smoking gun in her hand.

"You're sweet, Wiley," Casey said warmly.

Wiley seemed humored. "Remember that when I see you at the kissing booth," he teased.

"You get a freebie," Casey announced and leaned across the bar. She motioned him closer with a beckoning finger and kissed him quickly on the lips.

Wiley grinned proudly and possibly blushed. "Nope, no practice needed there."

"Got one more freebie?" Tucker suddenly asked while appearing a little too enthusiastic.

"Buy a ticket."

"One?" Tucker asked then laughed. "I'm cashing my entire paycheck."

Melanie appeared disgusted and walked away with a huff. Dina returned to the bar and appeared curious as she watched Melanie leave.

"Hmm? What did I miss?" Dina asked.

"Casey kissed me," Wiley cheerfully replied.

Grey, Ruger, and Diesel entered the tavern and approached them at the bar. Diesel stood behind Casey and massaged her shoulders, catching the attention of the men at the bar.

"What do they have to eat?" Diesel asked.

"You're a bottomless pit," Grey scoffed then looked at Casey, who enjoyed her shoulder massage from Diesel's massive hands. "Did you want to get a table?"

"Yeah, sure. Who's designated driver?" she asked.

Grey frowned and raised his hand.

Casey laughed then grinned at Wiley while indicating her group. "We're going to need a pitcher of martinis, three shots of tequila, and a soda for my poor brother."

Diesel spun Casey on her bar stool, picked her up into his arms, and carried her to the table. She let out a playful scream then laughed.

Ruger rolled his eyes and shook his head. "It's going to be a long night."

Chapter Twenty

*N*early an hour later, the tavern was quickly filling with locals who had finished bowling at the local bowling alley. Bowling league nights brought in large crowds even without live entertainment. There was no music, leaving the dance floor vacant. Casey, Ruger, and Diesel drank shots and laughed drunkenly at their table while Grey appeared bored and sipped his soda. Casey slipped her hand into Diesel's pocket and felt around for change. He grinned and held his hands up to allow her free access. He seemed disappointed she only went for the change. Casey took her newly found change and headed for the jukebox across the dance floor. She selected some songs and danced seductively to the first song as it played while scanning more titles. Diesel approached Casey from behind, placed his arms around her, and danced slowly and seductively with her. He spun her in his arms and they danced close to the slow song. Dina approached Grey from behind and rubbed his shoulders.

"I'm on break. Care to dance?" Dina asked.

Grey looked back at her, smiled as he took her hand, and joined her on the dance floor. They danced to the slow song, although not nearly as close and seductive as Casey and Diesel had danced. Melanie watched the couples dancing from her position at the bar and frowned. She was obviously bothered by their dancing. Tucker also felt compelled to watch Casey and Diesel dance close. He shook his head and looked back at Vaughn while frowning.

"No one can compete with that guy," Tucker muttered. "Look at him. He's built like a tank!"

Vaughn briefly glanced at them as they danced seductively. Diesel obviously knew no boundaries, and Casey didn't seem to protest.

"I always pictured her with someone smarter," Vaughn remarked lowly while casually sipping his drink.

Tucker looked at Vaughn with surprise and suddenly laughed. "You're jealous!'

Vaughn appeared embarrassed by Tucker's loud outburst and fidgeted in his chair. "Don't be ridiculous."

Tucker continued to chuckle softly and remained humored. "Whatever. I've had my limit," he announced with a sigh. "Want a lift?"

"No, I'll get a ride home with Wiley," Vaughn replied. "I want to discuss a few things with him."

"Oh, God, just let the bachelor auction go," Tucker groaned. "You'll be fine."

"It has nothing to do with that," Vaughn replied.

Tucker obviously didn't buy it. He chuckled softly while standing. "Beware of booze and Melanie. Remember what happened the last time you combined the two."

Tucker patted his shoulder and left the tavern. As the song ended, Diesel gave Casey a big bear hug then escorted her back to the table for more drinks. Grey approached Vaughn at the bar and took Tucker's seat.

"Why don't you join us, Sheriff?" Grey asked.

Vaughn glanced from Grey to their table then minded his drink and shrugged. "I don't want to intrude."

"Intrude on what?" Grey snorted. "Those three are already half wasted. I could use the conversation."

Vaughn considered his comment then nodded and joined him. Vaughn and Grey approached the table as the others laughed and did another shot.

"Okay, make room, you lushes," Grey announced loudly. "Darwood Falls' finest is joining us."

Casey moved from her chair to open up a space. Diesel grinned at her and patted his lap, indicating a free spot for her to sit. Casey bypassed him and casually sat on Ruger's lap. It was obviously non-sexual in nature, but Ruger proudly clung to her regardless.

"Every time," Diesel scoffed and shook his head. "How does this happen?"

Ruger smiled drunkenly and held up his middle finger to Diesel behind Casey's back.

Diesel smirked and chuckled softly. "One day, you little Muppet--"

✝

*I*t was over an hour later. Dina brought more shots of tequila to the table and placed one in front of everyone except Grey, who remained sober and appeared bored. Vaughn was almost as drunk as the others were and shook his head at the offer of another shot.

"No, no. I shouldn't. Really--" he insisted.

Vaughn picked up his shot glass along with the others, clinked glasses with them, and drank the contents. They all laughed and slammed their shot glasses down. Casey, still seated on Ruger's lap, glanced across the crowded tavern. She placed her arm over Ruger's shoulder and whispered something in his ear. He, too, glanced across the room. Wayne, Ryan, Blain, and Fred entered and stood just inside the doorway. They scanned the tavern as if looking for something in particular. Grey and Diesel glanced in the direction of the door as well now. The table became unusually quiet. Vaughn remained pleasantly drunk, noted the looks, and glanced behind him. The Harford boys looked at their table. Vaughn stiffened and sat straight while glaring back at the four by the door. Wayne nudged Ryan and motioned for his brothers to follow him to the pool area. It was unknown which occupant at the table they feared or were attempting to avoid.

Casey snorted a laugh and patted Ruger's chest. "I think you scared them away," she remarked drunkenly.

Ruger snickered in response. "I think that honor's all yours, my dear."

Vaughn started to stand. "I'm going to go back there and arrest them," he announced in a drunken tone.

"You're off duty," Grey casually reminded him.

Vaughn returned to his seat and felt his chest for his badge. He suddenly frowned. "Oh," he replied with a defeated sigh. A strange smile crossed his face. "In that case, I'll just kick the crap out of them instead."

"Maybe you should hold off on that tonight," Grey announced with a tiny grin on his face.

Vaughn appeared to consider the comment then sighed. "Yeah, maybe you're right."

Melanie approached Vaughn from behind and affectionately rubbed his shoulders. Vaughn grinned and caressed the hands on his shoulders without looking back.

"How are you boys doing over here?" Melanie asked.

Vaughn eyed the hands on his shoulders with bewilderment then looked at Grey. "Who's behind me?"

"That would be Melanie," Grey casually replied.

Vaughn quickly pulled away from her hands, turned in his chair, and glared at her. "No, no. You need to go away."

Melanie smiled sweetly, returned her hands to his shoulders, and clung to him from behind. "One dance for old times' sake," she cooed.

"No, just stay away from me," Vaughn announced firmly then looked at Grey. "A little help here."

Grey appeared surprised and held his hands up. "What do you want me to do? Rough up your ex-girlfriend?"

Vaughn pulled away from Melanie and stood drunkenly while facing her. "Just stay away from me, Mel."

Melanie placed her hands to his chest and attempted to cozy up to him while smiling seductively. "Oh, come on," she said sweetly. "Just one dance." Her hand traveled his body despite his attempts to keep her away.

Her wrist was suddenly grabbed, stopping her hands from traveling his body. Melanie appeared surprised and looked at Casey, who now stood before her. Casey glared at her with hostility and annoyance.

"He's off limits," Casey scoffed.

Melanie smirked and pulled her wrist from Casey's grip. All four men watched the exchange in silence.

"Not to me, sister," Melanie snapped and gave Casey a quick once over. "We used to date."

Casey's glare was cold and unpredictable. She wasn't in the mood to deal with the little bitch. Not tonight. "No, you got him drunk, seduced him, and made him think you were pregnant to keep him around."

"This doesn't concern you, bitch," Melanie lashed out.

Ruger, Grey, and Diesel laughed and 'ewe' softly, which only encouraged the situation. Vaughn just watched with possible surprise and sank back into his chair. Casey may have been drunk, but she certainly didn't show it now.

"These are my boys," Casey informed her with a stern glare while casually indicating the table of men. "You stay away from my boys, or I'll show you just what kind of bitch I really am."

Melanie appeared unimpressed and sneered at her. Casey maintained her glare and moved into a fighting stance with her eyes locked on Melanie.

"You should probably back away slowly," Grey announced with a tone of concern. "She doesn't have real good control when she's drunk."

"You wouldn't dare," Melanie scoffed with a snort.

Casey kicked for Melanie's face. Melanie suddenly gasped. Ruger yelled something in Mandarin. Casey stopped her kick short of her face and collected herself. Melanie appeared alarmed, gasped, and hurried away.

"Now sit down and relax," Ruger firmly said.

Casey obediently sat on the first available lap and helped herself to the drink on the table before her. Diesel watched her and chuckled. Grey groaned and shook his head. Casey eyed Ruger's disapproving look from across the table and appeared bewildered. She suddenly realized she was sitting on Vaughn's lap. Casey laughed, leaned against Vaughn, and playfully clung to his neck.

"Well, good evening, Sheriff Holt. How did you get there?" she teased.

Vaughn grinned and laughed drunkenly at her. "You are so wasted."

Casey smiled, patted his chest, and giggled. "And *you* are seriously aroused."

Diesel and Grey burst out laughing, while Ruger just rolled his eyes with disgust. Vaughn drunkenly grinned and clung to her with his face nuzzling her chest. Melanie stood near the bar and watched Casey cling to Vaughn while sitting on his lap and laughing. Vaughn caressed her leg through her jeans without care and received little to no protest. Melanie sneered with disgust, shoved past Dina, and headed into the backroom. Dina watched Melanie storm off then glanced at the table containing her friends. Sheriff Holt appeared to be holding little back, as he was obviously enjoying Casey's presence on his lap. Dina grinned and laughed softly. Melanie entered the pool area and pushed past the few patrons brave enough to hang out in the pool area with her four cousins. She approached Wayne with a disgusted look on her face.

"What are you going to do about Casey Remington?" she demanded to know.

Wayne straightened from making his shot and glared at her. "I don't know what you're talking about."

"She beat the crap out of the four of you," Melanie snapped. "What do you intend to do about it?"

Wayne snorted a laugh and mocked her. "Step on your tiara, did she?"

"You could say that," Melanie huffed while folding her arms across her chest.

"Fight your own battles, princess," Wayne snorted. "We have better things to do."

Melanie glared at them, appeared disgusted, and returned to the bar. They laughed at her as she walked away.

Chapter Twenty-one

The Remington farmhouse was well-lit in the night setting with Grey's jeep parked out front alongside Ruger's car. Casey rode her horse at a leisurely walk along the driveway toward the barn. She stopped the horse before the hitching post, attempted to dismount, and fell onto her backside by the horse's front legs. Casey giggled while looking up at the horse from where she sat on the ground by his hooves. The gray horse looked at her on the ground and snickered.

"Stop laughing at me."

She clung to the stirrup to pull herself up to her feet and stumbled toward the house. Storm followed her to the porch. As she walked onto the porch, she heard the strange, hollow thump. Casey suddenly realized she was being followed. She looked back at her horse with his front hooves on the second step of the porch. She burst out laughing.

"Oh, that wouldn't have gone over well," she remarked in a drunken tone. "Ruger would flip if he found you in the living room tomorrow morning."

She motioned for the horse to follow her as she stumbled back toward the barn. Storm casually followed at a leisurely walk and stopped near the gate. She unsaddled the horse, leaving her saddle on the hitching post, and opened the gate to the paddock. Storm excitedly ran through the open gate, crossed the pasture, and immediately rolled on the ground, grinding dirt into his once clean coat. She knew he did that on purpose. Casey stumbled back toward the house and entered the dimly lit kitchen. She was about to walk across the kitchen toward the backstairs when she suddenly stopped. Vaughn sat on the floor before the island counter in the exact spot he had held her the night she was stabbed. He held his head in his hands with his elbows resting on his bent knees and stared blankly at the floor. Casey watched him a moment in silence. Seeing him like that almost instantly sobered her. A flood of bad memories swept over her.

"Sheriff?"

Vaughn drunkenly looked at her then stood with some difficulty. "Grey said I could sleep on the sofa."

"That's not the sofa," she casually informed him.

"Yeah--"

Vaughn stared at her with a strange look. Casey attempted to read his look but she couldn't get past his dark eyes. His drunken state was concerning.

"Haven't I always looked out for you?" he suddenly asked.

"Are you okay?" she asked softly.

Vaughn moved closer to Casey and looked into her eyes. She stared back at him even though she wanted to avoid looking into his dark eyes. She didn't need the memories from that night haunting her tonight.

"I would have taken care of you," he informed her gently. "Why didn't you let me take care of you?"

His comment stunned her. She tensed and became uncomfortable. She wasn't sure how to respond. What he was saying didn't make any sense. Perhaps it was just because he was drunk.

"I think we're both too drunk to be having this conversation," she informed him gently. "You can sleep it off in my parents' bedroom."

Vaughn took a step toward her. Casey immediately took a step away and backed into the island counter. Without warning, he pulled her into his arms and held her against him. Casey appeared slightly surprised, tensed, and braced her hands against his chest to hold him back. His hands firmly caressed her back and shoulders as he buried his face into her neck. Memories from that night flooded back into her consciousness. She'd been attempting to suppress those memories, but her drunken state and his actions brought them all back in a tidal wave of emotion. She remembered him holding her.

She heard him crying. The memory was sobering and one she had tried hard to forget. Her dreams in the cemetery weren't dreams at all! They were memories of Vaughn. He had been holding her. He was the shadowy dark figure who gave her so much comfort. She had heard him in her unconscious state! His was the voice that pulled her back from the light! Although he never admitted it, he must have been in ICU with her when her condition deteriorated. Casey remained tense in his arms as she attempted to sort out a flood of emotions and memories. Her head was spinning from too much alcohol and this new realization. It was almost too much for her to take in! Despite her weak attempt to hold him back, Vaughn held and caressed her.

As he nuzzled her neck, he whispered softly, "I only slept with Melanie; because I was so drunk I thought she was you."

His words stunned her. Casey exhaled a soft groan and shut her eyes. She uncertainly slipped her arms around his neck and returned the embrace. Vaughn slowly lowered his mouth to hers and trembled as he brushed his lips past hers. Casey tensed but didn't pull away. He kissed her warmly but passionately, sending shockwaves through her nearly numb body. She suddenly felt defenseless as she sank into his comforting arms. Casey uncertainly returned the kiss with few inhibitions in her drunken state. His kissed turned more aggressive as he firmly ran his hands along the curves of her body. She couldn't seem to convince herself to stop his traveling hands, and she didn't know why. After all, she hated him! Didn't she?

†

Early the next morning, sunlight flooded Casey's bedroom. Vaughn slowly moved beneath the covers and groaned softly while holding his head. He slowly sat up, realized he was naked, and appeared bewildered then startled. He looked around the empty room and uncertainly shook his head. He again held his head while reaching for his pants on the floor. He dressed and wearily stumbled from the bedroom. Vaughn walked onto the porch while still holding his aching head. Casey sat reclined on the railing in a tank top and her sleep shorts, looking slightly disheveled. She glanced at him as he approached her on the railing.

She snorted a soft laugh. "God, you look like I feel," she muttered and hid her smile.

Vaughn slowly and uncertainly sat on the railing across from her, shut his eyes, and groaned softly while placing his head to the support beam behind him.

"I don't remember much about last night, but should I be apologizing?" he asked softly as he glanced at her.

Casey snorted a laugh and appeared humored. "Any fun you had in my bed last night was a solo act."

He seemed surprised by the statement and stared at her. "So we didn't sleep together?" he asked softly.

"Yes and no," she replied teasingly. "You were supposed to take my parents' bedroom, but I found you passed out in my bed instead. Since there was no way in hell I was going to sleep in my parents' room, I opted to sleep in my bed. You just happened to be there."

He didn't seem convinced and pressed further. "And you're sure nothing happened?"

"You were already naked and passed out long before I got there," she assured him.

Vaughn groaned softly and shut his eyes with possible embarrassment. "Can you possibly not mention to anyone that you found me naked in your bed?"

"I'm sure I could, but what fun would that be?" she teased, taking pleasure in his embarrassment.

He cast a look at her and grinned despite his aching head. "You love torturing me."

"You're a big boy," she said firmly. "You can handle it."

He snorted a laugh and stared at her a moment longer. Casey stared back at him briefly then felt compelled to look away. After their conversation last night, she found it even more difficult to look him in the eyes. Apparently, he didn't remember much of it. He continued to study her then finally looked away and across the secluded property. The farm seemed completely isolated from the rest of the world.

"It's so peaceful out here," he remarked softly.

As he stared off, she was finally able to look at him where he sat. Last night was burned into her mind, and she was having a difficult time dismissing it. She no longer knew how she felt about Sheriff Holt. Her mind was cluttered with the past and last night's events. She didn't like how confused she felt. Being angry was easier. When he looked back in her direction, she looked out across the pastures and again avoided eye contact. She felt his stare on her for a long moment. She pretended she didn't notice. Grey walked onto the porch, startling both. He was up early, even for him. He paused just past the doorway, stared at both, and grinned deviously.

"I'm not interrupting anything, am I?" he teased.

Vaughn shifted and appeared uncomfortable. "No, and do you have to be so chipper?"

"It's the sworn duty of the designated driver to torment those hungover the next morning," he replied then chuckled. "You look like shit, Sheriff."

"Thanks," Vaughn replied. "I wish I felt that good."

Grey again laughed and appeared too enthusiastic for the early hour. He then shifted his attention to Casey, who didn't appear nearly as hungover.

"Sometime after lunch, when the lushes roll out of bed, we're running to Dina's apartment to pick up her things," Grey informed her. "Tucker offered Dina his truck, so we can move the bigger stuff."

"Dina's moving in?" Vaughn asked from his reclined position against the railing.

"We thought it was best," Casey informed him.

"I know she brightens my mornings," Grey announced while grinning.

Casey rolled her eyes. Vaughn remained baffled by the comment.

"You still haven't figured out who attacked Dina in the parking lot the other night?" Grey asked as he collapsed into the rocking chair.

"She said he was wearing a mask, and she didn't really get a very good look at him," Vaughn replied. "She was almost positive it wasn't Wayne. His build was wrong."

"Yeah, but it could have been one of his brothers," Casey informed him.

"Ernest alibied Ryan, Blain, and Fred," Vaughn replied with a sigh. "Supposedly they were all together at home from midnight until morning."

"That's bullshit," Grey scoffed.

"I don't have any evidence to bring them in for further questioning," he replied.

"That's also bullshit," Grey added.

"Sometimes it goes that way," Vaughn informed him.

Grey appeared disgusted and defeated. "Did you want a ride to town this afternoon?" he asked then hesitated. "I could run you back now, if you're in a hurry."

Vaughn remained peacefully reclined, smiled, and shook his head. "No, I think I'll wait until my head stops spinning. I have nowhere to be."

"All right then," Grey announced with a little too much enthusiasm. "I should probably get some coffee started. Sounds like we're going to need it around here today."

Grey entered the kitchen and approached the coffeemaker on the counter. He hesitated, leaned on the counter with both hands, and appeared to sink deep into thought. He finally straightened, removed a bag of coffee from the cupboard and tossed it onto the counter near the coffeemaker. He again hesitated. Vaughn and Casey were heard talking softly on the porch. Grey's lips curved into a sneer. He violently and repeatedly punched the bag of coffee on the counter while grunting with anger and rage. After the tenth hit, the sturdy bag ruptured, sending coffee grounds scattering along the counter. Grey again placed both hands firmly on the counter, hunched over the spilled coffee grounds, and attempted to control his breathing as his psychotic look remained fixed on the ruptured bag of coffee. Dina wearily entered the kitchen and stared at the scattered coffee grounds. He saw her and quickly straightened. His look immediately turned innocent and possibly charming.

"What happened?" she asked with surprise.

"It slipped from my hand," he replied timidly.

†

$\mathcal{I}$t was early evening. Dina removed clothing on hangers and hung them in the closet of the spare bedroom while Casey removed clothing from a box and placed them in dresser drawers. They busily worked in near silence. Dina looked back at Casey several times between trips to the closet. She bypassed the box, sat on the foot end of the bed, and watched Casey.

"I really appreciate you doing this for me, you know," Dina announced softly.

Casey glanced at Dina and shrugged but kept her attention on filling the drawers. "We have the room, and after what happened at the tavern, it didn't seem right to let you stay in your apartment alone."

"I've been thinking about your routine for the talent show," she announced.

Casey snorted a laugh without looking at her. "I'm glad someone is," she announced. "I'm certainly not."

"They're letting us practice on stage tomorrow afternoon," Dina informed her. "You should come along and practice, you know, get a feel for the stage. It's different being on stage."

"I don't know," Casey announced then shut the drawer and finally turned to face Dina. "I'm having stage jitters as it is."

"All the more reason to practice on stage," Dina informed her then smiled deviously. "We'll also get a chance to scope out the competition."

"I know Melanie is good," Casey snorted. "I don't need to be reminded of it."

Grey entered the bedroom and set a box down on the floor with a grunt. "What do you have in here? Bowling balls?"

"Close," she replied. "They're family photo albums."

She received odd stares from both.

"From my grandparents," Dina replied to their silent question. "When they were still living and before my father took off, there were a lot of fond memories."

Casey glanced at her brother and appeared curious. "I thought you left with the guys," she said to Grey.

"Ruger and Diesel can handle the rest of the boxes in Dina's apartment," he announced. "I thought I'd pick up a few pizzas for dinner."

"I thought I saw both cars leave," Casey remarked.

"Yeah, last trip," Grey replied.

"Then what do you intend to drive to get pizza?"

Grey suddenly grinned and raised his brows suggestively.

Casey appeared horrified and shook her head. "Oh, no," she said defensively. "You're not driving my car."

"Oh, come on," Grey pouted childishly. "You never let me drive your car."

"You own a car?" Dina asked her friend with a look of near surprise.

Grey looked at Dina and grinned. "Not just a car," he announced. "It's a 1969 Chevy Camaro Z/28 classic muscle car with an engine the size of a freight train."

Casey rolled her eyes as Grey boasted about her car. Grey seemed disappointed that neither shared his enthusiasm for the car. He sounded oddly like their father for one fleeting moment.

"Sheriff Holt was drooling over it when I showed it to him in the garage," Grey announced proudly.

"You were showing him my car? Why?"

He stared at her with an oddly dumbfounded look. "Because, it's the only cool thing about you."

She again rolled her eyes. Dina hid her smile to keep from laughing.

"Fine, take the car," Casey scoffed. "I don't know why Dad gave it to me in the first place."

"Yeah, he knew you drove like an old lady," Grey announced and appeared to pout. He then looked at Dina and flashed a smile. "It was supposed to be a surprise high school graduation gift, but it took him longer than anticipated. It turned into her college graduation gift. He worked on restoring that car every weekend for seven years."

Casey sank against the dresser, appeared distant, and frowned. "It was a surprise all right," she said with a sigh. "Ruger found my graduation card on the dashboard of the car when he was packing up things the day we moved out." She glared at Grey. "You know where to find the keys."

"I'll be back in an hour," he announced and darted from the room.

"That means he'll drive around half the county before getting pizza," Casey informed Dina.

"I wasn't really hungry anyway," Dina announced gently.

Casey straightened and sighed. "I'm going to make some tea. Did you want some?"

"Actually, I'd like to take a bath before the guys return," Dina informed her. "I've been feeling grimy all day."

"That's actually not a bad idea," Casey replied. "I might take a shower myself. I'll make tea afterwards. Just come downstairs when you're finished."

Casey left the bedroom, shutting the door behind her.

Chapter Twenty-two

The black Chevy Camaro appeared at the end of the dimly lit gravel driveway from the Remington farm. The engine revved as the car burned out in the dirt and the tires squealed on the paved road. The Camaro jetted down the road with a roar. A truck's headlights suddenly came on. The pickup truck drove along the road and turned into the Remington farm driveway. The headlights went out as the truck pulled off to the side of the driveway just out of view of the house. Wayne and Ryan got out of the truck and looked at the house in the near distance beyond the barn. There were several inside and outside lights on.

"Was that all of them?" Ryan asked.

"Except for Casey and Dina," Wayne announced. "The others should be gone at least an hour."

"Remember," Ryan said firmly. "We're just sending a message. If anyone gets hurt, Uncle Lance will have our heads."

Wayne removed a cord of rope from the back of the truck, glared at his brother, and shook his head. "You're starting to sound like a little girl. If I wanted to hear nagging, I would have let Fred tag along."

"Let's just get this over with," Ryan snapped. "I'm not thrilled hanging around out here."

"Relax," Wayne snorted. "We need to case the place first. Make sure they're both inside."

Both men stood near the front of the truck and watched the house in the distance. Everything seemed quiet. There appeared to be no signs of life within the big farmhouse.

"Someone's in the upstairs bedroom," Wayne announced. "I didn't see anyone else moving around." Both hurried around the back of the truck. "We have to do this quick. Once I catch Casey's horse, you need to tranquilize it."

"Yeah, I know what I'm supposed to do," he huffed.

"We'll leave the horse's head on the porch," Wayne said while grinning. "That should send them running out of Darwood Falls."

Ryan removed an ax from the back of the truck and took a deep breath. "Let's go."

Both men hurried along the darkened driveway while keeping in the shadows. They approached the barn with its vapor light brightening the entire paddock. Both peered around the corner of the barn to the horses grazing in the pasture. Casey's gray horse stood near the fence separating him from the mares and attempted to get female attention. The mares weren't interested tonight. Storm's head suddenly lifted. He looked toward the barn and snorted. Nothing moved. The horse minded his own business and returned to snickering at the mares. Wayne and Ryan kept their backs to the barn and appeared to contemplate their next move.

"I swear, that horse knows what we're up to," Ryan said softly to Wayne.

"It's just a dumb animal," Wayne scoffed.

"I remember that dumb animal kicking our ass once before," Ryan reminded him. "Maybe we should go after one of the others."

"No, it has to be Casey's horse," Wayne insisted and looked back around the edge of the barn toward the gray horse in the paddock. "The message has to hit her where it counts."

Wayne looked back alongside him. Ryan was gone. The barn door gently swayed. Wayne looked around and appeared bewildered.

"Ryan?" he asked. "Where'd you go? Now's not the time to be taking a piss."

There was no response. Wayne stared at the open barn door and the darkness beyond it. He slowly approached the barn door, set the rope down, and clutched the ax in his hand.

"Ryan, you'd better answer me," Wayne snorted softly.

Someone moved within the darkened barn. Wayne lifted the ax to his shoulder and slowly entered through the open barn door. He looked around the near darkness of the wide aisle. Stall doors on either side lined the dark barn. Each stall door was open to dark stalls. Ryan wasn't seen.

"Ryan?" Wayne whispered.

The sound of a tiny whinny was heard from one of the nearby stalls. Wayne clutched his ax and approached the stall. The sounds of a small animal thumping around within the stall was heard along with what sounded like a foul snickering softly. Wayne paused by the closed stall door, peered inside, and grinned.

✝

*I*t was over an hour later. Casey entered the kitchen in a pair of comfortable shorts and a worn tank top. She looked out the kitchen window toward the well-lit barn and wondered where all her guys were. At the very least, Ruger and Diesel should have returned with the rest of Dina's belongings. There was no telling when or if she'd ever see Grey again. He was probably in the next county with her car by now. A car's headlights appeared in the driveway. She couldn't make out the car, but it was driving too slowly to be Grey in her car. She appeared relieved that someone had finally returned. Dina entered the kitchen wearing a thin t-shirt and shorts that left little to the imagination. One look at Dina, and Casey knew Grey was going to be tripping over his tongue.

"Okay, now I'm hungry," Dina reported. "Where's the pizza delivery boy?"

"Daytona, probably," Casey retorted. "One of the guys just pulled up though."

"Oh, fuck!" Diesel was heard yelling from outside.

Both women were suddenly alerted by the sounds coming from the usually unflappable man. They ran for the front door. Casey opened the door and stepped onto the porch. She stared off the porch and appeared horrified. Dina stared past her and suddenly gasped. The baby horse had Diesel's jacket sleeve in its tiny teeth while tugging on his arm. Diesel attempted to hold the box he held while fighting off the frisky foul.

"It's attacking me!" Diesel shouted. "Get it off me!"

Casey suddenly laughed then ran off the porch for the little foal. She gathered the baby horse around the chest and hindquarters and gently pulled it away from the big man. It finally released his jacket sleeve and attempted to pull free from her. She struggled to contain the baby horse while Storm snorted playfully at his little boy from his front row view at the gate.

"Isn't that thing supposed to be on a leash or something?" Diesel demanded while juggling the box in his arms.

"He's just a baby," she informed him and tried not to laugh. She then appeared curious. "I wonder how he got out of his stall."

Casey kept her arms around the baby horse and scooted him toward the barn. She disappeared inside the darkened barn. Diesel carried his box to the house and set it on the porch. He returned to the car for another box and glanced at the silent, dark barn. He removed another box from the car and again looked at the dark barn. His head tilted as he stared suspiciously. A moment passed before Casey finally came out of the barn. Diesel returned to acting disinterested. Casey approached Dina on the porch.

"Is everything alright?" Dina asked.

"I guess," Casey replied but wasn't convinced. "Mom was in the aisle eating hay. I don't know how they got out of their stall, but the door was wide open."

"Maybe you didn't latch it right," Dina replied.

"I don't make those mistakes," she replied dryly. "That's more Grey's department. He must have gone in there for some reason and didn't latch the door right." She shrugged. "No harm done, I suppose."

"I hope there's something for dinner," Diesel announced as he passed them with a box and no longer paid attention to Casey's dilemma. "I'm starving."

Casey eyed him and shook her head. "When aren't you starving?"

†

*R*uger carried a large box down the outside steps from Dina's second floor apartment and onto the sidewalk. He approached Grey's jeep parked out front and placed the box in the back with the rest. Several people ran down the sidewalk toward Town Square while chattering excitedly. Ruger watched the people rushing past him. On the other side of the street, more people ran in the same direction. The commotion was louder now. Ruger appeared curious and followed the crowd. There were dozens of people collected around Town Square.

Ruger saw Wiley and approached him. "What's happening?" he asked, faking a serious tone. "Did someone's cow go into labor?"

Wiley glanced at Ruger and gave him an odd look. Ruger grinned in response. Wiley shook his head and pointed in front of Town Hall.

"No, I'd say it's a little more entertaining than that," Wiley reported.

Ruger moved through the crowd to see what had everyone's attention. He found a part in the crowd and suddenly stopped to stare at the sight. Ryan and Wayne were bound and naked facing each other on either side of the old cannon in front of Town Hall. They attempted to scream through their socks stuffed in their mouths. Deputy Mitchell attempted to untie them while Ernest screamed at him and the crowd, who took pictures with their cell phones. Ruger stared at the sight with a look of mild shock. He suddenly grinned and laughed while shaking his head. He removed his cell phone and snapped his own picture.

✝

*I*t was Thursday morning. There was a lot of activity around town with the fair coming up on Saturday. Vendors filled the streets on their way to and from the fairgrounds in preparation for the upcoming events. Traffic jams and loud horns blowing awoke the town early. Larger vehicles were having difficulty navigating the streets to get safely to the fairgrounds. Two temporary police officers attempted to direct traffic alongside Mitchell, who appeared frantic. The sheriff's police blazer pulled alongside the road several yards away. Sheriff Holt joined Mitchell and helped the temporary officers direct traffic so the larger trailer could pass through the intersection. Several locals stood on their porches and enjoyed the free show. Most of the people in town were easily amused, and the annual fair brought plenty of entertainment, particularly the week before and the days after the fair. Once the large trailer was able to pass through and traffic began moving again, the onlookers from their porches teasingly applauded Sheriff Holt and Deputy Mitchell. Vaughn smirked and waved back at them.

Vaughn left his blazer parked in front of the pharmacy and walked the two blocks back to the police station. It would take longer to navigate traffic and wasn't worth the effort. He crossed the traffic and headed into the police station. Vaughn entered the mostly quiet office and approached Jeannie's desk before his office with a pleasant smile.

"Good morning, Jeannie. Did I miss anything yesterday?"

"Hmm, I don't know," she replied and held back her giggle. "Did you hear about the Harford boys' naked romp in Town Square last night?"

Vaughn groaned softly and tried not to laugh. He attempted a more serious look and raised his brows. "Yes, and I intend to look into that."

"Should I forward the photos of the *incident* for your investigation?" she teased.

"No, that's okay," he replied. "Everyone in town sent me a copy last night."

Jeannie noted his good mood despite the commotion outside. "I assume you enjoyed your day off."

"Actually, I was hung over the entire day," he replied, "but I had a good time drinking with the boys Tuesday night."

Jeannie suddenly appeared concerned and her eyes widened. "Oh, God, you didn't hook-up with Melanie, did you?"

Vaughn held back his laugh and firmly shook his head. "Not in this lifetime," he replied. "Apart from the disaster outside, is everything else set up for the fair? Extra officers, security, permits in place?"

"Yes, Sheriff," she replied. "The remainder of your police force will arrive later this afternoon, and we have plenty of security guards arriving Friday night." There was an odd silence between them. Jeannie grinned. "And, yes, you're covered for the bachelor auction, so stop worrying about it."

He appeared surprised by her candor and looked innocent. "Did I say I was worried? I'm not worried," he announced. "I'll be in my office--not being worried."

Vaughn headed into his office, poured a cup of coffee from the coffeepot on the nearby table, and collapsed behind his desk. He looked over some papers then glanced at the revised flier for the fair that had somehow made it to his desk. He glanced at Casey's name listed under the kissing booth and hid his grin. There was a knock on the door. Tucker opened the door without awaiting a response and stood in the doorway. He wore a cheap grin on his handsome face.

"You aren't going to believe the rumors I'd heard around town," he announced while barely being able to contain himself.

Vaughn groaned softly. "I'm sure I won't," he announced then smirked. "Let me have it."

Tucker flopped into the chair before the desk and raised his brows suggestively. "You and Casey Remington--"

The sheriff shook his head while appearing humored. "There is no me and Casey."

"Not what I heard," Tucker teased. "A little bird told me our sheriff got plastered Tuesday night and was seen with a drunken Casey on his lap. Apparently there was some serious groping and possibly a little tongue action."

Vaughn shifted in his chair and was obviously embarrassed. "You may want to double check your sources."

"You were seen leaving with her."

"No, Casey left on her horse," Vaughn informed him. "Her brother gave me a ride home."

"You didn't get home until noon yesterday," Tucker announced then grinned. "Come on, Vaughn, I'm your best friend. Give up some details. Did you bang Casey or what?"

"No, I didn't *bang* Casey," he scoffed. "Grey let me sleep it off in a guestroom. There were three other men in the house including her ex-boyfriend."

Tucker shook his head and frowned. "I'm disappointed in you."

There was another knock on the door. Mitchell walked into the office, eyed Vaughn, pointed, and chuckled.

"Congratulations, Sheriff!"

Vaughn suddenly groaned. "Nothing happened."

"According to Wiley something happened," Mitchell announced cheerfully.

"Wiley?" Vaughn asked then frowned. "Why does he hate me so much?"

"Hate you? He's proud of you," Mitchell said. "Guess you and Casey finally kissed and made up--or is that 'made out'?"

Vaughn again shifted in his chair. "Okay, Tuesday night if officially closed for discussion."

"We can always discuss Wednesday morning," Tucker teased.

"The two of you are like a couple of horny teenage boys. Moving on--"

Both deputies appeared disappointed that there wouldn't be any details or even an admission to what happened. It was back to business as usual.

"June stopped by with the bachelor auction schedule," Mitchell informed him. "She was adamant about keeping us last in line. She is also quoted as saying, 'Sheriff Holt needs to suck it up and shake his thing for charity'."

"That's really nice--coming from a seventy-year-old lady," Vaughn scoffed.

"Earnest Harford was looking for you," Tucker informed him. "He seemed pissed."

"When doesn't Earnest seem pissed?" Vaughn remarked with little interest. "I assume it has something to do with the incident in Town Square yesterday evening."

"How did you guess?" Tucker teased.

"Dumb luck," he replied. "Did you get a straight answer out of either of his boys?"

"They said they were minding their business when someone got the slip on them," Mitchell replied. "When they came to, they were naked and tied to the cannon."

"Yeah, I'm sure they were minding their own business," Vaughn scoffed.

"A couple of people reported seeing Ernest's car cruising slowly past the Remington farm driveway several times since Casey kicked the crap out of his boys," Tucker added.

"When the rest of our rent-a-cops arrive, I want them to include the Remington farm in their sweeps," Vaughn informed them. "I also want them to keep an eye on Ernest and his boys. I don't want any trouble out of them during the fair."

"You've got it," Tucker said.

Both Tucker and Mitchell stood and left the office. Vaughn leaned back in his chair and appeared to sink reflectively into thought. He finally leaned forward and worked on his computer. He checked his email messages from yesterday. Most were photos of the incident with Wayne and Ryan outside Town Hall. He held back his laugh then opened a confidential file. As he read, his expression suddenly dropped and concern swept over his face.

"Oh, Casey. What have you done?"

Vaughn printed out the report, grabbed his jacket, and hurried from his office.

Chapter Twenty-three

The fairgrounds entrance was guarded by a rental cop to keep non-essential people out of the way while vendors set up rides and games in preparation for their busy week. Anyone entering was required to provide their name in order to gain access to the extremely busy area. Workers and vendors milled around in preparation for the upcoming events in two days. Casey's horse was tied just inside the gates. Despite the commotion, the horse wasn't the least bit affected by cars and trucks coming and going. Toward the back of the fairgrounds, there was a bustle of activity surrounding the stage area. Grey talked with Wiley toward the back of the bleachers by the sound system while the talent show contestants rehearsed their routines on stage. Casey, Dina, and several other contestants sat on the front row bleachers before the stage and watched Melanie practice her tap dance routine in workout clothing.

Casey appeared tense and leaned closer to Dina, who sat alongside her. "She's better than I remember."

Her comment seemed to be the same sediments shared by the other contestants. They all whispered while watching the very talented and attractive Melanie perform. Abby sat on the bleachers on the opposite side of the aisle and proudly watched her daughter's dance routine.

Dina leaned closer to Casey and whispered back, "It's all about how you look up there. Remember, the judges like to see a little leg and cleavage."

"Are you sure we need to be here?" Casey asked softly. "I don't see the point to this. Grey didn't see the point."

"Practicing at home and being on the actual stage are completely different," Dina insisted. "It has a different feel, makes different sounds, and the elevation sometimes throws performers off. Trust me."

Casey frowned and attempted to relax. As Melanie finished her act, the other participants exchanged more comments with disgust. Abby applauded enthusiastically. Melanie walked offstage and smirked at Casey as she passed. Their new rivalry was almost baffling to Casey. She knew she'd gotten into it with Melanie the other night at the tavern, but it seemed as if the rivalry had been going on much longer than that. Casey was almost certain it had something to do with Sheriff Holt. Abby handed Melanie a towel as she approached and praised her.

Wiley was heard speaking into the microphone from behind the stands. "Casey, you're up next."

Melanie appeared interested and remained to watch her performance. Casey eyed Dina for reassurance. Dina grinned and nodded her toward the stage. Casey reluctantly walked on stage and awaited her music. Wiley turned on the music from the sound system while Dina coached Casey on dance steps. Casey made an effort to dance to the music but got the steps wrong. She appeared very stiff and awkward. Her dance routine was borderline embarrassing. Melanie hid her humored smile and exchanged a few words with her mother. Both took pleasure in Casey's obvious failure. The other contestants talked quietly and appeared equally stunned by Casey's unprepared routine. Once the song ended, Casey was quick to exit the stage. Dina hurried to join her and tried to reassure her that she just needed a little more practice.

Toward the back of the bleachers, Wiley stood with Grey and watched in silence. Wiley's smile was twisted into a slight grimace, but he appeared unable to say anything negative about Casey to Grey. Grey had his arms folded across his chest and held his chin. The look on his face was something between horrified and embarrassed.

Wiley spoke into the microphone. "Dina, you're up next."

Dina nodded, gave Casey a reassuring pat on the shoulders, and then hurried onto stage for her rehearsal. Casey ignored the looks and whispers from the other contestants and returned to the bleachers to watch Dina's performance. Wiley turned to Grey and offered a timid smile.

"I know we schedule contestants according to when they sign up," Wiley began, "but perhaps Casey would be less nervous if she went on closer to the beginning. Most of our performers feel intimidated following Melanie."

Grey appeared to fume silently and could barely look at Wiley. He finally collected himself and managed a smile. "No, we're fine with last spot," Grey announced with conviction. "She was better at home. She has another two days to get the routine down. She'll be fine."

Wiley smiled and nodded. "I'm sure she'll be terrific."

Once Dina was finished with her routine, she joined Casey and they approached Grey and Wiley near the back. Grey glared at Casey then turned and walked away. Wiley smiled cheerfully at both women.

"You were both terrific," he announced. "Why don't you take these last two days to polish your routines? You'll be fantastic on Saturday night."

Casey managed a weak smile. Wiley hadn't changed any since she'd been gone. She could do no wrong in his mind. It was sweet and troubling at the same time. It may have taken two years of absence, but she'd grown to love Wiley and understood his *fatherly* feelings for her. Casey and Dina left the stage area and hurried after Grey, who appeared reluctant to wait for them. They caught up to him and walked across the bustling fairgrounds in the direction of the main entrance. Once they were out of earshot of the busy vendors, Grey suddenly stopped and turned to face Casey with the rage evident in his eyes.

"What the hell was that?" Grey demanded, as the vein in his temple appeared ready to explode.

Casey appeared surprised by his tone toward her but contained her reaction. "Dina said we should practice on stage."

"That wasn't part of the plan," he snapped hotly while throwing his arms around in a fit of rage. "You almost got moved from last spot. If Wiley wasn't so hot for you, he may have bumped you altogether!"

"It's my fault, Grey," Dina announced timidly.

He spun toward Dina and pointed a warning finger at her, startling her. "Things have to go according to plan," he lashed out. "I won't have anyone messing this up!"

Dina stared at him with surprise and a look of possible concern. She appeared unable to respond at first. She timidly replied with a soft, "I'm sorry."

Grey's mood softened as he fidgeted. He appeared to be wrestling with some particularly unpleasant demons. "No, I'm sorry," he said more gently while running his fingers through his hair. He avoided looking at either woman. "I'm just a little tense. This is very important, that's all."

He turned and continued toward the main entrance with both following. There was a long silence. Casey then looked around and realized something was missing.

"What happened to our partners in crime?" Casey asked.

"Off doing whatever it is they do that I don't want to know about," Grey muttered.

Vaughn was seen approaching from the main entrance in the near distance. All three saw him heading in their direction.

Grey suddenly groaned softly and rolled his eyes with disgust. "Great, just what I need," he scoffed softly. "One of you needs to distract him with a blowjob or something. I can't deal with him right now."

Casey and Dina glared at Grey. Neither was humored by the comment. As Vaughn approached, Grey immediately turned on the charm.

"Sheriff Holt, I see you survived those tequila shots," Grey announced pleasantly.

Vaughn paused before them and glanced at Dina. "Dina, would you mind excusing us?" he announced firmly.

Dina appeared surprised then concerned and shifted nervously. "I'll meet you guys at the shop." She continued toward the main entrance.

"Is something wrong, Sheriff?" Grey asked while giving him an innocent look. "If it's about what happened at the tavern, I swear, I didn't show those pictures to anyone."

Vaughn lacked patience and appeared unusually authoritative. "Drop the good brother, bad sister act," he firmly announced, surprising both. "I want to know why you're here and what you brought into my town."

"What are you talking about?" Grey asked innocently.

Vaughn removed the folded paper from his pocket and handed it to Grey. Grey unfolded the paper and glanced at it. His expression twisted into something resembling a sneer.

"I'm talking about your 'family friends'," Vaughn remarked sternly and glared at both. "Former Special Ops with sealed military records. There's a string of charges against those two from assault to attempted murder."

Grey glared at Vaughn and carelessly returned the paper. "I don't see anything about arrests or convictions."

Vaughn was losing his patience with them. "I think the two of you came back for revenge, and you brought your little friends to help you."

Grey smirked with a strange look on his face. He looked like a cobra preparing to strike. "Revenge is an ugly word, Sheriff," he remarked lowly. "I'm sorry if we're still a little pissed about our parents' being butchered." Grey stiffened while glaring at Vaughn. Grey appeared to be restraining himself from reacting, but it came off frightening all the same. "Now, if you'll excuse us, we have work to do." Grey nodded to Casey. "Come on."

Casey turned without hesitation and headed toward the main gate with her brother. Grey headed through the gate and into town while Casey untied her horse. Vaughn approached her. She didn't look at him.

"I don't like being played, Casey," Vaughn boldly informed her. "I really thought you'd finally stopped blaming me for what happened that night."

Casey mounted her horse without comment and appeared ready to ride away. She then hesitated and looked at him as he stood near her horse.

"I don't have to blame you," Casey informed him. "You're doing that enough for both of us."

Vaughn stared at her in silence. Casey looked past him and frowned. Melanie and Abby were approaching from across the fairgrounds.

"Great, here comes your girlfriend," she muttered.

Vaughn didn't even look back. He stared into Casey's eyes, despite her refusal to look at him. He placed his hand on her leg, catching her attention. She stared into his sorrowful eyes from her elevated position on her horse.

"Please, Casey," he said gently. "Assure me you don't intend to do anything stupid."

"No, I already did that the other night," she announced simply, removed his hand from her leg, and sent her horse into a gallop across the fairgrounds toward the woods.

Vaughn watched her ride across the back of the fairgrounds. She disappeared onto the trail in the woods. He frowned and groaned with disgust. Melanie and Abby approached him from behind and stared after Casey as well.

"Poor Vaughn," Melanie announced with a sigh. "Casey Remington slipped through your fingers once again." She then smiled slyly. "When are you going to learn your lesson?"

Vaughn didn't bother looking back at either, although his look conveyed his emotions. "Go to hell, Mel," he scoffed and headed toward the gate and his police blazer.

Melanie hurried after him while Abby walked behind in less of a rush. Melanie walked alongside him, kept stride, and maintained her grin. He refused to look at her.

"Face it, Vaughn," she announced. "You and I were meant to be together."

He didn't stop and refused to respond. Melanie remained persistent and followed him to his blazer. She stepped in front of his police cruiser, stopping him from opening the door with her body. He finally looked her in the eyes.

"Get out of my way," he growled.

"I'm not giving up on this relationship," she replied.

"There is no relationship," Vaughn retorted hotly. "There's just you being a bitch as usual."

Abby hung back to give them some privacy. Melanie was a little surprised by his tone but brushed it off and managed a smile.

"I'm willing to forgive you for dumping me," she informed him.

"Well, good for you," he remarked, "but I'm not willing to forgive you for that shit you pulled on me."

Melanie suddenly became offended and sneered at Vaughn. "She's going to bomb in the talent show."

"What are you talking about?" Vaughn remarked impatiently.

"Casey's act for the talent show," she replied. "She's going to embarrass herself in front of the entire town and possibly the whole county."

"I don't have time for this, Mel," he announced. "Go bother someone else." He pushed her aside.

Melanie purposely fell to the ground and clutched her shoulder.

Vaughn looked at her and appeared unimpressed. "I'm not falling for that," he informed her.

Abby ran to Melanie's fallen side and helped her to her feet. She turned and glared at Vaughn. "What's wrong with you?" Abby launched hotly. "What sort of man assaults a defenseless woman?"

"I didn't push her that hard," he snapped. "She threw herself to the ground."

"You threw her to the ground!" Abby appeared enraged while clinging to Melanie, who milked the sympathy for all it was worth. "I'll have your badge for this!"

Vaughn climbed into his blazer, slammed the door, and glared at Abby. "Be my guest," he scoffed then drove out through the main gate.

†

*T*he Remington farm was peaceful early Saturday morning. It was nearly three o'clock in the morning and the fair was starting in just a few hours. Grey sat on the porch railing and stared out across the moonlit pasture. The porch door opened, alerting him. Dina walked onto the porch in a camisole top and floppy shorts. Her hair was slightly mussed, and she appeared exhausted. Grey shifted on the railing and appeared slightly uncomfortable.

"Trouble sleeping?" he asked.

Dina sat on the rocking chair with her legs curled beneath her and clung to her slightly chilled, bare arms. "Bad dreams," she replied softly.

Grey snorted a soft laugh and returned his head to the support beam behind him. "That's the only kind I ever have anymore," he replied with some humor to his sad existence.

"I don't doubt our nightmares are similar," Dina replied gently. "I think about that night constantly. Your mother and father were the closest thing to parents I'd had since I was little." She inhaled deeply and stared off at nothing in particular. "After you and Casey left, I felt like I lost everything."

Grey took a deep breath and avoided looking at her. "Yeah, Casey felt bad about leaving you like that, but she was in a really bad place for a long time. There were times I didn't even want to know her."

Dina looked at him. He met her gaze. She stared at him a long moment with a strange look. "It wasn't just Casey I was missing," she said gently. "You were a bigger part of my life than I'd realized."

He stared back at her with some surprise but didn't comment.

She smiled timidly and shrugged. "After Melanie dumped Deputy Tucker for Vaughn, I had my chance with him," she announced gently then snorted a soft laugh. "I couldn't do it. I passed up my opportunity with Tucker, because I couldn't stop thinking about you. I just wanted you back in my life, so I could make things right."

Grey uncertainly straightened on the porch railing while staring at her with his mouth hanging open. "You *liked* me?"

"I still do," she said softly while staring at him.

He slowly moved off the railing, approached her in the rocking chair, and held out his hand to her. She accepted his hand, allowing him to pull her up from the chair and into his arms. As he held her against him, she ran her hands along his chest while staring into his eyes. Grey gently touched her face then kissed her warmly but passionately. Dina immediately returned the kiss with added aggression. He became tense, broke off the kiss, and appeared embarrassed.

"I, uh, haven't been on a date in over two years," he told her gently and avoided looking into her eyes. "I'm not really sure what I'm supposed to do."

Dina smiled warmly and caressed his chest, causing him to meet her gaze. She smiled lustfully and appeared unaffected by his admission.

"Well, we could start by lying naked together in your bed and see what happens," she cooed softly and brushed her lips past his.

Grey stared at her while nearly speechless and unable to move. He fidgeted then grinned like a schoolboy. "Uh, okay."

Dina smiled, took his hand, and led him back inside.

Chapter Twenty-four

$\mathcal{I}$t was late morning on Saturday. The Darwood Falls Annual Fair was filled with people from visiting towns as well as locals crowding the fairgrounds. There were games, food, and entertainment of every kind. Small children crowded midway for the overpriced rides that attracted them with lights and sounds. Excitement was everywhere. Vaughn was seated in the dunking booth, completely dry, in a pair of shorts and a white t-shirt with the sheriff's logo printed on it. The soaking wet mayor stood near the counter with a towel around him. He joked with some of the locals about purchasing balls to dunk the sheriff. A young man pitched balls and got nowhere near the target.

"Come on, Tim," Vaughn egged him on. "College is making you soft."

He missed all three attempts. Vaughn appeared humored and possibly a little arrogant as the boy walked away.

"And the sheriff stays dry once again," Vaughn announced cheerfully. "What kind of farm boys do we have around here? Can't even pitch a decent softball."

Diesel and Ruger approached the dunking booth. Diesel handed his funnel cake to Ruger, who attempted to juggle the funnel cake and several stuffed animals under his arms. Vaughn eyed them, groaned softly, and managed a smile. Diesel played with the first ball and grinned.

"Sheriff--"

"Diesel--"

Diesel threw the ball. It struck the target with tremendous force. Vaughn's seat fell out from under him, and he plunged into the cold water. Vaughn surfaced with a loud gasp.

"Oh, shit! That's cold!"

Diesel chuckled softly and played with the second ball while Vaughn reset the seat above the water. He wiped his face as he positioned himself on the seat and looked at Diesel.

"I know Casey put you up to--"

Diesel threw the second ball. It again struck the target. Vaughn was once again dropped into the tank of cold water. Vaughn surfaced with a gasp, wiped his face, and nodded.

"Okay, I see where this is going."

Vaughn set up the seat and returned to it while wiping his hand over his face. Diesel played with the third ball and slyly eyed Ruger, who watched with little interest.

"I like this game. What's it called?" Diesel asked Ruger.

"Drown the sheriff," Ruger casually replied.

Diesel grinned. "Okay--"

He threw the ball. It again struck the target and Vaughn once again fell into the water. He surfaced with a gasp and appeared reluctant to reset the seat.

"Do we have time for another three?" Diesel asked.

"Not if we eat our way to the horse show," Ruger simply informed him. "We want good seats."

Diesel grinned at Vaughn. "Later, Sheriff."

Vaughn gasped for air and gave them a slight wave as they walked away.

✝

*T*he horse show was already in progress by the time Diesel and Ruger arrived. Diesel had even more plates filled with junk food. They joined Grey in the stands. There were eight events at the horse show, although Casey was only participating in the advanced events, leaving the easier events for children and teenagers. She entered barrel racing, pole bending, walk/trot/canter, and the keyhole race. All three men cheered on Casey in the speed events. She had the shortest time for barrel racing and pole bending, but her horse stumbled during the keyhole and added precious seconds onto her time. During the walk/trot/canter, both she and Storm were flawless, and the professional judges were impressed with the horse's beautiful canter. She won first place in three of the events and second in the keyhole race. After her events, Casey rode up to Grey, Ruger, and Diesel, with his plates of food. She handed Grey her three first place ribbons and one second place ribbon. Grey eyed the second place ribbon and shook his head.

"Second," he scoffed. "You're such a loser."

She just sneered at him. Casey stretched in the saddle and suddenly felt anxious about her next project. A frown crossed her face. "How much time do I have before pimping out my lips?" she asked dryly.

"Forty minutes," Ruger replied while giving her a quick once over. "You may want to clean up a little. No one's going to want to kiss you smelling horsey."

"Speak for yourself, man," Diesel announced.

"Relax," she muttered. "I have a change of clothes and there's a shower in the locker room. One of you will have to unsaddle Storm for me and put him in one of the stalls in the arena barn."

"If it helps you smell better, I'm on it," Grey informed her while grinning.

She effortlessly dismounted her large horse with style and grace, landing near Diesel. He leaned closer, sniffed her ponytail, and grimaced.

"Oh, that's rank," he announced.

She snatched one of his French fries, glared at him, and bit into the fry. He glared at her for having touched his food. It was just something you didn't do. Casey turned and walked away. Diesel and Ruger headed in the opposite direction, making their way toward more game and food vendors, while Grey led Casey's horse to the arena barn. Ernest and his four sons stood nearby and watched the others go their separate ways.

"Well, I know what I'm doing," Ryan scoffed. "I'm taking out my revenge on Casey at the kissing booth."

"You'll do no such thing," Ernest growled in response while glaring at his son. "Sheriff Holt is already sympathizing with her. If you do anything out in the open, you'll be giving him cause to point blame at us."

"Then what the hell are we doing here?" Wayne demanded. "If my wife catches me here after I told her I wouldn't come with her, she's going to kill me."

"Still a little pissed about that video, huh?" Blain teased.

Wayne glared at his brother. "Shut up."

"All of you shut up," Ernest snapped and looked at his four sons. "According to what Abby told me, Casey's going to bomb in the talent show, so she doesn't need any help from us to look stupid. That leaves Dina. We'll make our point by sabotaging her performance. She's Melanie's only real competition anyway."

"I don't know," Fred announced softly and appeared tense. "Maybe we should let it go."

His father and three brothers suddenly glared at him. "What's your problem, boy?" Ernest demanded.

"That new girl of his has him whipped," Ryan scoffed then meowed like a cat.

"She does not," Fred protested. "After what happened the other night, I'd think you'd learn your lesson."

"What are you talking about?" Wayne demanded.

"I know you were up to something at the Remington farm," Fred replied. "Someone saw you and got the slip on you. Do you want to end up naked and tied to a cannon again? I think they're just watching and waiting for you to try something else. Face it; they're smarter than we are."

"And maybe they're getting some help," Wayne growled and took a step closer to Fred.

"Not from me," Fred protested. "I wasn't included in either of your recent attacks."

"What do you mean *either*?" Ryan demanded to know while giving Fred a strange look.

"That thing at the tavern with Dina," Fred announced. "Slashing her tires and then stalking her. Now I hear Sheriff Holt is trying to link her attack to the murders. Dumb things like that could raise suspicion about our alibis for the night of the murders."

"We had nothing to do with what happened to Dina," Ryan suddenly protested. "And you better watch what you say."

"I'm not saying anything that Sheriff Holt isn't already investigating," Fred informed them. "I overheard Deputy Tucker and Deputy Mitchell discussing it."

Ernest stared at Fred a long moment then looked at his other three sons. "Fred's right," he announced. "It's too public here. If we're seen, it could open a whole other can of worms. We need to do something they can't trace back to us. I'll need time to give it some thought." He glared at his boys. "Until then, Dina and the Remington's are off-limits."

Fred appeared relieved. His three brothers reluctantly nodded without sharing Fred's sediments.

"We'll get even with them," Ernest promised. "We just need to be smart about it."

"I'll agree to that," Ryan sulked, "but I think I should be allowed to take out a little frustration on Casey and Dina at the kissing booth then."

Ernest groaned and reluctantly shook his head. "Knock yourself out, but I want no part of it."

Ryan glanced at Wayne.

Wayne vigorously shook his head. "If my wife sees me kissing another woman, I can kiss my marriage goodbye."

He then looked at Blain.

Blain held his hands in the air and took a step back while shaking his head. "Casey nearly broke my jaw the other night," he announced. "I'm not putting my face that close to her. She probably bites."

Ryan glanced at Fred, but he was already walking away. He groaned with disgust. "You're all a bunch of pussies."

"I need to find Lance," Ernest remarked. "I'll catch up with you later."

As Ernest walked away, Ryan glanced at his two, remaining brothers. "Are you at least coming along?"

"No," Wayne replied. "We'll catch up with you later."

Both walked away. Ryan appeared disgusted and headed toward the row of port-a-potties heading away from the arena and back toward the main fairgrounds. He entered one of the port-a-potties and shut the door. The 'occupied' sign was turned. Someone approached the port-a-potty. A zip tie was placed through the metal lock loops and was tightened. A moment passed. The sign turned to 'vacant' and the door was jolted.

"Damn it," Ryan was heard from inside.

The door jolted harder. Ryan was heard pounding on the door from inside.

†

*Y*oung and old men alike began collecting around the kissing booth, but they remained at a safe distance to give the appearance that they weren't anxious for their dollar-a-kiss. Melanie appeared relaxed in her short-shorts and hot pink, lacy camisole top as she leaned against the booth while inspecting her nails. Dina, who wore a short sundress, nervously paced the area before the booth while Wiley eyed his watch several times and looked around the surrounding area. Casey hurried toward the kissing booth wearing a white, low cut tank top and a pair of jean shorts. She carried her shoes, allowing her to jog the entire way. Dina glared at her from her position at the booth and appeared irritated with her. Wiley appeared overly pleased. Casey eyed the look she received from Dina and slipped into her shoes.

"I made it--relax," Casey scoffed.

"Barely," Dina snapped.

The booth had three sides, providing a side for each girl, and a counter to keep the men from getting too close. Melanie cast a loathsome glare at Casey and Dina. Dina fussed over Casey's hair that was still damp from her rushed shower. Ruger, Grey, and Diesel approached. There was still five minutes before the booth was officially open. Wiley made an announcement over the PA system, alerting all men that the kissing booth was about to open. Casey rolled her eyes and groaned.

"I can't believe you guys talked me into this," Casey muttered under her breath.

Ruger smiled and held up a tube of breath freshener. Casey groaned with a tense smile and allowed him to spray some into her mouth. Dina quickly approached and opened her mouth as well. Ruger gave her a squirt. Dina returned to her side. Grey joined Dina and smiled.

"I think I'm first," Grey announced.

She grinned her response. The small crowd of men now moved closer to the booth with an overwhelming majority lined up on Casey's side. Melanie appeared annoyed while folding her arms across her chest and huffed softly. Vaughn, now changed back into his uniform, maintained his distance and watched with disgrace as Deputy Mitchell and Deputy Tucker stood in Casey's line. Wiley stood nearby, looked at his watch, and grinned.

"One minute until the booth opens," Wiley announced with a little too much enthusiasm. "And since I'm in charge, I'll start things off."

Wiley placed a ticket in Casey's jar and quickly kissed her. He did the same for Dina and Melanie then looked at his watch and grinned proudly.

"The kissing booth is officially open," Wiley announced to the crowd of men.

Diesel approached Casey, grinned deviously, and dropped a stack of tickets into her jar. He patted the table. Casey eyed him, smiled, and moved across the counter to join him on the other side. Diesel pulled her into his arms and kissed her warmly but passionately. Dina also kissed Grey longer than she should. Melanie passed out the standard, quick kiss. The men on Melanie's side saw the other kisses occurring and quickly switched sides, opting for the longer lines. Ruger stood to the side of the booth, glared at Diesel kissing Casey, and appeared annoyed.

"Okay, break it up," Ruger muttered. "You're embarrassing me."

Diesel broke off the kiss and grinned at Casey, who hid her smile. She had to admit, he was a handful. Casey remained outside the booth as the men in her line approached. She allowed each one to kiss her above the standard and even place their arms around her. Ruger remained only a few feet away and closely watched each man's hands. Dina finally moved outside the booth as well. Toward the end of the hour-long kiss-fest, the men finally moved along. Wiley approached while looking at his watch and then smiled at the three women.

"Five more minutes, ladies," Wiley informed them.

Dina eyed hers and Casey's jars, which were filled with tickets and cash. Casey and Dina exchanged grins. Ruger approached Dina and placed ten dollars in her jar. She appeared pleased, smiled, and kissed him quickly but warmly on the lips. He then approached Casey, grinned, and placed fifty dollars in her jar. Casey smiled as Ruger pulled her gently into his arms and kissed her passionately. Casey returned the kiss without hesitation. Everyone surrounding the booth stared with surprise, including Dina. Ruger brook off the kiss, smiled lovingly, kissed her hand, and then walked away. Diesel glared at him, frowned, and shook his head.

"Show off," Diesel scoffed.

Casey appeared slightly flustered. Dina stared at her with her mouth hanging open and silently questioned the kiss with her eyes. Casey smiled and shrugged.

"One minute, ladies," Wiley informed them.

Casey casually leaned her back against the counter and looked across the fairgrounds. Vaughn patrolled the nearby area while keeping an eye on the kissing booth and finally approached her side. Casey eyed him with some surprise then smirked.

"Business or pleasure, Sheriff?"

Vaughn placed a ticket in the jar and appeared to mock her with a look. Casey casually straightened.

"All business, huh?"

"Consider it payback for all the crap you've put me through," Vaughn informed her.

Vaughn pulled Casey against him and kissed her passionately and aggressively, startling her. Her heart raced as the erotic kiss sent shockwaves through her entire body. He broke off the kiss before she could react and released her.

"Have a nice day," he remarked with a smirk.

Casey hid her smile as Vaughn left. She couldn't help but stare after him as her mind raced to make sense of his actions. She didn't know what his game was, but she sort of enjoyed playing it. Dina leaned on Casey's shoulder and dreamily watched the sheriff walk away. Melanie watched him leave as well and appeared disgusted or possibly embarrassed.

"What was that all about?" Dina asked.

"I doubt he even knows," Casey said and shook her head. "But he's one hell of a kisser."

It was no secret. In all his years behind a badge, Sheriff Holt had never participated in the kissing booth. He was always image conscious, especially while wearing his badge. Wiley officially announced the closing of the kissing booth, collected all three jars, and made himself comfortable at the counter to count the money and tickets from each jar. Melanie hovered over Wiley as he tallied up the small fortune they'd raked in. Dina excitedly clung to Casey's arm as she practically counted along.

Wiley sat back in his chair and smiled. "We have Melanie at one hundred thirty; Dina at two hundred ten; and Casey at four hundred sixteen."

Dina jumped excitedly. Wiley appeared pleased, stuffed the tickets and money into one container, and stood while looking at all three women.

"Nicely done. That's a new record for the kissing booth. Rest those lips until next year," Wiley teased.

"Casey cheated," Melanie announced with hostility while lunging forward.

"What?" Wiley suddenly demanded.

"Her friends put in twenty dollars each, and there's a fifty dollar bill in there from that one guy. That should only count as one," Melanie protested.

"That's not how it works," he replied. "It's all for charity--not ego boosts." Wiley gave a polite nod and left.

Melanie glared at Casey, wrinkled her nose, and sneered. "The day's not over yet."

Dina looked at Casey and grinned deviously while raising her brows. "Sheriff Holt has never participated at the kissing booth before. You must be special."

The look on Melanie's face was priceless. Her look turned hostile. "Not that special," she snapped with a snort. "He wants children. Casey's just an itch he's scratching."

"You bitch!" Dina gasped with horror and attempted to hit Melanie as she walked away.

Casey grabbed Dina's arm and had to stop her from chasing Melanie. "It's okay, Dina," she gently assured her. "We already hit her where it counts."

Dina attempted to compose herself, but she still had an unpredictable look of hostility in her eyes.

"Come on," Casey announced. "The bachelor auction is about to start, and we don't want to miss it."

Chapter Twenty-five

The bleachers in front of the stage were nearly packed for the bachelor auction. There were a lot of locals but also some visitors who just wanted to catch a peek at an authentic bachelor auction. It was actually the town's way of balancing out the sexism surrounding the kissing booth. Now it was the women's turn to objectify the men in town. Truth be told, the women enjoyed the bachelor auction possibly more than the men enjoyed the kissing booth. Most times, women bid on the guys just so they could watch neighborhood men clean their houses. Casey and Dina found a spot off to the side near a tree, while the guys had already secured their spot in the bleachers. Wiley took his position at the podium off to the side of the stage and looked at the large crowd with a pleased smile.

"Good afternoon, Darwood Falls."

"Afternoon, Wiley!" the crowd yelled back.

"Oh, I can feel the love here this afternoon," Wiley announced with a chuckle. "We're about to start our annual bachelor auction. This year we have some fine new additions, and of course, the old favorites. Our first bachelor is new to Darwood Falls. Let's have Diesel Mann on stage."

Vaughn, Tucker, and Mitchell suddenly exchanged looks from where they sat near the stage. Diesel jumped up from his seat while dumping his food onto Ruger's lap, made his way from the bleachers, and jogged onto stage. Wiley eyed Diesel and possibly thought the same thing as every other man in town. There was a soft murmur from the crowd, particularly from the women, to the brawny newcomer.

"Diesel is a thirty-six-year-old ex-Marine. He enjoys working out and--" Wiley hesitated then read from the index card, "--good food." Wiley grinned and looked back at the crowd. "Should we start the bidding off at one hundred dollars?"

Diesel removed his shirt and tossed it across stage. His massively toned chest, muscular shoulders, and six-pack abs were revealed to the crowd. There was a round of gasps from the women. Numbers began flying up in every corner.

Vaughn shut his eyes and groaned softly. "I'm going to pretend I'm not here."

"Huh, Jeannie's even bidding on him," Tucker remarked.

Vaughn suddenly looked up with surprise. "That better be her money."

Wiley was having a tough time keeping up with the bids as the numbers flashed from around the bleachers. Casey and Dina looked at each other and exchanged smiles as Diesel flexed his muscles in every thinkable way. He was enjoying the attention, which was evident from the grin on his face. The bidding continued to climb as the female chatter rose. Ruger casually ate popcorn and appeared disinterested in the spectacle. Vaughn had his hand over his eyes and no longer watched.

"Two thousand twenty dollars--going once, twice, sold to the lovely Jeannie," Wiley cheerfully announced.

Vaughn suddenly looked up with horror on his face. "What? No, no, no."

Tucker and Mitchell laughed at Sheriff Holt's reaction to Jeannie bidding on Diesel with his money. Jeannie jumped up and down excitedly. Vaughn collapsed into his seat and groaned lowly. Diesel left the stage with a pleased smile and met Jeannie at the payment table off to the side of the stage. Casey and Dina excitedly cheered him on. The next few guys went for the usual purchase of a couple hundred dollars.

"Next up, we have a former resident returned home," Wiley said cheerfully. "Let's hear it for Grey Remington."

Grey trotted onto stage, smiled with some embarrassment, and waved. He was obviously self-conscious having to follow Diesel's performance. The crowd happily cheered to him.

"Grey is co-owner of our antique shop due to reopen this summer," Wiley announced. "Many of you probably remember him for his famous streak at the church picnic."

Grey smiled at Wiley, raised his brows, and pointed at him while laughing. In Grey's defense, he was only fourteen at the time and did it on a dare. The crowd was getting into Wiley's storytelling about the bachelors.

"We'll start the bidding at one hundred dollars," Wiley announced. "Do I hear one hundred?"

A few numbers raised. Despite Grey's non-impressive physic, it was obvious he was more popular than first imagined. Everyone knew about the murder of their parents and possibly wanted to get to know him a little better now because of the mystery surrounding his departure. Wiley continued with the bidding on Grey.

Dina finally raised her number. "Five hundred."

There was a round of gasps from the crowd. All eyes were now on Dina standing with Casey by the tree. Grey looked at Dina, smiled warmly, and blew her a kiss.

"We have five hundred. Do I hear five hundred and ten?" Wiley banged the gavel and grinned. "Sold to our lovely kissing queen, Dina."

Dina grinned at Casey, who handed her the money. Dina took the money and hurried to the desk near the stage. Grey met her there, pulled her into his arms, and kissed her.

Wiley watched them kiss then laughed. "Well, folks, I don't think Grey will be a bachelor much longer."

Grey and Dina left the payment desk and joined Casey by the tree. Ruger also joined them with Diesel's box full of food.

Grey looked around and appeared curious. "Where's Diesel?"

"I haven't seen him since he went off with the lady who bid on him," Ruger replied.

Several bachelors went up for auction. During bidding on the fifth bachelor, faint female moans were heard. Several people in the crowd looked around to the sound. As the bidding continued, the moaning turned to cries of ecstasy. Wiley continued the bidding but was obviously distracted and now looked around as well. Vaughn and Tucker were alerted to the sound, left their seats, and searched the area for the source. A loud banging came from the nearby, closed ticket booth followed by a loud scream.

"Oh, God--yes!" came Jeannie's voice.

The sound suddenly stopped. Vaughn approached the closed ticket booth and was about to open the door when Diesel casually walked out. He eyed Vaughn with little emotion.

"What's up, bro?" Diesel announced.

Diesel walked past as Jeannie appeared from the ticket booth looking worn-out and rumpled. She attempted to fix her hair and looked at Vaughn with some embarrassment. She gently cleared her throat and scurried past him.

"Sheriff--"

Half the town saw their departure and stared after them with astonishment.

Wiley's mouth hung open. He gently cleared his throat and attempted a smile. "I'd like to reiterate that the bachelor auction in no way promotes prostitution," he announced and received several knowing chuckles.

Diesel approached Casey and the others by the tree. All four stared at him with shocked looks.

"What the hell was that?" Ruger suddenly demanded.

Diesel took his food from Ruger and gave him an irritated look. "What? She got her money's worth."

"You weren't supposed to *service* the winner," Ruger lashed out. "It's not *that* kind of transaction."

"Oh? No one told me that," Diesel remarked casually. "Well, she was happy with the transaction."

All four rolled their eyes and groaned. Sometimes Diesel was unbelievable. That it didn't bother him was the most disturbing part. The bachelor auction continued. After Mitchell went for the standard couple hundred, Tucker was finally up for bid. The bidding started at the usual one hundred dollars and rapidly escalated. Young women bid on him with fury. His popularity hadn't waned any in the last two years. Melanie was unusually silent. It was obvious that ship had sailed a long time ago.

"We have five hundred forty--sold for five hundred and forty to Mrs. Ridgeway," Wiley announced.

The mayor laughed and patted his wife's leg. She seemed proud of her purchase. Tucker waved to the crowd and headed for the payment table to meet Abby. Wiley consulted his sheet and grinned with pleasure.

"And last up is our fine sheriff," Wiley announced cheerfully. "Let's hear it for Sheriff Vaughn Holt."

The crowd cheered for him. Vaughn reluctantly walked onto stage and stood tough. His discomfort was obvious but unfounded. Who wouldn't bid on the sheriff?

"For those of you who are unfamiliar with our sheriff's early years as a deputy; he was the only deputy to successfully get Mrs. Wilson's cat out of the tree," Wiley informed them. "He was also the first deputy to fire his weapon while responding to a call." Wiley grinned. "Unfortunately for Mrs. Wilson's cat, they were both on the same call."

The crowd laughed along with Wiley. Vaughn groaned, lowered his head, and covered his eyes.

"The cat was fine," Wiley assured them. "Although his tail was a bit shorter."

Vaughn was severely embarrassed and attempted to leave stage. Tucker and Mitchell grinned as each grabbed an arm and escorted him back onto the stage. The crowd laughed and applauded.

"Our sheriff is just a bit bashful, ladies," Wiley informed them. "So let's make him feel better and start the bidding at two hundred dollars. Two hundred for the most important position in town, if I may say so."

Melanie grinned slyly and bid on Vaughn. Vaughn immediately frowned. Abby playfully bid against Melanie, allowing the price to escalate for their amusement. The two women smirked and played along for a few minutes.

"We have three hundred. Do I hear three twenty for our sheriff, who can shoot the tail off a cat at fifty yards?" Wiley announced.

Abby finally stopped bidding, allowing Melanie to claim victory.

"Three twenty?" Wiley again announced.

There was silence from the crowd.

Casey casually raised her number. "Four hundred."

All eyes suddenly shifted to Casey, who didn't react. Vaughn stared at her with some surprise.

Melanie appeared flustered and immediately held up her number. "Four fifty."

"Five hundred," Casey said without hesitation.

Melanie fidgeted and appeared to consider her response. "Six hundred," she finally called out.

There was silence again. Several stares were now on Casey, who still showed no emotion while casually leaning against her tree.

"Do I hear--" Wiley began.

"One thousand," Casey interrupted without batting a lash.

The crowd suddenly gasped. Wiley was equally surprised, although no one was as stunned as Vaughn was. Melanie was momentarily paralyzed by the large amount. She looked desperate.

"Any more bids?"

"Fifteen hundred," Abby announced, breaking the silence and invoking loud murmurs.

Melanie appeared relieved and smiled gratefully at her mother.

Casey casually folded her arms across her chest while leaning against the tree. She showed no reaction then responded, "Two thousand."

The crowd continued to gasp and looked back at Abby, who appeared tense. Diesel, Grey, and Ruger casually ate popcorn and appeared disinterested.

"Twenty-five hundred," Abby finally called out, her voice crackling.

Melanie excitedly clung to her mother's arm. The mayor just stared at his wife with a stunned look. All eyes were again on Casey, including Wiley. Casey casually held up her hand showing five fingers.

Wiley appeared shocked. "Five thousand?"

Casey gave him a thumbs up along with a tiny grin. The crowd gasped and looked at Abby. The mayor suddenly jumped on his wife and held her down.

"Five thousand going once, twice, sold to our town darling, Casey," Wiley announced cheerfully while laughing.

Vaughn appeared stunned and stared at Casey with his hand propped on his gun belt. The crowd clapped and cheered. Casey stole some popcorn from Diesel, flashed a smile, and headed to the payment table near the stage. Vaughn crossed the stage, hurried down the steps, and met her by the table.

"What the hell was that?" Vaughn demanded.

She didn't bother looking at him, but she knew his look was priceless. "Payback for all the crap *you've* put *me* through," Casey teased while smirking.

"You do realize you're buying a worker not the law," he informed her firmly.

"I have a college degree," she said matter-of-fact. "I think I know how these things work." Casey wrote out a check and glanced at him. "You know, I just saved you from a fate worse than Melanie--her cougar mother. Try kissing my ass a little."

Casey paid the elderly woman, June, at the table and turned to Vaughn with a smile. "By the terms of the auction, you're mine from seven to three tomorrow," she said with a look of humor on her face. "Be at my house dressed to work. It's going to be a very long day. Like 'boot camp' long."

She flashed a smile, cheerfully patted him on the chest, and walked away.

Vaughn shook his head and watched her leave. "How can something so small make my life so miserable?"

"Nothing a good, sturdy romp won't cure," June informed him from where she sat behind the payment table.

Vaughn slowly turned his head and looked at June behind the table. She smiled and seductively waved the check.

"And for five thousand dollars, you should be flattered," the elderly woman continued. "Why I remember giving blowjobs to boys behind the stage for cotton candy."

Vaughn stared at June with surprise, shook his head, and walked away.

June called after him, "I still like cotton candy, Sheriff!"

Chapter Twenty-six

The crowd had returned to the stage area for the evening talent show. They were packed into the bleachers and sat on lawn chairs and blankets on the grass in an endless sea of spectators. The talent show was a huge draw for locals and visitors alike. Men and women from neighboring towns also participated in the show. It was open to anyone. Vaughn patrolled the area with some of the hired security. With that many people, things could get out of hand quickly, and it was their job to keep everyone safe throughout the show. Contestants showed off their singing talents, dancing skills, and various other talents. A comedian performed and had the crowd laughing so hard some were in tears. A magician attempted to pull off some amazing magic acts but failed miserably. His jovial commentary entertained the crowd, and no one knew it wasn't part of the act. There were several singing acts that drew applause from the crowd. One women's slinky attire may have had something to do with the tremendous applause she received.

Dina was up next with her singing and dancing routine. She wore a top hat, tuxedo style jacket with a white, low-cut top, and a short, black skirt while tap dancing and singing to "Putting on the Ritz". The crowd applauded for her. Most would believe she had taken years of tap dance lessons, but she was actually self-taught. As

Dina exited from behind stage, Sheriff Holt approached her. She eyed him and grinned.

"No autographs, please," she teased.

"I caught your performance. You were great, Dina," he replied but obviously had another motive for stopping her short of the locker rooms. "Have you seen Ruger or Diesel?"

"They're with Casey," Dina casually informed him. "I guess she's having last minute performance jitters. I have to change before Casey's performance. Why don't you find a good spot and enjoy the show?"

"Yeah, I think I'll patrol, if it's all the same to you."

"Have it your way," Dina announced then muttered. "You usually do."

Dina hurried toward the women's locker room. Melanie was up next and performed her tap-dance routine in an extremely short dress and low-cut top. She looked fantastic on stage and her routine was flawless with amazing dance moves that would put even the professionals to shame. The crowd went wild over her amazing routine. She appeared pleased with herself and the wild applause she received. Another woman performed a gymnastic routine for the crowd. Her routine was then followed by another magic act that was better than the first. There were more singers who performed. Most did well, although one was cringe worthy. Wiley appeared on stage after the last act left and applauded the young woman.

"Wasn't she terrific?" he announced. The crowd applauded mechanically, but it was obvious her performance wasn't very good. "Now, for our last performance of the evening, we have a last minute addition," Wiley announced cheerfully and looked at his cue card. "We have 'Casey and Company' in a non-specified dance routine. Let's hear it for 'Casey and Company'."

The audience applauded along with Wiley, who hurried offstage. Melanie, still dressed from her performance, slipped into a seat alongside her mother and father and maintained a devious grin. Dina rushed back to the stage area and squeezed in where she could. Vaughn paused alongside one of the nearby trees, casually leaned against it, and watched the stage. He failed at looking casually disinterested. The stage curtains opened to reveal Casey in a low-cut, sequin dress with tassels just covering her thighs and sequin heels. The scar on her left thigh was clearly visible even through her stockings. She stood facing Ruger, who wore dress pants and a flashy vest. Diesel casually leaned against the stage in what appeared to be an old-fashioned gangster's zoot suit complete with hat and shoes. "Land of 1000 Dancers" began to play. Ruger and Casey started dancing Latin Jive to the music without missing a beat. They were amazing! Ruger spun Casey around in his arms as she danced wildly and seductively around him. They continued with an amazingly choreographed routine in a fast tempo. Casey flipped backwards over Ruger's arm several times, and he spun her around his body with speed and grace. The audience appeared stunned. Melanie stared at their flawless dance routine with her mouth hanging open. Abby shared the same look of horror and clung to Melanie's hand. Vaughn also watched with surprise and uncertainly straightened.

The dance continued with high impact moves and flips that stunned the audience. Two minutes into the routine, the song "Beat It" grew louder as their song faded. Diesel walked across the stage as Casey spun. She turned into him and immediately stopped. Diesel began dancing slow and seductive with Casey. Casey pulled away as part of the dance routine. Ruger slid over in a dance move and attempted to rescue Casey. Casey was slung to the side as Diesel and Ruger danced a fight sequence, which ended with Diesel grabbing Ruger by his arms. Ruger jumped onto Diesel's bent leg and made it appear as if Diesel had pulled him up. Ruger back flipped away from Diesel, landed on his feet, and immediately threw himself into a roll across stage where he lie motionless. Diesel again danced sultry with Casey, who attempted to reach Ruger and get away from Diesel. Not even two minutes into the song, he slung Casey around him and gracefully onto her hip across the floor without releasing her hand. She avoided looking at him. "I Need a Hero" began drowning out "Beat It". Everyone looked around. Grey ran through the audience and leapt onto stage wearing a vintage black suit and hat with black and white saddle shoes. He ran up to Casey on the stage floor, took her arm, and spun her around him and gracefully to her feet. Diesel and Grey started a fighting dance sequence with kicks, punches, and flips that stunned the crowd. Casey slid to Ruger's side and pretended to revive him.

In an amazing dance sequence, Grey flipped Diesel over his hip then pretended to kick him. Diesel threw himself onto his back, rolled, and then scrambled to his feet and took off backstage. Grey danced over to Casey and helped Ruger to his feet. The three of them finished out the song with an amazing dance sequence that excited the crowd. As the song ended abruptly on the lyric, "I Need a Hero", Ruger dipped Casey back with her leg high on his side, and Grey spun and landed on one knee with his hat in his hand. A massive confetti tube erupted, shooting confetti across the stage, and a banner dropped behind them that read, "Grey for Mayor". The audience jumped to their feet while wildly applauding and cheering.

Everyone applauded except Melanie, who appeared somewhere between stunned and disgusted. The mayor sneered and clapped his hands together with disgust in a failed attempt not to seem bitter. Vaughn laughed, shook his head, and clapped as well.

Wiley hurried from the judge's table and onto the stage. He yelled excitedly above the crowd. "It's unanimous! Casey and Company are the winners of this year's talent show!"

The crowd continued to applaud. The mayor slipped away through the crowd. Diesel joined them on stage to take a bow. Casey jumped into Ruger's arms and hugged him. Dina joined Grey on stage and gave him a kiss of congratulations. People swarmed the stage, shook Grey's hand, and expressed their support for him for mayor. Diesel grabbed Casey, pulled her up and into his arms, and playfully kissed her. He then tossed her back into Ruger's awaiting arms. She kissed Ruger on the lips. He held her against him and smiled with embarrassment. People continued to congratulate them on their performance and the mayor run. Grey clung to Dina as they made their way offstage and through the excited crowd. Melanie remained in her seat with her arms folded across her chest and a look of annoyance on her face.

Casey nudged Grey as the crowd continued to swarm him. "I'm going to change, get Storm, and head home."

"You want us to come along?" Grey asked between greeting people and shaking hands.

"No, this is your moment," she announced with a proud smile. "You enjoy it."

Casey headed for the changing rooms at the nearby pavilion. Ruger watched her walk away then became surrounded by several women praising his performance. Some were a little overly enthusiastic to meet him, which startled him. Just beyond the crowd toward the back of the stage, the mayor was seen arguing with Ernest, who threw his hands in the air then pointed a warning finger at him. Sheriff Holt stared across the crowd and watched the exchange between the two men. He appeared curious and slowly made his way through the crowd to get closer.

"I guess you're happy," Abby was heard from behind him.

Vaughn turned and looked at Abby. Her expression was that of rage and possible embarrassment.

"What do you mean?" Vaughn asked with a puzzled look while tilting his head.

"Grey running for mayor," she retorted. "He's going to give Lance a good run, I'm sure, and I don't doubt you couldn't be happier."

"I won't argue that," Vaughn replied matter-of-fact while placing his thumbs down the front of his gun holster.

Abby sneered at his candid response. "You're just going to toss Melanie over for our darling, little Casey, aren't you? You really don't care how much you hurt Melanie. She's the one who really loves you."

"We're not having this conversation," Vaughn boldly informed her while shaking his head. "Whatever my intentions regarding Casey don't concern you or your daughter."

Abby stared at him a moment, considered something, and then suddenly grinned. "Can it be?" She laughed softly in her throat. "Nothing happened between you and Casey the other night. Melanie was worked up over nothing! Casey Remington still hasn't forgiven you!" Abby shook her head and maintained her superior attitude. "Poor, poor Vaughn. That little, teenage crush Casey had on you is just a faded memory. She'll never be yours."

Vaughn maintained a look of limited emotion, but his thumbs tensed beneath his holster in response. "More importantly," he announced, "I'll never be with Melanie." He removed his thumbs from his holster. "If you'll excuse me--"

He proudly walked past her. She glanced after him while attempting to look disinterested, but she was obviously bothered by his statement.

†

Casey stood before an open locker within the women's changing room. She was once again wearing her jeans and the tank top she had worn at the kissing booth. She carelessly stuffed her sequin dress and shoes into the locker before her. She honestly didn't care if she ever wore it again, and she hoped to God that she never saw those shoes again. Tossing them in the garbage crossed her mind only once, but she knew Grey would have something to say about it. It had been a long day, and, despite the positive outcome, she was glad it was over. A hot bath was what she wanted most, even if that meant using the whirlpool tub in her parents' bedroom. She turned and nearly collided with Melanie, who had almost silently appeared behind her. Casey was startled to see her then relaxed. She was actually the last person Casey was expecting to see tonight. She thought she'd be off somewhere pouting or licking her wounds. Melanie's look conveyed hostility and possible embarrassment. Whatever Melanie's reason for confronting her, it undoubtedly wasn't going to end well for her. Casey wasn't in the mood, and there was the very real possibility that she was going to vent some of her hostility on Melanie if she provoked her.

"You humiliated me in front of everyone!" Melanie suddenly exclaimed while nearly down to tears.

Casey was surprised by her emotional state. She was expecting a different kind of argument, one where she would finally get to hit the little bitch. She was almost uncertain how to respond.

"Don't be ridiculous, you performed wonderfully," she replied, no longer feeling the need to get into an altercation. It was clear Melanie was fighting an emotional battle deep inside her. "Just because you didn't get first place--"

"I hate you! I've always hated you!" Melanie lashed out as she became wildly animated. It was the first time she'd ever come out and said it. "Everyone loves Casey Remington, the little town darling!" Her tone was sarcastic and mocking. "I was *always* second best!"

Casey stared at her with an astonished look. She couldn't believe Melanie resented her because she was jealous! It didn't even seem possible. She suddenly felt as if she entered some bizarre world where nothing made sense.

"You were dating Tucker, the most popular guy in town," Casey informed her. "You won the talent show five years in a row."

"Four," Melanie scoffed while folding her arms across her chest and appeared to pout.

Casey shook her head with disbelief. She couldn't believe she was actually coddling the spoiled, little girl who always tried to find new ways to insult and humiliate her.

"How does that make you second best?"

Melanie remained disgusted but appeared less hostile while frowning. "Tucker used me to get in good with my father," she retorted with some embarrassment. "I really only wanted Vaughn, but he never wanted to be with me. He always wanted you; even when he thought I was carrying his baby."

Casey was surprised by the comment. He had said some things that night while drunk in her kitchen, but she didn't realize how deep it went. She now lost all enthusiasm to fight with Melanie and took a different approach.

"Resenting me isn't going to solve anything," Casey gently informed her.

Melanie appeared to lose her strength, groaned softly, and held her head. "You're right," she said softly. "I should have known he'd always want you. Tucker told me how Vaughn saved you from that sexual assault, and how emotional he got when he thought you'd died. Not that Vaughn ever shared those emotions with me." Melanie frowned and appeared to pout. "The most emotion I ever got out of him was relief that I wasn't pregnant and anger that I'd lied about it." She stared blankly at the floor and appeared distant. "After you'd left," she said softly, "Vaughn would actually go to your house and sit on your porch for hours."

"I didn't know that," Casey said softly with surprise. "Did he tell you that?"

She snorted a laugh. "No, he never shared anything with me, especially how he felt about you." Melanie frowned with a look of embarrassment. "I'm ashamed to admit it, but I followed him a couple of times. When he caught me, I questioned him. He said he was hoping to find some clue to solve the murders, but I know it was because he never got over you," she remarked sadly.

Despite the thoughts and emotions running through Casey's head, she knew she needed to say something. She could easily crush Melanie's frail ego after what must have been the worst day of her life, but she no longer wanted to destroy this woman.

"You need to move on, Melanie," Casey said gently. "There are plenty of guys out there who are crazy about you."

"You think so?" She smiled weakly and appeared tense. "So, uh, what's the deal with the big guy?"

"Diesel?" Casey asked with surprise then snorted a laugh. "If you're looking for some fun time in the sack, he's your man. Anything more serious, avoid him at all costs."

"Were you and he--?"

"Never," Casey quickly interjected, appeared almost humored, and then added an uneasy chuckle.

Melanie suddenly appeared pleased. "Would you be willing to give him my number?" she asked timidly. "I think I could use a little casual fun."

Casey smiled and nodded. "Absolutely."

Her look again turned serious. "I'm sorry for being a bitch toward you," Melanie announced and attempted a smile. "I know why everyone in town loves you; I just could never admit it to myself." She appeared awkward but sincere. "Could we maybe start over?"

"I'd like that," Casey replied.

It was possibly the strangest day Casey had ever had. She kissed over one hundred men, helped elevate her brother onto a pedestal she feared from which he'd never come down, overpaid for a slightly used sheriff, and now she was actually having a grown-up conversation with the woman who'd dedicated her life to making Casey miserable. Did she just suddenly turn into her mother? Casey reconsidered. She wasn't sure if she was ready to sheath her claws just yet.

†

*D*eputy Tucker made his way through the crowd still surrounding Grey, who was discussing his mayor campaign. He was in his glory talking with different business owners, mill workers, and farmers, all eager to show their support. Dina stood by Grey's said and appeared proud to be with him. Ruger and Diesel were conspicuously missing, possibly to change out of their dance costumes. Tucker approached Dina and pulled her aside, startling her. His look was serious and immediately made her nervous.

"Is something wrong?" Dina asked the handsome deputy.

He appeared reluctant to respond. "I don't know if I should say anything," he began then fidgeted, "but one of our temp police officers arrested your mother."

Dina rolled her eyes and snorted a laugh. "That's not news, Deputy Tucker," she replied callously. "Was it prostitution? Drunk and disorderly? It's not like I haven't heard it before."

Tucker drew a deep breath and stared at her with uncertainty. "A little of both, I'm afraid," he informed her. "But it turned into an altercation. She'd been beaten pretty badly outside the tavern. They took her to the police station. She asked for you."

She stared at Tucker and appeared uncertain how to respond. Grey slowly approached while observing the exchange.

"Everything okay?" Grey asked.

"Uh, yeah," Dina informed him while fidgeting. She attempted a smile and affectionately patted his chest. "I, uh, need to go see my mother."

The look on Grey's face was almost shocked. "Your *mother?*" It was as if he immediately felt her conflicted emotions. She hadn't referred to Olivia as her mother since she was in high school. "Do you want me to come along?"

"No," she said almost too quickly then attempted a smile. "I mean, that's not a good idea. I should probably go alone."

Grey uncertainly nodded.

"I could give you a ride," Tucker announced. "I should find the arresting officer and get the report from him."

"Actually," Dina said softly, "I think I'd rather go by myself. I need time to think, and the walk will do me some good."

"Yeah, sure," Tucker replied. "I understand." He attempted a smile and walked away.

Grey took her hands in his and appeared sympathetic. "Take my jeep. I'll walk you to the parking lot," he firmly announced. "I'll ride home with the guys."

"Are you sure?" Dina asked.

Grey smiled and nodded. He kissed her quickly on the lips then caressed her shoulders. "And if you need me, just call."

Chapter Twenty-seven

*T*he stable area beyond the bustling fairgrounds was quiet in the darkened, evening hours. The fair was still going strong, and, as far as Casey could tell, there was still a large crowd surrounding the stage area. Grey was going to be busy for a few more hours while playing it up to his adoring fans. As she saddled her horse, she couldn't help but be happy for her brother and the evening he was enjoying in the spotlight. She saw Vaughn approach with his baton flashlight. Casey offered a tiny smile and finished saddling Storm. Now that the talent show was over and Grey was officially throwing his hat into the political arena, she no longer felt the need to spar with Sheriff Holt. Was she one step closer to being declawed?

"Sheriff--"

Vaughn stopped near her and patted the horse's large rump. His eyes strayed to the massive scar along his hindquarters. He looked back at Casey.

"Are you sure you want to ride through those dark woods? You can leave your horse here. I'll give you a ride home." He offered a teasing smile. "I'll even let you ride up front for a change."

"Thanks, but Storm had a long day, and I sort of promised him a little playtime with the mares tonight," she replied.

Vaughn leaned on the horse's rump and studied her. There was obviously plenty on his mind. "That, uh, was quite a show you and your friends put on tonight. So, uh, how long have you been planning that?"

"Nearly two years."

Vaughn snorted a laugh and shook his head. It was as if the world suddenly made sense. "Is that why you and Grey came back? So he could run for mayor?"

Casey grinned in response. "While he was recovering, it became his obsession to realize our father's dream and end the corruption in Darwood Falls."

"And you couldn't have told me that?"

"Corruption runs deep, Sheriff," she announced firmly. "I never believed you were involved, but your history with Melanie didn't sit well with the others."

He appeared uncomfortable and straightened. "Melanie was a drunken one-night stand followed by several weeks of lies to keep me in her life."

"I know," Casey said gently while staring into his dark eyes. "What she did to you was wrong, but her mistreatment of you was nothing compared to mine."

Vaughn appeared bewildered as his arm slipped off the horse's rump and watched her without comment. She shrugged and was no longer able to look him in the eyes.

"I was consumed with guilt over my parents' death, and I took it out on you." She finally met his gaze with a strange but sincere look in her eyes. She released a shaken breath. It was difficult even talking about the attack. "You shot that man three times in the chest even though we both know he was surrendering."

Vaughn suddenly tensed to the comment. He had led the entire town, including Wiley, to believe he shot the man after he stabbed Casey, but he conveniently left out the part that the killer had been surrendering.

"Don't worry, Sheriff. No one will ever hear it from me," she softly informed him. "I know you did that for me. I was wrong for blaming you." She stared into his dark eyes with all sincerity. "Deep down, I always knew I was wrong, and I'm sorry for the way I treated you. You saved my life, and I never even thanked you." She gently placed her hand on his badge without taking her eyes from his. "Thank you, Vaughn."

Vaughn stared at her a moment as if uncertain how to respond then suddenly pulled her against him and held her in a tight embrace. Casey uncertainly returned the embrace. Vaughn buried his face in her hair and sighed softly as if some terrible burden had finally been lifted.

"Thank you, Casey," he said softly with a quiver in his voice. "You have no idea how much that means to me."

Casey pulled back just far enough to meet his gaze. She was in no hurry to pull away from him. She wanted to be in his arms, and she was no longer afraid to admit it. She caressed his badge and smiled timidly. "You know, I never told anyone except Dina, but when I was fifteen and saw you in your uniform for the first time, I had such a crush on you."

Vaughn appeared surprised by the comment and, without warning, kissed her passionately. She was startled by the aggressive way he kissed her. Her heart immediately pounded in response. Before she could react, he just as quickly broke off the kiss. He pulled away from her, appeared embarrassed, and had no idea what to do with his hands.

"I'm sorry; I've been a little--" Vaughn considered his mood and groaned softly, "--out of my mind lately."

Casey fidgeted slightly. She knew it was time to admit what she couldn't or *wouldn't* admit before. "There may be a reason for that," she said timidly and grimaced. "When we were drunk the other night, we sort of had sex in the kitchen."

Vaughn stared at her and appeared unusually tense. "Oh--" he replied gently and fidgeted as well. "I, uh, didn't think you remembered."

Casey was surprised by his admission. "You knew?"

"It took most of the next day, but I eventually figured it out," he replied then gave her a strange look. "If you knew, why didn't you say something?"

"Like what? That you'd bent me over the counter and--"

"Okay," he quickly interrupted with embarrassment. "I was a mutt in heat and hoped you wouldn't remember. I didn't want to make things worse between us."

"You didn't make things worse," she assured him.

"I was drunk and aggressive," he replied and again debated what to do with his hands. "There was potential for things to get really bad between us."

"You may have been aggressive, but I wasn't exactly protesting," she informed him then grinned almost lustful. "You're sort of missing the point."

"What point?"

"You transformed a horrible memory into a wildly sexual one. I'm no longer haunted by my own kitchen." She suddenly laughed. "Guess you should have thought of trying that when you had me locked in the back of your cruiser two years ago. We probably would have gotten along a lot better." She suddenly hesitated then muttered, "Oh, God, I sound like my mother."

He stared at her with a strange look on his face then snorted a laugh. His hands finally settled in his pockets, giving him an insecure look. "I'm pretty sure you would have killed me at the mere suggestion."

Casey offered a tiny smile and shrugged. "I probably would have been more open to the offer than you think."

Vaughn stared at her a moment in silence then suddenly groaned, pulled her into his arms, and kissed her passionately with some added aggression. Despite that he took her by surprise, Casey immediately returned the kiss this time, which quickly turned aggressive as they caressed and groped each other. There was no hesitation on either of their behalf, and it was quickly escalating. She held him back and broke off the kiss before things got out of hand. Casey remained in his arms, lustfully caressed his chest, and looked seductively into his eyes while grinning.

"There's room for two in the jetted tub at my house."

Vaughn suddenly groaned and failed at an attempt to hide his lustful grin. He was reluctant to release her as he held her close and firmly caressed her body.

"I'll make an excuse to leave," he said with a soft moan. "I can be there in an hour."

Casey grinned and seductively raised her brows while caressing his shoulders. "Don't be late, or I'll start without you."

Vaughn groaned again and kissed her wildly. His lust was rising fast, and his hands started traveling her body. Any moment, she was certain he'd start undressing her. Casey pulled away, smiled warmly, and held him back.

"One hour."

She kissed him quickly on the lips then mounted her horse before he could react and rode away. Vaughn groaned while smiling lustfully, watched her ride across the fairgrounds, and collapsed against the barn. Everything finally seemed right in his world.

"Sheriff," Ruger was heard from nearby.

Vaughn straightened and looked at the corner of the barn. Ruger casually approached with an emotionless expression. It was almost obvious he had witnessed some or most of what had just happened. Ruger was the dreaded fatherly figure, and his reaction could have a huge impact on their future. Vaughn appeared tense then resumed his authoritative demeanor.

"You just missed Casey," Vaughn replied simply.

"Yes, so I see. I wanted to make sure she got off okay," Ruger informed him then sneered, "but it sounds like you're taking care of that later."

Vaughn's entire body stiffened, and he appeared instantly annoyed. "Nice of you to eavesdrop, Ruger," he muttered lowly while hiding his displeasure to the comment.

"I think you should know; Casey's only been with one other man," Ruger boldly informed him. "She's not the sort of woman who sleeps around."

"Grey had mentioned her past relationship," Vaughn replied and appeared uncomfortable with the subject.

"So you understand why I'm protective of her."

Vaughn glared at him with arrogance. "She nearly died in my arms, so you'll understand why *I'm* protective of her," he informed Ruger and showed he wouldn't be intimidated. "I fell in love with Casey the day I'd met her only to be devastated when I learned she was only fifteen. I've waited a longtime to be with her, and I finally have my one chance. Trust me; I'm not going to blow it, and I'm certainly not going to be intimidated from pursuing her either."

Ruger appeared unimpressed with Vaughn's candor. "Being like a father to her, I'd be very displeased if you did anything to hurt her. However--" Ruger's look suddenly turned cold and harsh. "--as her former lover, I wouldn't hesitate to break your neck without thinking twice."

Vaughn stared at Ruger with a stunned look. "You?" he gasped. "I thought Diesel--?"

"Diesel? Seriously?" Ruger announced with a somewhat shocked expression. "She'd never go for his type. I'm surprised you'd think she would." He shook his head while maintaining his serious look. "What happened between Casey and me was a mistake that ended over a year ago. That relationship was probably my biggest regret, and, believe me, I have quite a few."

"Why would you regret it? You're obviously very close," Vaughn announced.

"Sleeping with your commander's daughter is one of those lines you just don't cross," he informed him. "Our relationship was complex. She was filled with so much anger and rage, that I opted for the radical solution. I know it was wrong, but it was my last option to bring her back." He took a deep breath and stared at Vaughn. "Our current relationship is as it should be."

Mitchell was heard talking over Vaughn's radio. "Sheriff, we have a situation at the rabbit building."

Vaughn groaned, removed his radio, and responded, "What's the situation?"

"Someone opened the pens," came Mitchell's reply. "We have rabbits everywhere."

Vaughn groaned softly and appeared defeated. "Okay, I'm on my way," he said into the radio then looked at Ruger with irritation. "You'll be happy to know that I won't be keeping my date with Casey. That should give you some added time to successfully turn her against me."

Ruger shook his head with defeat. "You really haven't been paying attention, Sheriff. I know how Casey feels about you even if she refused to admit it to even herself. Honestly, she could do a lot worse," he informed him. He straightened proudly. "Diesel and I will take care of your bunny situation. You keep your date."

Vaughn stared at him and appeared surprised. "Seriously?"

"I'm only concerned for her welfare," Ruger replied. "I'd never stand in the way of her happiness. It's in her best interest that you keep your date. Diesel and I can handle your bunny related emergency."

†

*W*hite rabbits hopped around the fairgrounds just outside the rabbit building. They looked confused and uncertain what to do with their newly found freedom. Mitchell, two rental cops, and a couple of workers attempted to catch the rabbits, which darted away every time they got close. Grey, Diesel, and Ruger appeared at the small animal barn and watched the others attempting to catch the remaining rabbits. It was almost hysterical to watch. Mitchell narrowly missed catching one of the rabbits, saw the three men while straightening, and appeared surprised.

"Where's the sheriff?" Mitchell asked.

"He had an emergency call, so you're stuck with us," Ruger informed Mitchell.

"Huh? Well, if you're here to help, start catching rabbits," Mitchell informed them.

Diesel looked around with bewilderment then eyed the deputy. "Wouldn't it be easier if you just used your gun?"

Mitchell glared at Diesel. Grey frowned, smacked Diesel on the arm, and pointed to the rabbits. Diesel rolled his eyes and pursued one of the white rabbits. The rabbit ran from him and led him in circles.

Mitchell removed his cell phone, placed a call, and spoke into the phone. "Hey, it's me," he announced. "The sheriff sent some additional help, so we have the situation here pretty much under control." Mitchell was silent while listening to the person on the other end. "No, he was taking care of something else. If he needs backup, I'm sure he'll call."

Ruger overheard the conversation, glanced at Mitchell, and hid his humored smile.

†

*D*ina entered the police station bullpen. There were several temporary police officers milling about with drunken men in handcuffs, who were adamantly insisting they didn't do anything wrong. Most of those being arrested were non-locals who indulged a little too much at the annual fair. It wasn't uncommon, although it wasn't something Dina had ever seen before. She immediately noticed her mother sitting alongside one of the desks with her hands cuffed behind her back. She looked disheveled, which was actually normal for her, but her worn, tired face was bruised and scratched. Dina stared at her profile a moment from a distance then uncertainly approached her and the arresting officer, who sat behind the desk and typed on the computer before him. She paused several feet before her mother and saw the scratches and bruises more clearly. Olivia looked oddly like roadkill. It was possibly the saddest moment Dina had ever had with her mother. Olivia looked at Dina in her usual drunken manner, but this time, she actually made eye contact.

"Are you okay?" Dina finally asked.

"I need five hundred dollars for bail," Olivia remarked with little emotion. "If I don't make bail, they're going to make me spend the night in jail."

Dina stared at her while searching for a response. "That's it? You need money?" she suddenly asked. What should have been hurt was actually anger. "You haven't spoken to me in almost ten years and when you finally do, it's to ask me for money? Is that why you called?"

"I didn't call you," Olivia scoffed and attempted to hold up her head, although it was obvious she would soon pass out. "Do you have the money?

Dina shook her head with disbelief. "No, I'm not posting your bail. I don't even know you."

"I'm your mother," she snorted with hostility.

Dina stared at her and looked stunned by the comment. "No," she replied and vigorously shook her head. "The only mother I knew died two years ago. Spend the night in jail. I'm sure you'll find it more comfortable than your usual corner table at the tavern."

Dina stormed from the bullpen leaving Olivia staring after her with her mouth hanging open. Dina hurried out of the police station and paused just on the quiet sidewalk. She allowed her head to fall into her hand. She lifted her head, took a deep breath, and fumbled with Grey's car keys. She was about to approach Grey's jeep when she suddenly stopped and looked back at the police station with a bewildered expression. She removed her cell phone and pressed a button while heading for Grey's jeep.

†

The fair was winding down by the time the rabbits were caught and returned to their cages. Grey, Ruger, and Diesel walked across the nearly deserted fairgrounds toward the parking lot. There were still some visitors playing last minute games, although most of the food stands were already closed. Many vendors were getting ready to enjoy a night on the town, which consisted of the tavern or the bowling alley. Ruger's cell phone rang. He glanced at the caller ID, appeared puzzled, and answered the phone.

"Hello?"

Ruger suddenly stopped and listened to the mysterious caller on the other end. "Who is--?" He pulled the phone away from his ear and stared at it with a puzzled look. The caller had apparently hung up. He hurried Grey and Diesel toward the parking lot. "That was an anonymous call. Someone broke into the store."

Grey removed his cell phone as he followed them and pressed several buttons. "I'll call Sheriff Holt."

"I'll call Casey," Ruger quickly announced then looked at Grey as they continued toward the parking lot. "Tell the sheriff to stay with her."

Grey appeared bewildered by the comment. Ruger pressed a button on his cell phone as they hurried across the parking lot.

"Damn it, it went to voicemail," Ruger announced then spoke into the phone. "Casey, we have a situation. Stay alert."

All three hurried through the parking lot and toward their car. Grey appeared frustrated while on his cell phone and disconnected the call.

"I got the sheriff's voicemail too," Grey announced.

"Someone needs to go to the house and make sure Casey's okay," Ruger said.

Grey looked around the parking lot. There was a long run-in shed with saddled horses tied to a hitching post. "I'll borrow my

197

friend's horse," he informed them. "I can ride through the woods and be there in ten minutes."

Ruger nodded. Grey hurried for the shelter with the tied horses. Ruger and Diesel jumped into his car and drove away. Grey untied one of the horses, backed it out of the shed, and placed the reins around its neck. He touched the horse's face and pointed a warning finger at it.

"This is important," Grey sternly informed the horse. "I don't like riding at night, so I want you to be on your best behavior, got it?"

The horse appeared disinterested.

"As long as we've got that straight," Grey muttered and clumsily mounted the horse. He sent the horse into a trot across the fairgrounds, and, despite his anxiety, he appeared to ride rather well.

Chapter Twenty-eight

Sheriff Holt drove along the dark back road to the Remington farm in his police blazer. He glanced at himself in the rearview mirror several times and attempted to fix his hair while driving. He casually placed both hands on the steering wheel and smiled dreamily to himself. He could barely contain his smile and shook his head while sighing. Life was finally as it should be--with Casey by his side. He hummed the wedding march then appeared embarrassed and shook his head.

"Getting a little ahead of yourself, Vaughn," he muttered softly. His grin again returned. "Ah, who cares."

A car's headlights were seen in the rearview mirror behind him. The headlights flashed. Vaughn studied the car behind him and appeared curious. Perhaps it was a drunk driver. Who the hell would flash a police blazer? The car sped up and rode up the back of the police blazer. Vaughn looked in both mirrors and appeared to contemplate his next move. The car suddenly picked up speed and started to pass him. He glanced in the side mirror. It was Casey's black Camaro. He smiled and laughed while shaking his head.

"She's going to be the death of me," he teased but maintained his grin.

Vaughn slowed to allow her to drive alongside him, but she didn't pass only kept pace with his blazer by the back quarter panel.

Vaughn appeared concerned and looked at the curve coming up ahead. Now she was just being plain dangerous. Giving her a ticket for reckless endangerment would certainly put a damper on their romantic evening. Her car didn't back off. Vaughn looked back several times.

"What the hell are you doing?" he firmly demanded aloud to himself.

The car suddenly revved and rammed into his back quarter panel as they neared the curve. Vaughn attempted to control his blazer but there was a tree just up ahead. He slammed on his brakes, but it was too late. The blazer struck the tree head on. Vaughn was thrown forward as the airbag deployed and then his head hit the side window. Casey's car sped past and continued through the curve and out of sight. The sheriff's police blazer was partially in the woods with the front end smashed against a tree. The entire back driver's side panel was smashed in as well. All the lights remained on outside the vehicle. The driver's side window was cracked with blood smears. Within the blazer, Vaughn was slumped back against the seat with blood running down the side of his left temple as the air bag hung shriveled from the steering wheel.

†

*T*he Remington farmhouse was well-lit with the outside barn light and the porch light on. Several lights were on within the house both upstairs and downstairs. Storm grazed in the pasture among the mares. His head suddenly lifted and he appeared to be watching someone or something. The horse suddenly snorted and galloped across the pasture for the gate near the barn. Storm appeared alert, snorted several times, and then pinned his ears back and reared up with aggression. He ran along the fence as someone moved through the shadows toward the house. Through the outside window of the house, Casey was seen walking across the kitchen with her shirt open, revealing her black, sexy undergarments. She poured two glasses of wine then looked at her vibrating cell phone. She glanced at the caller ID, picked up the phone, and put it on silent mode without answering it. She left both glasses of wine on the counter and headed up the back kitchen stairs. The intruder moved away from the window and walked onto the porch. A black, gloved hand turned the doorknob and slowly opened the door. The intruder entered the kitchen and silently headed for the backstairs.

†

*T*he woods were dark and spooky that night despite the clear skies. Strange sounds seemed to come from every direction. Grey rode the slightly excitable black horse along the path in the woods at a fast gait. He was having a difficult time controlling the horse, which obviously didn't want to be in the dark woods. Even the sounds of the leather saddle creaking seemed to spook the nervous horse. Small animals were heard roaming the woods and the faint sounds were almost deafening while riding a horse that heard everything. The horse suddenly spooked at something and wildly spun around. Grey collected the horse and appeared shaken while attempting to soothe the snorting horse. The horse's head was raised, his ears perked, and his eyes were wide just waiting to find something else to be frightened by. Once the horse settled, Grey encouraged the horse along the path at a trot. A small animal crossed the path just up ahead. The little, brown rabbit may as well have been a bear. The horse suddenly sidestepped in sheer panic. Grey attempted to regain control of the horse. The horse spun wildly several times at the frightening rabbit, which had just crossed the path. Grey mimicked every move he'd ever seen Casey do while on a spooking horse, but it wasn't working. The horse suddenly reared up. Grey toppled off the horse and roughly struck the ground. The horse ran back for the fairgrounds and it would eventually end up back at its farm. Grey groaned, slowly moved to his hands and knees, and watched the horse run away.

"Horses suck!"

t

*T*he antique store along Main Street appeared quiet in the town that had settled in for the night after a long day at the fair. The glass on the front door was shattered inward just near the handle. As Diesel cautiously approached the partially open door, a man was seen standing just inside the alleyway opening. Diesel looked at the man. Fred stared back at him and gave a slight nod to the broken door.

"You don't want to go in there alone," Fred said softly. "They have crowbars and baseball bats."

"I've got this," Diesel replied and nodded him away. "You'd better go before they see you."

Fred slowly nodded and hurried across the street for an old pickup truck. He jumped in and drove away. Diesel gently pushed open the front door and caught the bell above before it could ding. He slowly entered the mostly dark store while stepping over the broken glass. A dim light was seen in the next room over and soft voices were heard. Diesel removed a small, twelve-inch baton and carried it with him. Where most men would appear frightened, Diesel seemed more curious and almost enthusiastic to meet those who broke into the store. The sound of items being smashed was heard within the next room. Diesel followed the dim light and approached the opening. Several men in dark clothing smashed china and other valuable items. Diesel watched them a moment then casually flipped on the lights. Wayne, Ryan, and Blain jumped with surprise and spun toward Diesel, who now casually leaned in the doorway with the baton in his hand.

"I hope you realize you're going to pay for that," Diesel said simply.

Ernest sat in one of the antique chairs like a king on his throne and looked at the big man in the archway. He casually stood and glared at Diesel with a smirk.

"Just leaving a little message for your friend, Grey," Ernest announced with a little too much arrogance. "Stay out of our way, and you may not get hurt."

The look on Diesel's face was that of humor. The threat was almost laughable. He just grinned and shook his head. "You're going to hurt me?" His smile was frightening. "That would be quite an achievement, considering all four of your boys couldn't even handle one, small girl." He didn't move from where he leaned in the archway. "You'd need an army to defeat me." His smile suddenly twisted. "And I'm not even the dangerous one--" Diesel smirked and nodded across the room. "--he is.

All five men looked across the room to Ruger, who stood just outside the office with an oddly emotionless expression on his face. Ernest and his boys appeared humored by the less than impressive man.

Ernest gave a nod to Ruger. "Show him what happens when you mess with a Harford," he announced then looked at Wayne. "You take care of the muscle."

Blain and Ryan approached Ruger, while Wayne lunged for Diesel with a baseball bat. Diesel suddenly straightened, flicked the baton in his hand, and it extended to three feet. He defended the bat with his baton. The two men lunged for Ruger with their crowbars. Ruger spun into a series of forward and backward roundhouse kicks and knocked the crowbars from each of their hands. It was easy to see who finished Casey's martial arts training. Once they were disarmed, Ruger grabbed Blain by the arm and kicked him several times in the side then flipped him over his hip as Ryan came to his brother's aid. Ryan threw a punch. Ruger blocked his fist, grabbed his wrist, and kicked him in the chest. Ryan crashed into the old settee and appeared momentarily dazed. Ruger casually picked off a speck of dirt from his shirt while Ryan got his second wind and finally sprang to his feet. Blain was back on his feet as well. Both men lunged for Ruger from opposite directions. Ruger spun into a roundhouse kick and knocked Blain to his hands and knees. He catapulted across Blain's back, using him as a springboard, and flew into a roundhouse kick while airborne, striking Ryan in the head. Ryan immediately dropped to the floor. Both men lie on the floor, writhing in agony, while Ruger casually stood over them.

Diesel knocked the baseball bat from Wayne's hand, tossed his baton aside, and began punching him with all the skills of a Marine in Special Forces. Wayne was down before he even realized he'd been hit. Ernest watched in horror as Wayne hit the floor. Ruger casually stepped over Ryan and approached Ernest. Ernest backed away with the horror evident in his eyes then attempted to bolt past him. Ruger spun into a ground spin and swept his legs out from beneath him. Ernest painfully struck the floor. Ruger moved over him, grabbed him by the throat, and stared into his eyes. Ruger's eyes were void of any emotion.

"I vowed to never kill anyone again, but the next time you force me to put my hand on your throat, I'll rip out your windpipe," Ruger casually informed him. The look in his eyes conveyed the seriousness of his threat. "Do we understand each other?"

Ernest stared at Ruger with a look of horror while gasping beneath his grip. He slowly nodded. Ruger released Ernest's throat and casually straightened.

"Video surveillance captured your destruction, so I'll expect prompt payment for damages," Ruger said. "And in case you're thinking your brother-in-law will interfere, you should know we have friends who are worse than me."

Ernest scrambled to his feet, ran for his sons, and hurried them from the shop. Diesel and Ruger watched them flee the scene. Diesel folded his arms across his chest and gave Ruger a curious look.

"We know someone worse than you?" Diesel asked.

Ruger shrugged and appeared humored. "Probably not, but a man can dream."

Diesel chuckled softly and patted Ruger's back. "I was surprised," he remarked. "One of those boys almost got a punch in. You're going soft, old man."

Ruger glared at the big impressive man standing alongside him. "Call me old man again, Diesel, and I'll permanently crack your nuts."

Diesel turned to face him and appeared serious. "Now, see, that's what I mean," he announced. "You didn't even take one cheap shot. None were clutching their boys in total agony. I mean, who are you? Casey's made you soft. You didn't used to be so gentlemanly."

Ruger sank into thought then looked at Diesel with realization. "You're right," he remarked then shook his head and sighed. "I am getting soft. I didn't used to be this nice."

"Exactly," Diesel chimed in while slapping his shoulder.

Ruger smacked Diesel in the groin with the back of his hand. Diesel gasped and clutched himself. He didn't hit him hard enough to drop him, but it obviously stung. Diesel glared at Ruger with disapproval. Ruger grinned in response and sighed.

"Yes, that did make me feel better," he announced cheerfully. "Thank you."

"Yeah, any time," Diesel said in a higher than normal pitch.

†

*G*rey's jeep pulled into the crowded tavern parking lot. Dina jumped out of the jeep and hurried inside. The tavern was packed to maximum capacity with fairgoers, vendors, and locals alike. The noise level was staggering and the mood was extremely enthusiastic. Dina easily maneuvered her way across the crowded tavern with years of waitressing practice on her side. She slipped between two men and stood before the bar. Mack busily tended to the thirsty patrons and temporary waitresses, who had their hands full attempting to serve customers. Despite the crowd, Mack approached when he saw her, apparently surprised to see her on Saturday night following the talent show.

"Hey, Dina," Mack announced cheerfully. "I hear Casey rocked at the talent show."

"More like an earthquake," Dina replied then immediately fidgeted. "What happened tonight?"

Mack appeared bewildered. "What do you mean?"

"With my--with Olivia."

He glanced across the bar to her mother's usual table then looked around the tavern with some surprise. "Actually, I haven't seen her in a few hours."

"That's because she's been arrested," Dina informed him then shook her head and appeared surprised. "You don't know about that?"

"No," Mack replied. "I hadn't heard about that. Where did it happen?"

"Right outside," she replied with rising anxiety.

He again shook his head. "Nope, I hadn't heard. Is she okay?"

"You have no idea what happened?" she asked with surprise.

He again shook his head. She stared at him a moment. Mack returned to his customers and busily filled mugs. He looked back at Dina, but she was already heading through the crowd for the door. Dina left the tavern and immediately removed her cell phone as she crossed the parking lot. She pressed a button and held the phone to her ear. She groaned when she got Casey's voicemail. She approached Grey's jeep and pressed another button. She paused before the jeep and waited. She groaned with disgust as Grey's voicemail picked up.

"Grey, it's me," she announced into the phone. "It was no accident. I think I was lured away on purpose--"

She saw Casey's black Camaro pull into the parking lot. Dina sighed with relief and disconnected the call as the car drove closer to her. She immediately noticed the damage to the right front fender and appeared alarmed.

"What the hell--?" Dina gasped and hurried for Casey's car as it stopped.

†

Dina opened her eyes and stared at the steering wheel beneath her head. The only light in the darkness was from the vintage dashboard of the Camaro. She attempted to sit up and immediately groaned in agony. She touched her bleeding temple and looked around with disorientation. She was behind the wheel of Casey's car! Dina made a second attempt to sit up, but something was holding her back. She uncertainly looked out the windshield and immediately appeared horrified. The hood of the car was severely crumpled and a tree was only a few feet in front of the windshield. Beyond the windshield was the deep ravine. Casey's Camaro was vertically inclined on the hillside and the only thing that kept the car from plummeting nose first into the ravine was a single, large evergreen tree beyond the treacherous curve's busted guardrail. Dina gasped with alarm and uncertainly looked around the empty car. Her purse lie on the dashboard, although how it got there was a mystery. She didn't have it with her when she left Grey's jeep. How she even got in the car was a mystery. She made another effort to sit up, although gravity and her own injuries held her back. She contained her sobs and slowly reached for her purse. The tree groaned beneath the weight of the car, and she felt a slight jolt. Dina gasped and stared frozen out the windshield. There was no telling how long she had before the car plummeted, taking her to her death in what was sure to be a fiery crash. That was exactly what someone wanted when they put her behind the wheel.

Chapter Twenty-nine

A black, leather gloved hand slowly pushed the master bedroom door open. The intruder entered the quiet, dimly lit bedroom that once belonged to Catherine and Brandon Remington. The Remington's bed was neatly made, and, although the comforter and decorative pillows weren't the originals, they were painstakingly close to it. The room looked just as it had with the exception of the empty gun cabinet. The bathroom door was partially open, revealing the glow of a light. The jets from the whirlpool tub were heard circulating. Romantic music played softly from within the bathroom. The intruder quietly crossed the bedroom, paused before the bathroom door, and slowly pushed it open to reveal the large white, bright bathroom. The intruder looked at the circulating jetted tub. It was empty! Deputy Tucker stood in the doorway with his gun in his hand and a surprised look on his face. He quickly turned within the doorway to the bedroom and came face-to-face with Casey, who was now dressed in a black stalking outfit. She swiftly kicked the gun from his hand, caught it mid-air, and aimed it at his face. Tucker stared at her holding his gun and appeared alarmed while holding his hands up in front of him. From the look in her eyes, it was almost surprising she hadn't pulled the trigger.

"Casey, put down the gun," Tucker said gently.

Casey stared at him with no emotion and cocked her head slightly. "What are you doing in my bathroom, Deputy?"

"Sheriff Holt said we should patrol your farm," he sternly informed her. "The front door was open and no one answered when I called. I don't know what you're thinking, but I need you to give me the gun."

Her expression didn't change. "So you heard the tub circulating and just decided to have a look-see?" she asked. "Wouldn't you assume I was in the tub? A courtesy knock would have been appropriate."

"This is all a misunderstanding, Casey," he said firmly. "Don't do anything stupid."

"Trust me, anything I do will be smart and deliberate," Casey scoffed. She nodded to the window. "If you were patrolling, where's your cruiser? You weren't driving it when I saw you sneaking to the house on those cute little spy cams Diesel installed."

His expression suddenly dropped. "You saw wrong," he insisted and looked more nervous now.

"Don't fuck with me, Tucker," Casey growled. "I'm still a little pissy about the last time I ran into you in this bedroom."

Tucker stared at Casey and appeared stunned. For a moment, he was unable to speak. He slowly shook his head. "I don't know what you're talking about."

"Sure you do," she insisted. "Remember, that's the night you murdered my parents and gutted me." She casually indicated the bedroom door. "That's the door I blew out with the shotgun when I nearly took off your head." She smiled innocently. "I would think that would still be fresh in your mind," she announced then suddenly sneered. "It's *fresh* in mine."

"Casey, you're making a mistake."

"I don't think so," she insisted. "You told Melanie that Vaughn interrupted a rape attempt, but Vaughn never told you that. He never told anyone that."

"No, of course he didn't," Tucker replied. "I read it in his police report."

"It wasn't in the report, because he arrived after the fact. Vaughn didn't know anything about it," she informed him and again smiled sweetly. "The only people who knew about that were the two people in the kitchen that night. Me and the killer."

Tucker suddenly tensed while staring at her. Her look was cold and frightening. "You can't prove anything," he informed her. "I have an alibi for the time of the murders. I was with Melanie."

"Oh, please, Tucker," she scoffed. "As deputy, you could easily manipulate the time. I doubt anyone ever questioned your whereabouts. You probably showed up at Melanie's house right after your little side trip here." Her look was now oddly psychotic. "Besides, I don't care what I can prove." Casey raised her brows while tilting the gun. A twisted smile crossed her face. "I'm just looking for revenge."

Tucker's look slowly faded to fear. Casey was on the edge, and it wasn't going to end well for him.

"Let's see," she announced reflectively. "An eye for an eye, right? Now what would be the male equivalent to my reproductive organs?" She grinned most sinister. "I think you know what's coming next--"

Casey cocked the hammer and aimed the gun at Tucker's crotch. He suddenly cried out. A car was heard pulling up the gravel driveway. Casey frowned and pulled the gun back.

"Damn, that's Sheriff Holt here to ruin my fun."

For some odd reason, the sound of the approaching car allowed Tucker to regain some of his arrogance. "I doubt Vaughn will be making your date tonight. He met with an unfortunate accident on his way over," Tucker bluntly informed her and smiled deviously. "Some drunk driver in a stolen car ran him into a tree."

Casey's look suddenly changed from sinister to concern. She removed her cell phone and pressed a button. The phone rang on the other end. Vaughn's voicemail picked up. Casey disconnected the call then glared at Tucker.

"For your sake, you'd better be lying," she growled. "Toss your handcuffs and keys to me."

Tucker tossed both to the floor near her. As Casey reached down to pick them up, Tucker suddenly lunged for her. Casey spun into an upward kick from the floor and struck him in the face. Tucker fell harshly against the dresser then collapsed to the floor. Casey casually collected the handcuffs and snorted a laugh.

"Thank you," she announced to the unconscious deputy. "That was actually easier than telling you what to do." She sighed while grinning. "And ten times more satisfying."

Moments later, within the kitchen. Deputy Mitchell poked his head in through the open door and cautiously looked around with his hand on his gun within his holster.

"Hello? Anyone home?" Mitchell uncertainly called out while scanning the empty kitchen. It was too quiet. "Casey? Grey? Big, *brawny* dude?"

Mitchell slowly entered the kitchen while continuing to scan the area then uncertainly approached the living room archway. He cautiously entered the dimly lit living room and looked around. Nothing moved. He slowly headed toward the main stairs. Casey emerged from the shadows, slinked across the floor, and entered the dark dining room. Mitchell hesitated, looked back from where he stood near the bottom of the stairs, and scanned the room. Nothing moved. He focused his attention on the stairs and headed up them. Mitchell quietly walked along the upstairs hallway, glancing into each dark room as he passed. He uncertainly peered into the dark, master bedroom. There was a thump. Mitchell removed his gun and fumbled with the light switch. Tucker was naked and standing facing the bedpost. His wrists were handcuffed to the canopy, his ankles were tied to the bottom post, and his sock was stuffed in his mouth. Red lipstick scribbled across his buttocks read, "Vote for Grey". Mitchell hurried toward him while appearing alarmed and removed the sock from his mouth.

Tucker spit several times then glared at Mitchell. "Untie me," he cried out in mild panic. "She's in the house!"

Mitchell quickly removed his handcuff keys and unlocked the cuffs on Tucker's wrists. "You said you could handle her," he protested with the alarm evident in his voice.

"Are you sure you didn't see her?" Tucker demanded.

"No, she must have slipped out." Mitchell removed his knife and cut the ropes binding Tucker's ankles while avoiding looking at his naked body.

Tucker grabbed his clothing and quickly dressed. "Guard the door," he ordered.

Mitchell hurried to the bedroom door and watched the hall as Tucker dressed. Casey appeared in the bathroom doorway and somersaulted across the room.

Tucker saw her and suddenly cried out, "There she is!"

Mitchell spun with his gun aimed. Casey was already in front of him, spun into a roundhouse kick, and knocked his gun across the room. Mitchell gasped and ran from the room. Tucker lunged for the gun on the floor. Casey flipped through the air, struck him in the head with her foot, and gracefully landed near the gun as Tucker was thrown onto the bed. He groaned and appeared disoriented. Casey picked up the gun and shook her head with disappointment.

"You're not even making this sporting," she scoffed. "I'll be back to deal with you."

She darted across the room and disappeared into the hallway.

†

*D*ina held back her sobs while she half lie frozen against the steering wheel of the vertical car. She again looked at her purse on the dashboard. She had to reach it. She had to get her cell phone. It was her only hope for survival. The Camaro suddenly jolted and the tree creaked loudly. Dina screamed. The large evergreen swayed slightly as the car pulled away from it. She stared out the windshield as the front of the car was pulled backwards and away from the tree. She clutched the steering wheel in both hands as the car was pulled up the ravine. Within seconds, the car was pulled through the mangled, metal railing that resembled torn tinfoil. The driver's side door was pulled open with a loud creak. As Dina looked at the open door, Ruger stared back at her with fatherly concern.

"Are you alright?"

Dina held back her laugh, clutched her bleeding temple, and slowly shook her head. "Honestly? No."

Ruger helped her from the car. She leaned heavily on him while holding her head.

"What happened?" she asked.

"I'm guessing you had an accident and ran off the road," Ruger replied.

Diesel removed the tow cable from the Camaro and returned to Grey's jeep. Dina stared at Grey's jeep a moment then looked back at Ruger with alarm.

"No," she announced firmly. "I was driving Grey's jeep."

"We found it abandoned at the tavern with the keys in the ignition," Diesel informed her as he approached.

Dina remained disoriented then looked at both men. "Someone hit me as I approached Casey's car!" She was now horrified. "We need to find Casey. I know who's behind this!"

Chapter Thirty

Mitchell ran down the backstairs, crossed the Remington's kitchen, and ran for the partially closed door. He threw open the door to reveal Grey, who was out of breath and clinging to the doorframe. Grey looked at Mitchell, appeared surprised to see him, and uncertainly straightened.

"I thought Sheriff Holt was here," Grey said.

Mitchell was in a state of panic. "Casey's gone crazy. You've got to stop her!"

Grey appeared surprised while staring at him. There was an eerie silence. "Did you do something to her?"

"No--"

A twisted smile suddenly crossed Grey's face. His look was oddly psychotic. "Did she *accuse* you of something?"

Mitchell slowly backed away from Grey. He entered the house while grinning in a creepy manner. Mitchell appeared frightened and continued to back up. Casey appeared in the living room archway and casually leaned against it. Mitchell saw her behind him, panicked, and lunged for Grey, the obvious lesser of two evils. Grey spun into a high, roundhouse kick, and struck him in the chest. Mitchell flew backwards and into Casey. She caught him, smiled sweetly, and brushed the dirty footprint from his chest.

"How about you start by telling us what you did with Sheriff Holt?" Casey demanded to know with a look that immediately sent chills through the deputy.

Mitchell was now terrified. In her state of mind, there was no telling what Casey would do. "I didn't do anything with Vaughn, I swear," Mitchell cried out. "It was Tucker! He had someone run him off the road. I swear; it wasn't me!"

Casey looked at Grey. Her expression changed to that of concern. Grey gave her a firm look and a quick nod. Casey resumed her slightly psychotic attitude and forced Mitchell to look her in the eyes.

"Was it Tucker who killed our parents?" Casey demanded to know.

"Yes, it was Tucker," Mitchell stammered while attempting to keep watch on both. "Tucker did it to keep the mayor in office. Your father was a threat to his position."

"And what was your part in it?" Grey demanded, causing Mitchell to gasp and look back at him.

"I was supposed to keep an eye on Vaughn at his speed trap, but I fell asleep," he announced nervously. "I didn't know he was going to kill anyone, I swear."

"And the mayor ordered the hit?" Grey asked.

"There wasn't supposed to be a hit," Mitchell protested. "It was supposed to be a warning." He suddenly hesitated. "He said he was just going to rough up Casey and her mother to frighten Brandon. He never said anything about killing anyone." Mitchell remained tense and looked from Grey to Casey. "That's why I volunteered to go after Dina the other night. I didn't want to see anyone else hurt, but then someone jumped me--" He suddenly eyed Casey with an odd realization.

She grinned and shook her head. "Sorry," she replied. "That wasn't me. If I came across a man in a mask, I probably would have shot first and asked questions later."

"If it wasn't you--" Mitchell gasped softly then looked at Grey.

Grey grinned. "Sure, blame it on the psycho brother," he teased.

"I knew it!" Casey suddenly announced with a twisted smile. "You were acting a little too innocent. You were behind the Harford boys and the cannon too, weren't you?"

"We all vent in our own way, sister dear," Grey replied.

"And here I was blaming Ruger," she scoffed while hiding her smile. "I'm proud of you."

A gun was suddenly heard cocking just behind Casey. She tensed to the familiar sound near her head. Mitchell darted away from her, turned to look back, and held his chest. Tucker stood behind Casey with a small, semiautomatic pistol to her head.

"Look what I found in daddy's nightstand beneath the dirty magazines," Tucker teased.

Casey remained still as horror crossed her face. She didn't chance looking back at him but knew it was a gun against her head. "The twenty-two?" she asked softly.

"That's right," Tucker said with a chuckle.

Casey groaned softly and shut her eyes. She then muttered, "Forgot about that one."

Grey appeared stunned while staring at her with his mouth hanging open. "Good job, Casey!"

"They know everything, Tucker," Mitchell informed him and appeared less nervous now.

"Of course they do, thanks to your big mouth," Tucker snapped. "We'll continue with the original plan."

"How do you intend to explain your missing guns?" Casey asked while resuming a little of her earlier confidence.

Tucker suddenly glared at Mitchell. "Cuff Grey to the banister and find our weapons. Check the upstairs bathroom."

Mitchell removed his handcuffs and kept a safe distance from Grey while subconsciously rubbing his chest. He nodded him to the stairs and tossed him the cuffs.

"Cuff your right wrist to the banister," Mitchell ordered.

Grey hesitated and eyed Casey. She raised her brows in silent response. Grey frowned then groaned as he cuffed his right wrist to the banister. Mitchell took a wide birth around Grey then darted up the stairs.

"Who ordered the hit on our family?" Grey asked while glaring at Tucker across the kitchen. "Was it the mayor or that bastard Ernest?"

"The same person who stole Casey's car and ran Vaughn off the road tonight," Tucker informed him while grinning slyly. "Although an investigation will reveal it was Dina behind the wheel, that is, once they identify her body."

Casey and Grey exchanged horrified looks. Grey sneered and gave a firm tug on the handcuff attached to the banister. His look was once again psychotic. Abby appeared in the open kitchen doorway and stared at Tucker with a strange look on her face. He looked at her and appeared surprised. A clearly visible cut on the corner of her mouth bled freely.

"Abby?" Tucker gasped. "What are you doing--?"

Vaughn forced Abby into the kitchen while holding his gun to her head. She was obviously frightened by her run-in with him.

"You know, I never hit a woman before," Vaughn said firmly. He casually looked around the room then eyed Casey. "I wasn't expecting quite so many people on our date."

"Yeah, the party got a little out of control," she muttered while casting a sideways glance at the gun to her own head. "Nice of you to finally join us."

"Traffic was bad," he scoffed. "I saw Dina along the road with the 'auto club'. She seemed fine, but Diesel's a little pissed about the car." He then looked at his deputy and best friend. "You never were good at tying loose ends, Tucker. So I figured I'd help you out. You off my girlfriend; I off yours."

Casey and Grey stared at Vaughn with surprise.

"Really?" Casey gasped. "The mayor's wife and your deputy?" She managed to eye Tucker partially behind her and suddenly grimaced. "Ewe, you slept with your ex-girlfriend's mother! That is so nasty."

"Yeah," Vaughn announced and smirked. "She was surprisingly talkative after I bounced her head off the steering wheel. She was the driving force behind keeping her husband in office. It seems Lance had no clue what she and Tucker had been doing behind his back--in and out of the bedroom."

It seemed out of character for Vaughn to assault Mrs. Mayor, but he'd obviously had a rough night.

"When she stumbled upon my *accident*, something she said earlier about Casey's teenage crush on me finally registered. Half the town knew I had a thing for Casey many years ago, but only three people knew about her teenage crush on me. Casey, her mother, and Dina. Abby could only have known that if she read Catherine's journal, which she had stolen from my desk."

Casey stared at Vaughn with surprise and hostility. "She stole my mother's journal? When did you intend to tell me it was stolen?"

Vaughn sharply raised his brows at her. "I think we're getting a little off subject, Casey," he remarked.

She glared her disapproval. "Fine, but we'll finish this discussion later."

"Shut up, both of you!" Tucker appeared enraged while clutching the gun he held to Casey's head. "You won't shoot Abby, Vaughn, but you know I'll do Casey."

There was a tense moment. Casey stared at Vaughn and knew damned well Tucker was right. There was no way Vaughn would ever shoot Mrs. Mayor without being provoked. Casey showed no emotion while staring at Vaughn.

"Shoot him," she announced sternly.

Vaughn stared back at her and appeared stunned. "Are you crazy?" he gasped.

"I'm pretty sure she is," Grey remarked simply while casually leaning against the banister to which he was handcuffed.

"Do it," Casey said firmly.

"Shut up!" Tucker shouted while clutching her shoulder and dug the barrel of the gun into her temple.

Vaughn tensed but didn't take the gun from Abby's head. Casey stared into Vaughn's eyes from across the kitchen.

"There's one bullet in the chamber, but the clip is empty," she quickly informed Vaughn then raised her brows sharply. "Shoot him!"

Tucker suddenly appeared alarmed at the prospect of only having one bullet and aimed the gun at Vaughn. Vaughn shoved Abby aside and shot Tucker in the head as Casey ducked. Tucker's head snapped back as his gun clicked empty. Abby screamed and bolted toward the garage door just past Grey. Grey suddenly kicked her in the chest, throwing her backward. She roughly hit the floor and didn't move. There was a loud thump from upstairs. Mitchell tumbled down the stairs, landed roughly at the bottom, and lay unconscious. Ruger casually walked down the steps and assessed the situation in the kitchen.

Vaughn stared at Ruger with surprise. "Where did you come from?"

"From upstairs," he said innocently while pointing up the steps, "just now." Ruger casually tossed Grey the handcuff keys.

Diesel entered from the living room with Dina just behind him and looked around. "What did I miss?" he asked then eyed Tucker lying on the floor as blood spilled from his head wound.

Dina saw Tucker and gasped with horror.

Diesel nodded his approval and grinned. "Nice shot."

While avoiding the spilling blood, Dina ran past Tucker's lifeless body and toward Grey, who removed the handcuffs. He gathered her into his arms and clung to her while sighing his relief. Vaughn approached the dead man and glared at Casey. She innocently watched him as he picked up the small gun by the barrel.

"Did you know the gun was empty?" he suddenly asked.

Casey casually shrugged, folded her arms across her chest, and maintained an innocent look. "No, I actually thought there was one in the chamber."

"What former Special Forces keeps a gun with a bullet in the chamber but an empty clip?" Vaughn demanded.

All four looked at him while smirking but none responded. His question was silently answered. Vaughn rolled his eyes and shook his head. He crouched down alongside Tucker and unbuttoned his shirt to expose the bulletproof vest. He lightly ran his finger along the indents in the chest of the vest.

"Three indents," Vaughn remarked with a soft sigh. "Same vest he wore two years ago."

"Didn't do him much good tonight," Diesel muttered then grinned.

Vaughn stuck his finger in a hole near the side of the vest and glanced at Casey. "I think this was your handy work. Looks like a .357 Magnum. If he hadn't been wearing, he wouldn't have gotten up when you shot him."

"My shot was a little obstructed," she casually remarked. "If he had stuck his head out though, I would gladly have blown it off."

Vaughn slowly straightened and allowed his eyes to fall on her attire. He casually walked past her and murmured softly, "I like the outfit."

Casey grinned and raised her brows lustfully.

Ruger rolled his eyes, turned away, and scoffed, "I'm going to be sick."

Chapter Thirty-one

$\mathcal{O}$ne week later. There was a large crowd standing before the stage at the fairgrounds. Just about the entire town had showed up for what would be the turning point in history of their small town. They had been under a cloud of corruption for decades and finally things were going to be different. Grey stood behind the podium as the crowd cheered and applauded. He proudly looked over the cheering crowd while realizing his father's dream. Brandon would have been proud of his son.

"As acting mayor, I'm making a promise to end corruption in our town," Grey announced. He barely got the words out when the crowd cheered wildly.

Ernest was seen off to the side with his three sons. Fred was conspicuously missing. He motioned to his sons and all four walked away.

"And in order to do that," Grey continued from behind the podium, "we need a strong police department. At this time, I'd like to call to the stage our very own Sheriff Holt, who bravely saved mine and Casey's life not once but twice now."

The crowd applauded and cheered as Vaughn made his way onto stage, once again embarrassed by the spotlight. He approached Grey at the podium and shook his hand.

"Mayor Remington," Vaughn cheerfully announced.

Grey grinned in response. "Our town is going to be in the best of hands," he announced to the crowd then looked at Vaughn. "Sheriff Holt, would you please introduce our new deputies."

Vaughn stood behind the podium and looked out to the crowd, who waited anxiously for his announcement. "I'd like the good people of Darwood Falls to meet our new and *improved* police force," he announced cheerfully. "Please welcome Deputy Diesel Mann and Deputy Ruger Quinn."

Ruger and Diesel walked onto stage in their new police uniforms and badges. The crowd applauded wildly. Vaughn walked down the steps as both men soaked in the attention. Casey rode up to the stage on her gray horse and smiled at Vaughn. He grinned, climbed onto the horse behind her, and they rode across the fairgrounds as he clung to her. Grey watched them leave, smiled proudly, and stepped behind the podium.

"Let's hear it for Sheriff Holt," Grey announced cheerfully and clapped. "My soon-to-be *future* brother-in-law."

As the crowd cheered, Grey joined Dina offstage and hugged her affectionately. Diesel and Ruger also left stage. Melanie walked past Diesel, gave him a lustful smile, and nodded toward the ticket booth. She flashed a box of doughnuts. Diesel grinned and nearly trampled Ruger to get to her and the doughnuts. A group of women approached Ruger and swarmed him. He appeared startled by all the female attention and looked at Grey with Dina.

"Grey, a little help?" Ruger announced.

Grey smiled deviously at him and gave his best royal wave. Casey and Vaughn were seen riding off on her gray horse across the field and out of sight.

✝

Ernest entered the foyer of his mansion with Wayne, Ryan, and Blain following behind. All four appeared disgusted. Wayne slammed the door.

"Now what?" Wayne demanded.

"First, I want that traitorous brother of yours found," Ernest snapped then looked at his watch with a frown. "Lance has some nerve insisting he meet us here."

"I can't believe he resigned as mayor," Ryan snorted and collapsed onto a bench in the hallway. "Then to throw Aunt Abby under the bus like that--"

"I could kill him on that score alone," Ernest scoffed. "If Grey Remington gets his way, I'm going to be broke within a year."

"What can we do?" Blain demanded.

"We're going to finish what Abby and Tucker started," Ernest snapped. "We're going to get rid of those Remington kids once and for all. No kid gloves this time. I want them eliminated."

"That's not as easy as it sounds," Wayne retorted. "They don't roll over easily."

"So, we'll solicit some professional help," Ernest remarked. "I know some people. It won't be cheap, but it'll be worth it. I just need to make a few phone calls."

Blain suddenly sniffed the air and looked around. "Do you smell something?"

The other three looked at him then smelled the air. Ernest shook his head.

"You're imagining things," he remarked.

Blain walked into the living room, smelled the air, and approached the propane fireplace. "It's propane," Blain announced as the others approached. "There's something wrong with the fireplace."

Wayne looked at the coffee table and appeared puzzled. A cigarette rested on the ashtray with a book of matches holding it up.

"What the hell--" Wayne began to speak.

The book of matches caught fire and the propane fumes suddenly ignited, turning the entire living room into a ball of fire. From outside Ernest's mansion, there was a loud explosion as the front windows shattered and flames shot out of the house. Wiley stood casually on the sidewalk while watching the flames engulf the front of the house. He looked at the gray cat in his arms, affectionately petted its coat, and continued on his way past the mansion.

The End

Other books by Holly Copella!
Reviews left on Amazon are appreciated!

"Insanely Deadly"

When the dead return to life, it's up to an admiral's daughter and a mildly insane, former war hero to save their small town.

Jetta Cross, a Navy Admiral's daughter, is tasked with keeping her father's comrade, a former war hero turned town crazy, grounded in the real world. Capt. John Hunter is still fighting the war in his head, where imaginary dead people are part of his world. When a viral outbreak brings about a zombie uprising, Hunter is left to his own devices. He must resume his role as a one-man commando unit in order to destroy the ravenous undead. With Hunter still fighting his own inner demons as well as the undead, the townspeople fear their zombie neighbors may not be the only threat. Stranded at the island's luxurious resort with a handful of workers, Jetta is forced to live up to her father's reputation and take charge of the deteriorating situation at the hotel. She must wage her own war against the infected before the government declares her hometown a total loss.

"Deadly Institution"

A town recluse suspected of killing his wife teams up with a young woman in order to stop a killer.

After being accused of murdering his wife, Konrad Asher turns his back on the town that once adored him. Ten years later, he still holds his grudge and the title of the most feared man in town. With the reopening of the burned mental institution, where his wife had died, former employees are now murdered one-by-one, throwing suspicion back on Asher. A young local reporter, Jacey, is forced to reveal her long-time friendship with the infamous recluse in order to clear his name not only in the recent murders but to exonerate him in the death of his wife as well. Will Jacey's relationship with Asher invite the killer closer to her? Or is the killer already in her life?

"Death Displacement"

A grief-stricken man travels back in time to seek revenge on the woman who murdered his girlfriend but inadvertently falls in love with her.

Kane is about to marry the woman he loves. His life is perfect. A few weeks before the wedding, a vindictive woman from his girlfriend's past mysteriously arrives and kills her. He learns of a traumatic accident that happened five years earlier, which triggers Riley's hatred for his girlfriend. Distraught over his girlfriend's death, Kane uses an antique time machine to travel into the past in order to find and destroy the woman responsible. When he runs into Riley's younger self, he realizes she's not the monster she later becomes, and he can't bring himself to destroy her. With a little help from his oddball friend from the past, they formulate a plan to prevent the accident that sends Riley down her destructive path. Kane's plan backfires when he falls for the younger Riley. His new tortured existence is further complicated when future Riley, his girlfriend's killer, shows up with her own devious agenda that doesn't include him. Will he be able to stop the time ripple, which ultimately ends with his girlfriend's death? Or will future Riley take him out of the timeline forever--

"The Battle for Andrea Maria"

A cruise ship attack turns six survivors into overnight celebrities after they take credit for the heroic act of a stowaway who died saving them.

The cruise is just what Jess needed--a bit of harmless fun far from her daily grind. But what begins as a relaxing vacation turns into a desperate fight for her life when terrorists take over the ship and start piling up bodies. Teaming up with a mysterious stowaway, Jess attempts to send out a distress call but knows they cannot wait for help to come. If she or the few remaining passengers have any hope for survival, Jess must act now. The papers dub it "The Battle for *Andrea Maria*," but to Jess it is the moment she fought side-by-side with her enigmatic Romeo, saving the ship--and losing him. She thinks the story ends there, but really, the nightmare is just beginning...

"Screenplays: The Island Collection"
"Jungle Princess", "A.L.F. Resort", "Brighton Island"

Discover how romance and fun in the sun can be downright *chilling*!

"Jungle Princess" is a romantic/thriller that leaves a teenage girl stranded on an island with two male shipmates and a creature of "unknown" origin. She soon discovers the island is home to an abandoned prison with several prisoners roaming free. What really killed over one hundred prisoners? And is it still out there--?

"A.L.F. Resort" is a romantic/thriller set on an island resort with Artificial Life Forms as the main draw. At this resort, all your fantasies come true...until a malfunction removes safety inhibitors on the A.L.F.'s. Zombies, biker gangs, and mobsters run amuck, turning fantasies into nightmares. A young reporter gets more of a story than she anticipates, but will she survive long enough to write the story?

"Brighton Island" is a romantic/thriller set on a private island. When the owner's niece brings her psychic friend to the mansion, his presence awakens the spirits' tortured souls. As the psychic attempts to solve the old murders, the niece is confronted with the possibility that she's next to join the mansion ghosts. Stranded on the island with a crazed killer, he uncle wages his own war to save them. Will his "shock and awe" tactics actually save them or get them killed?

"Reaper of Souls" A fantasy short story

A young woman must outwit an evil sorcerer in order to save her brother or become one of his minions forever.

Unwilling to believe her brother is dead, Reggie discovers an underhanded deal made with Kahn, a less than ethical sorcerer, who collects humans to serve as slaves in his kingdom. In order to rescue her brother from his horrible fate, she must complete his failed task or be forced to serve Kahn forever. After being transported to his world, Reggie realizes that even if she beats Kahn at his own game, she's at his mercy for him to uphold his end of the deal. All seems lost until Kahn's discontented, self-serving brother, Helsing, arrives. Can Reggie convince Helsing to help her? And at what cost?

ABOUT THE AUTHOR

Holly Copella has been writing since the age of twelve when her frustration at a book's poor plot drove her to author her own story. Over the last decade, she's written a number of screenplays, some of which she's now adapting into novels. Her fascination with zombies and other darker material lends an edge to her writing, which tends to lean toward horror. As a fan of Agatha Christie, she appreciates the craft of a good plot and the importance of creating significant characters.

Hailing from Pennsylvania, Copella lives in the Endless Mountains on a farm with her rescue horses and other animals. In addition to writing and reading fiction, she enjoys riding horses and traveling to Las Vegas and Disney World.

www.ingramcontent.com/pod-product-compliance
Lightning Source LLC
Chambersburg PA
CBHW060916180626
46817CB00004B/1285